NEWLY UNDEAD IN DARK RIVER

GRACE MCGINTY

For Tash and Tegan.
Best. Stalkers. Ever.

ALSO BY GRACE MCGINTY

Hell's Redemption Series

The Redeemable: The Complete Novel

The Unrepentant: The Complete Novel

The Fallen: The Complete Novel

The Azar Nazemi Trilogy

Smoke and Smolder

Burn and Blaze

Rage and Ruin

Stand Alone Novels and Novellas

The Last Note

Bright Lights From A Hurricane

Castle of Carnal Desires

Treasure

NEWLY UNDEAD IN DARK RIVER

DARK RIVER DAYS
BOOK 1

GRACE MCGINTY

CHAPTER ONE

I woke to a rat scuttling across my chest, its tiny nose twitching as it paused to stare at me before scurrying off. Damn, I was hungry.

The fact that my initial reaction to a rat was hunger and not disgust was the first sign that something was very, very wrong. The second clue was that I was lying in a drain pipe in the middle of the night. Although it was hard to concentrate on anything but the hunger clawing at my stomach, I could hear the nocturnal animals shuffling around in the silence, smell the stale water that now soaked my clothes.

I tried to sit up and banged my head on the slimy concrete. Groaning, I rolled over and crawled my way out into the open. My body felt like I'd climbed Everest. Twice. I couldn't see my backpack anywhere. Panic began to fill my chest. Everything was in that pack. But it was pitch black, the moon not even visible behind the clouds. I became acutely aware that I was standing in the middle of the wilderness, at night, alone. I was a serial killer's wet dream right now.

I stared down the road, looking for the oncoming lights of a car or truck or something. Maybe I could hitch a ride into the nearest town. It was probably hitchhiking that put me in this predicament to start with. My mom was going to be pissed that I'd been so irresponsible.

I felt dazed like I'd been tranquilized, but I patted down my clothing with sluggish movements. Nothing was torn, and all my clothes were still on. I didn't feel violated in any way. My brain was cloudy, and I tried to sift through the fog to remember why I was lying in a ditch, outside of…

I looked up at the road sign. *Welcome to Dark River.* Where the hell was Dark River?

Hunger tore at my belly again, a burning ache so painful I moaned into the darkness like a wounded animal. First, I needed to eat something. Maybe then I'd be able to work out what the hell was going on.

I stumbled down the side of the road, and I could see the muted glow of the town lights once I was over the small rise.

Electricity surged up through my chest, and the edges of my vision dimmed. The last thing I felt when my body buckled was the rough gravel scraping my cheek.

. . .

I SNAPPED back to consciousness all at once, like when you dream you're falling. My head felt too full, and panic was beginning to mingle with the overwhelming hunger.

I was now in town, beneath the striped awning of Bert and Beatrice's Old Fashioned Diner. How the fuck did I get here? Everything was completely blank as if someone had plucked the memory from my brain like a bad apple. A clock tower sat in the middle of town, proclaiming it to be almost midnight.

I pushed through the glass door, and a little bell tinkled above my head. The place was filled to the brim, which was unusual seeing how it was basically the middle of the night.

Every set of eyes turned to look at me, and the old guy behind the counter dropped the soda glass he was drying, the smashing sound shooting pain into my skull. I must have really looked like hell. An elderly woman bustled out of the swinging doors, which probably led to the kitchen.

"What's goin' on out..." she trailed off when she saw me standing in the doorway. She nudged the old man out of the way.

"Lass, are you feelin' alright? Bertie, get the girl a drink. The house special," she said slowly, her accent a thick Scottish brogue. "Tilda, call the Sheriff, please. Get him down here, quick smart." She was rounding the counter now. "Here, Lass, take a seat."

I took the stool she indicated obediently. She had

a no-nonsense, matronly tone that soothed my panicked nerves.

"I lost my money and my passport." My voice sounded so weak that I hardly recognized it as my own.

The elderly lady just patted my shoulder.

"Not to worry, Sweet. It's on the house."

I could hear the sound of Tilda murmuring quietly into the phone down the other end of the diner.

"Yes Sheriff, just stumbled in the door. Looking like death, if you know what I mean."

The old man, Bertie I guess, slid a cardboard milkshake cup in front of me, complete with red and white straw. It smelled so good that I fell on it like a half-starved animal. When I'd sucked down the last drop, I looked up, embarrassed.

"Sorry. I was really hungry." Bertie just took away my empty cup and put a fresh one in front of me.

"Don't worry about it, Darlin'. Have another one." I was struggling to concentrate on her words. I found it hard to concentrate on anything but the milkshake in front of me.

The bell over the door tinkled, and everyone's eyes shifted in that direction again, even mine. A tall man in a chocolate brown uniform walked into the place, and everyone started talking at once. The cacophony after the complete absence of noise was hell on my eardrums. I pushed my palms over my ears to try and muffle some of the sounds.

"Quiet!" The guy was obviously the Sheriff, judging by the way that everyone's flapping jaws snapped shut with almost perfect synchronization. Silence again. The man strode over, his every movement elegant, to where I was sitting and gaping in his direction.

The man was hot. Like, spontaneous combustion, three-alarm, call in the National Guard, hot. He had sandy brown hair and deep green eyes. The uniform hugged his muscular body. He was so attractive it made my teeth hurt. Literally.

"Ma'am, my name is Sheriff Walker Walton, do you need some help?" His deep voice was gentle, almost as if he didn't want to startle me.

"I don't know how I got here," I whispered. It was all a blank.

I'd been backpacking my way through Canada with my friends, but they had gone home last week, while I continued to travel up through Alberta by myself. I'd missed my bus to Yukon, so I'd decided to hitchhike my way through the last stretch to the border of British Columbia. After all, what's life without a little adventure? I'd been picked up by a family with teenage sons, but they'd let me off near Grande Prairie. I walked down the highway a bit more, and then poof, everything else is blank.

"Do you remember your name?" the Sheriff asked in the same soft voice.

"Mika McKellan. From Boston."

"That's good, Mika. I'd like you to come down to the station with me, so we can get this all sorted out. The town doctor will meet us there, just to check you over."

I nodded absently, and followed Sheriff Walton out of the diner, clutching my take away cup to my chest like a lifebuoy. He walked me over to the squad car, and let me sit in the passenger seat, instead of the back.

We drove in silence around the block, and I took the town in. It was actually quite beautiful. Not the cemetery stillness of most small towns after dark. Fairy lights were strung around the town square, and people milled about. The lights were on in all the shops, and small clumps of people were talking to each other on well-lit sidewalks.

"Is there a festival going on or something?" I asked Sheriff Walton.

"Or something," he replied, letting silence fill the cab.

Within a minute, we had pulled up in front of a skinny brick building. There were shiny bars on the windows, and a police sign hanging over the front lawn.

Sheriff Walton moved around the front of the car and opened the passenger door. I heaved myself out of the seat. Moving wasn't as painful as it was when I first woke up, but I still felt sluggish.

A plain woman with sparkling eyes met us at the front door. She looked me over and then sent a pointed expression to Sheriff Walton.

"Mika, this is Doctor Alice Sommer. I'm gonna get the Doc to check you for any signs of, uh, injury."

He held open the door of the station for me, and I gave him a polite smile.

"Let's go into the conference room. We need to have a chat after the Doc has looked you over. I'll be out here doing some paperwork."

He opened the door to an interrogation room. No windows, just a metal table with two chairs. Conference room, my ass.

"Thanks, Walker. I'll give you a shout when we're done," the doctor said softly.

The door closed with a click. The doctor sat a leather doctor's bag on the metal table. "Have a seat, Miss McKellan."

"Mika."

"Okay, Mika it is. But you have to call me Alice. Now, let me have a look at you." She shone one of those penlights in my eyes, and I let out a little squeal.

"Ouch."

"Hmm, light sensitivity. You have a little bruising on your throat too." She got out a measuring instrument and measured the width of the bruise. "Anything else feel off to you?"

"Except for the starving feeling, my muscles aching, the weird blank spots and the passing out?" My sarcasm was obnoxious, but I couldn't seem to help it. "Other than all that, I'm as healthy as a horse."

The doctor clicked her tongue and wrote down the measurements. "Walker, can you get the cooler from the backseat of my car and come in here please?" She barely raised her voice, but the Sheriff must have heard because the front door of the station slammed.

"Don't worry, Mika. Your symptoms should lessen in a few days."

"Lessen?"

But the Sheriff was striding in the room, cooler in hand. Damn, he was fast.

"It's confirmed, Walker, though let's face it, it was obvious to everyone as soon as she walked through the door of the diner. You can smell it just as well as I can."

The Sheriff ran a hand down his face and sighed. "I know, but I didn't want to believe it. I didn't want to think someone we know could have done this."

What the hell were they talking about? I sniffed my armpit stealthily. I didn't think I smelled that bad, considering I'd been sleeping in a ditch. My nose twitched. A tangy metallic smell was coming from the cooler. A smell that was so familiar, but I couldn't quite put my finger on what it was.

"You know, I'm still in the room. Do you think someone could take me out to the ditch and see if I can find my wallet and my backpack? Everything I have is in that pack."

"Ditch?"

"The one I woke up in. Under the welcome sign."

The Sheriff's eyebrows knitted together, and I could basically see the cogs turning. "Sure. We'll go take a look out there first thing tomorrow night."

"Why can't we go in the morning?"

Alice laid a hand on my arm and rested her butt on the table. She was looking down at me sympathetically. In my experience, that was never a good sign.

"Mika, we have something to tell you. This is going to sound outrageous and frightening, but I want you to know that we are here for you."

My heart started to race, something in the back of my mind screamed that nothing was going to be the same again.

"Did my pet goldfish die? Are you two getting a divorce?" I deflected awkward situations with sarcasm. My therapist and I were working through it back home.

It was the Sheriff that answered. "No. Well, maybe, I don't know. I've never seen your pet goldfish, but I understand they die quite frequently." Walker ran his hand through his hair, and my hands itched to follow suit. "Look, Mika, I know this is going to sound strange, but it's our opinion that last night, you well, uh, you died."

I laughed. Maybe I'd stumbled into one of those reality TV shows. The producer was going to jump out any minute and make me sign a media release and a Non-Disclosure Agreement.

But the door never opened, and the two people opposite me never cracked a smile. "In case you guys didn't notice, I'm sitting right here, conversing with you. I haven't seen many dead people in my life, but I went to Great Aunt Milly's funeral when I was twelve, and she didn't talk back to me from the coffin."

Alice gripped my hand. There was something off-putting about a doctor holding your hand like you were about to get really bad news.

"What Walker is trying to say, Mika," they kept saying my name over and over like I'd suddenly forgotten it, "is that you are the undead. We believe you have been turned into a vampire. I should say, we *know* you've been turned into a vampire. It's the *how* that we don't understand yet."

I blinked. And then blinked again. They were actually serious. They thought I was a vampire. I'd definitely stumbled onto a TV set. It sounded like something the SyFy channel would come up with. But my heart was thudding, and I felt like I was going to throw up. It was like my body knew they weren't kidding, and it was just waiting for my mind to catch up.

"A vampire?"

Walker nodded sympathetically. "The hunger, the light sensitivity, even the blank spots, are all symptoms of the Turning."

"And you guys know this because..." No, that can't be right. My mind rebelled.

"Because we are vampires. The whole town is populated by vampires."

I stared at them dumbly, expecting something, I'm not sure what. For them to turn into bats, or broodingly sparkle in the overhead fluorescent lights. But nothing happened. They just looked like ordinary people. Not overly pale, their eyes weren't glowing red, they didn't have crooked, needle-like teeth. Nothing.

Alice had mocha-colored skin and smooth blond hair that went all the way down her back. She wasn't unearthly attractive by any means. She was pleasant and professional; exactly what you'd want in a physician. Okay, so Walker was hot, but from what I remembered of the diner, it wasn't like I'd stepped onto the stage at Milan Fashion Week or anything out of the ordinary.

"Do you have any questions?" Walker asked. Uh, yeah, I had a few. Like could he pinch me so I would wake the hell up from this bad acid trip?

"So, I'm a vampire, and you're a vampire. And she's a vampire." He nodded. "Do you, I mean I, have fangs?"

Walker bared his teeth, and there, gleaming white against his pink lips, were two pointed fangs. They were actually quite sharp, and I wondered how he didn't cut his mouth up with them. I looked at Alice, and she too was baring her fangs, which weren't quite as long as Walker's, and sat in her mouth with more ease. I eased my tongue over my own canines and found they'd elongated. I cut my tongue on them, and the blood dripped into my mouth.

Blood.

Hunger clawed at my stomach like a ravenous beast. Suddenly, I understood what the smell coming from the cooler was.

"Please." It was a half yell, half sob, as I dived for the cooler. Walker was around the table in a flash, his arms like iron bands around my body.

"Calm down. Alice is going to get you something to eat right now." As he said it, the Doc was getting a blood bag out of the cooler, like the ones you see in hospitals. She unscrewed the cap on the tube and handed it to me.

Walker released me from his hold, and I closed off the part of my mind that was grossed out at the thought of drinking blood, and let my body take over. I sucked that baby like it was my first cocktail on Spring Break in Cabo. All that was missing was the little umbrella and the frat boys trying to convince me to come to a snow party.

All too soon, the bag was empty. "I want some

more." My voice wasn't weak anymore, but it sounded slurred like I was drunk. Alice shook her head.

"With the two you had at the diner, and now this one, you've had enough. If you gorge yourself, you'll be vomiting for the rest of the night. I'll come see you tomorrow, and we'll discuss how everything works. For the remainder of the night, you need to rest." She picked up the cooler and her doctor's bag. "Are you taking her to your place?" she asked Walker.

He nodded. "I'll find somewhere more permanent for her to live tomorrow." He walked the doctor out, leaving me alone in the windowless room.

The shock settled over me like a numbing cloak. My mind spun as I tried to process, well, everything. I placed my hand on my chest, and my heart was slowly beating in there. Somehow, that made me feel better. I may have been dead, but my heart was still beating. The illogicality of that statement was something I'd deal with another day.

Walker was suddenly back, and his warm hand was on my shoulder. "There are a lot of things we have to discuss, and we can do it here, or back at my place. I know that sounds almost creepy, but I promise you'll be safe." He shifted from foot to foot, almost uncomfortably. "You are new to this world, and I wouldn't feel right about leaving you on your own. There are rules, life or death rules that you need to know. But, if you'd like, we could do it somewhere a bit more comfortable."

I nodded absently, every warning my mother uttered about going home with strange men now defunct. What was the worst that could happen? I was already dead. Plus the guy was the sheriff of a vampire town. If I couldn't trust him, who could a girl, err vampire, trust?

We hopped back into the squad car. I looked at the town through the window in a new light. I really studied the people, their inhuman grace, the fact that there were no children around. A guy stood on the pavement waiting to cross the road, and then magically was on the other side. I didn't even see him move in front of the car.

"Did that guy just teleport? Can we do that?" The thought was exciting. To just close my eyes and picture anywhere I wanted to be in the world, it would be amazing. Such freedom!

"I'm afraid not. He just moved really fast. As your vampirism settles into your body, you'll see him move as slow as a human. We can all move that quickly."

I was disappointed, though moving at super-speed was still pretty cool. "If we can move that fast, why the hell are we driving? Wouldn't we be wherever we are going almost instantly? Unless your house is in Alaska."

"Two reasons. Firstly, I didn't want to freak you out, plus you'll need a bit of time to get used to moving at that speed. Secondly, I enjoy the slower pace that a vehicle has to offer. Just because you can go at breakneck speed, doesn't mean you should." He sounded like my Dad teaching me to drive. Thoughts of my parents made me feel homesick.

"I need to call my parents and tell them I'm okay. Sort of."

Walker looked uncomfortable. "If you want, but just wait until tomorrow. Give everything you'll learn tonight time to process first."

He pulled up in front of a cute little whitewashed cottage, with a wrap-around porch and a perfectly manicured hedge. I looked at the man in the driver's seat and then back at the house. I saw him as the log cabin type of guy, not the gingerbread vibe that this place had going on.

I followed Walker up to the front door. I don't know when I started to think of him as Walker instead of Sheriff Walton, but it was probably around my third dirty fantasy.

When we walked in the space had a bit more of a masculine feel. Leather couches, a big-screen TV, and a scarred wooden coffee table occupied the living room. A large breakfast bar separated the living area from the kitchen, with three old diner stools tucked under the overhang.

Walker went over to the kitchen counter and poured two glasses of scotch into crystal tumblers.

"I can still drink?"

"Sure, you won't get drunk, but sometimes it's nice just to indulge in the nostalgia. You can also eat and go out in the sun. Though I wouldn't suggest going out in the daytime just yet. The increased sensitivity to light makes daylight extremely painful. It's something to work up to over time. Please, have a seat."

I walked over to the big scarred leather armchair. There was a burgundy throw rug over the arm, and I pulled it over my lap, even though I wasn't cold. The softness of the mohair was amazing. I could see the intricate pattern of the weave, the tiny flyaway fibers on each of the strands of wool. It was like my sight had become microscopic.

Walker handed me my drink and sat across from me, his elbows on his knees.

"I know this has been a lot to take in, but you have some serious decisions to make, Mika. This is a whole new world, with all new rules. Especially Dark River. We aren't your average community, as you know."

"Because everyone is the undead."

"Right, because we are all vampires. But it's not just that. Even within our own race, Dark River is rather unique. I'll explain the rules, and then it is up to you if you stay or you go. We can't keep you here against your will."

Well, that sounded ominous.

"Rule number one, there is absolutely no drinking from humans. Blood is delivered and distributed around the town by the Town Council, and no one goes hungry. The penalty is banishment from Dark River, forever."

That didn't sound so bad. It's not like I wanted to go around munching on people, giving them the hickeys from hell. I nodded for him to continue.

"Rule number two, you can never, ever, turn a human. The Town Council has decreed that the penalty for disobeying this rule is death. Because, in our eyes, turning a human is essentially murder." He looked at me imploringly. "This is what has happened to you, Mika. Someone has murdered you, and it is my job to find out who and bring them to justice. You are young, beautiful, and full of life. You should have had the opportunity to do everything you wanted to do. The opportunity to have children, get married, grow old with a loved one, live out in the light. You deserve retribution." His eyes lit up, and I don't mean sparkled with fervor, I mean literally started to glow.

"Uh, Walker, what's going on with your eyes?"

"Sorry. I didn't mean to freak you out. That sometimes happens when we get worked up. Plus I need to feed."

He walked over to the fridge and pulled out a bag of O positive. I knew it was O positive because there was a huge sticker on the side. He poured it into his tumbler on top of his Scotch. Ew.

He sat back down in front of me.

"Okay, the third rule and usually the most problematic for new vampires who want to join our community is that you must cut all ties with your old life, both for our safety and the safety of the people from before. You wouldn't know this yet, but being around humans is..." he let out a shaky sigh, "an overwhelming temptation. Especially when you are only just learning to control your new body."

I collapsed back on the couch. I'd have to cut ties with my family? Never see my mom smile again, or hear my dad tell a lame joke? Never watch my youngest brother graduate high school? Tears welled in my eyes as my death sunk in. My mind was in the denial stage of grief, apparently. I mean, I felt fine now that I'd drank that blood bag. Maybe I could go home and become a goth or something. I lived alone in my apartment, so I could keep the blood hidden.

"I know what you're thinking. Really, I do. But think about it. You will never look older than you do today. You will live hundreds, if not thousands of years. If you go home, you'll watch your parents die, and your siblings, and their children, and then their children's children. Trust me when I say that it is a soul-shattering experience to watch everyone you have ever loved whither and die." The level of pain in his eyes told me that he knew from experience.

I couldn't decide this now, I needed time to think it over.

"What if I choose to leave?"

Walker bit his lip, his fangs pressing into his full lower lip. "If you choose to leave, then you are subject to the rules of the Vampire Nation. No telling humans what you are, or revealing your nature in a way that could bring Vampires as a whole in the lime-light. If you feed on humans, you must do it in a way so that they do not suspect your true nature. Which basically means that unless you have the ability to wipe memories, which some vampires do, you have to kill them and dispose of their bodies discreetly. If you break these rules, Enforcers will come, and you will die. Trust me when I say that Vampire Nation always finds out if you break the rules."

Well, okay, then.

Walker's shaggy hair slipped over his eyes, and he combed it back with his fingers. The move made his shirt pull taut against his chest, and a completely different kind of hunger overtook me. The need to lean over and rip open his shirt was almost impossible to resist.

Walker's eyes met mine, and whatever he saw in them made him look nervous all of a sudden. He stood quickly and took a step away.

"Okay, I'll let you think it over. The guest room is the second door on the left, and the bathroom is right next door. Make yourself at home, if you need anything, just give me a yell." With that, Sheriff Walker Walton hot-footed it out of the room, faster than my eyes could follow.

CHAPTER TWO

When I was little, I was one of those curious kids. I needed to know the why's and how's of everything. It wasn't enough that my parents told me that the sky was blue, I wanted to know why it was blue. When my parents told me that little girls couldn't fly like birds, I'd had to test the theory myself, and broke my wrist jumping off my mother's kitchen counter.

Apparently, I hadn't grown out of this need to test every theory, because when I woke up the next day, I had to pull apart the heavy velvet curtains and check if being in the daylight really hurt as much as Walker had said.

It did.

The searing pain that burned at my eyeballs was excruciating, and I let out a loud screech. Well, I just had to know, didn't I? And apparently, Walker was a master of understatement because this was beyond extremely painful. Getting a tattoo was extremely painful. Childbirth was extremely painful. The pain I felt when I fell back against the floorboards was beyond that. It felt like someone had plucked out my eyeballs and set them on fire.

I thought I was going to vomit as I curled into the fetal position and moaned in pain on the floor. Everything was black, and panic overcame me. Had I just done irreparable damage to my eyes? Would I spend eternity blind because I was a foolish idiot that couldn't take anyone at their word?

The door crashed open, and the scent of Walker permeated throughout the room. "What happened? Oh. You opened the curtains." I looked in the direction of his voice and let out a choked sob. He picked me up off the ground and placed me back in the bed. "The pain will subside in a couple of hours, just relax. I'll get a cool washcloth for your eyes, it helps." His presence was gone from the room, and then returned so quickly, there was a slight breeze across my face. He laid the wet washcloth across my eyes, making tutting noises. His disapproval wasn't necessary; I already felt like an idiot.

He pulled the blankets up around me, tucking me in like a child. My moans of pain had subsided to pitiful whimpers.

"I should have known you were going to be one of those vampires. You turn up, against the odds, in what

I'm sure was a terrible situation, but you aren't a hysterical mess. No, you were all bravado and sass. You have a courageous heart and a stubborn chin. But you have to trust that what I'm telling you is the truth; otherwise, you are going to end up dead. And I don't want that for you."

All I could do was nod and try to stem the flow of tears from my eyes.

"Just rest. I have to go out and run some errands and check the spot where you said you woke up for clues. I'll be back at dusk, and then I'll take you out for dinner to meet the rest of the town."

"How can you go out in the daytime?" It came out like an accusation.

"I'm far older than you, and I have some damn good sunglasses. And a really big hat." I couldn't see his face, but the amusement in his voice led me to believe he was laughing at me.

I huffed as another whisper of wind told me he left the room.

MY SIGHT STARTED to return about four in the afternoon. Although they still stung, I could see enough to make my way out of the room and into the shower. Having a shower with my new senses was beyond divine. I felt each droplet of water pulse against my skin like a lover's caress. When the water eventually ran cold, I reluctantly left the bathroom.

With the exception of my sight at this particular moment, all of my senses had increased tenfold. I could hear someone laughing in the house down the lane. I could smell the roses in Walker's front garden from my bedroom, without a window open. I found myself running my fingertips against every surface because the range of textures had changed so dramatically.

But the inevitable downside was that I was bombarded with stimuli my brain had no chance of processing. I couldn't block anything out. The perfume of the soap in the shower nearly knocked me out. The pipes rattling in the walls was a cacophony. If I couldn't learn to control my senses, I was going to have to live my days in a padded, soundproof room.

I was still wrapped in a towel when the front door opened and closed.

"Mika?" Walker called from the living room.

"In the bedroom," I yelled back.

I eyed my filthy clothes that smelled musty and dirty from lying in a ditch. The smell made me want to heave. There was no way I could put those back on.

Walker strode into the bedroom and stopped dead when he saw me in just a towel. He quickly turned his back.

"Sorry. I see you found the shower." He sounded a little flabbergasted, and for some reason, that made me smile. "I bought you a change of clothes from the boutique in town. Tonight we'll go and pick you up some more, but I thought you'd appreciate a fresh set sooner." He held out the plastic shopping bag and placed it on the floor near the door. "I'll leave you to it. When you're ready, we'll head into town and get you acquainted with the place, and grab a bite to eat."

The mention of food made my stomach growl loudly. I was ravenous again, and even Walker's slow heartbeat sounded enticing. I finally realized what he was trying to tell me yesterday about the temptation of humans. If Walker, another vamp, made my mouth water, then I shuddered to think about my reaction to a human.

Walker left and shut the door, and I picked up the plastic boutique bag. Inside was a soft cotton T-shirt, a cashmere sweater and a pair of jeans, in exactly my size. I briefly wondered how he'd known my size, and decided that it didn't matter. For all I knew, it was a special vampire ability. There was no clean under-wear, which was fine with me because that just would have been weird, but the idea of putting on dirty ones also repulsed me, so I decided to go commando, at least until I could pick up some new ones myself. I pulled on the t-shirt and then slipped the sweater over my head. Its softness was unbelievable.

I lost fifteen minutes just standing there, stroking my sweater like an idiot.

I quickly pulled my hair into an elastic and brushed my teeth with one of the new toothbrushes

Walker had in the bathroom cabinet. I looked at myself with my new sharpened eyesight. My wild hair was still a riot of blond waves, and my skin was still creamy-white with a few freckles across my nose. If only vampirism had gotten rid of my freckles. The biggest change I guess was my eyes. My greenish-blue eyes seemed wider, and the pupils were abnormally large, like a cat at night, or a dancer at a rave party.

I didn't look different, or any more perfect, as Hollywood would have you believe. I still looked like me.

I walked out into the living room to see Walker relaxing in the armchair, his eyes closed and his head tipped back, exposing the long line of his throat. The slow thump of his heartbeat made my limbs tingle, and my stomach churn. It wasn't as lively as a normal heartbeat. It only beat every few seconds, but that was enough to stir a new primal need deep within me. I felt the caged predator that now resided in my blood raise its head and whisper to me.

I let out a cry as my fangs slid down and cut my lower lip. Ouch, dammit!

Walker's eyes snapped open, and he took a deep breath in. Something wild appeared in his eyes, and he inhaled deeply. Holy crap, he could smell my blood. He stood and walked toward the window, and I could see his back heaving as he took several deep, steadying breaths.

"What would happen if you were to drink from me?" My voice sounded too loud in the room.

Walker's shoulders stilled. He turned to look at me, but I could still see him struggling with his nature. "We can drink from each other, but it's not something that should be done without ample preparation. Extra sustenance would have to be taken, control would have to be firmly in place. It is possible for a vampire to be killed if another takes all the blood in their body." He shifted uncomfortably from foot to foot. "Plus, it usually isn't done unless the two vampires are in some kind of relationship. Taking blood can be an extremely intimate act." A blush lit his cheeks, and I resisted the urge to laugh. I had the feeling he was giving me the vampire version of the birds and the bees talk.

"Good to know," I said, trying to keep the smirk off my face. "I'm ready to go now."

Walker looked relieved that that line of questioning was over, and picked up his hat from the floor beside the armchair.

The trip to town was quiet, as I took in everything I could in the fading light. Not that the lack of light seemed to be a problem for me; I could see everything with a clarity that startled me. It was like watching high definition after a lifetime of the fuzzy goodness of Betamax.

"Did you find my stuff?" I was hopeful. My camera, my passports, my life, was in the backpack.

He shook his head.

"There was no sign of it. I got a few scraps of material, and a shoe print from the area, but otherwise it was clean. I have no idea how you ended up in a drain outside the town limits." He sounded frustrated. Well, that made two of us.

I still hadn't decided what to do with my... uh, death. The thought of never seeing my family again tore at my heart. However, the thought of literally tearing at their hearts with my fangs was even worse. So I was doing what I did best. I was stalling until the last possible moment. It was an innate talent. Instead of choosing someone to go to prom with, I went stag. Instead of choosing a Major in college, I'd set out to backpack my way around Canada. Look how well that ended.

He eased the car into a spot outside of Bert and Beatrice's Diner. "Let's go grab something to eat, then we'll figure out the rest." He pushed open the diner door and stood to the side to let me through.

Every set of eyes turned to look at me, and I was getting a strange sense of deja vu. Beatrice was manning the counter today, and she gave me a warm smile.

"Evenin' Mika, Sheriff. Just grab any table, I'll be over to get your order in a minute." She bustled down the other end of the counter to refill the coffee of a man in a tight cable knit sweater with shoulder-length black hair. He was the only person in the room, not staring at me.

Walker placed a hand on my lower back and directed me to an empty booth. There were some hushed murmurs, and then everyone descended at once.

People were in my space, shaking my hand and introducing themselves in a blur of names and faces that I'd have no chance of remembering. Walker was equally as bombarded with questions: who made me, were there any leads in my murder case, did he think it was one of the townspeople?

Two women, who looked to be in their late thirties, were hanging off Walker like two extra limbs.

"Well, I think it's that drifter. When I watch CSI, it's always the drifter." One, I think her name was Lynette, said to the people surrounding our table.

"I thought it was always the husband? Are you married, Honey?" Lynette's shadow asked. I dazedly shook my head. "Well then, maybe you are right. Maybe it is the drifter." Both of their eyes swung to look at the guy in the cable knit. I could see his shoulders were tense, and I was guessing that a) he was the drifter and b) that he had heard every word Lynette and her parrot had said.

I stared at his back and wondered if that was the truth. Was he my murderer?

In a town full of carnivores, anyone could be the

person who stole my life. The people crowded around me now seemed a lot more ominous.

"Ladies, please. What the town doesn't need is idle gossip pointing the finger at innocent people. I will do a thorough investigation, and only when I have found hard evidence, will anyone be charged. This isn't the Wild West, where you string up the new guy first and ask questions later." He gave them a stern look. "Now, if you'll excuse us, I think Mika would like to eat in peace. There's no need to overwhelm her on her first day."

Everyone left us alone for the time being, though I could still feel their collective gaze like a weight on my skin. Beatrice finally made her way over to take our orders.

"Don't worry about it, Lass. By next week, you'll be old news. Now, what can I get you two?" I hadn't even had time to look at the menu in all the hubbub, so when Walker ordered a burger and fries, and a type-O float, I ordered that too.

I was glad I could still eat food. The idea of sustaining myself entirely on blood gave me the heebie-jeebies. I'd always loved food, and you could tell by the snug way I fit into my size twelve jeans. My motto had always been, why deny yourself dessert, when there was a chance you'd be hit by a bus the following day? Luckily, I loved to go running nearly as much as I loved chocolate, so I was still more fit than flab.

"So if I'm immortal, can I still get fat?" It was a shallow question, but there had to be a silver lining to the dead thing, right? If I couldn't grow older, or get sick, surely I couldn't put on weight?

"You remain exactly the way you are when you are turned. Your body ceases all growth. Alice would be better explaining all the medical mumbo-jumbo though."

I resisted the urge to do a little happy dance. Instead, I waved my hand at Beatrice. "Could I get an extra serving of cheese fries and a piece of lemon meringue pie as well please?" Beatrice nodded and scribbled it on her notepad.

I grinned from ear to ear, and Walker shook his head. "You can still get stomach aches, you know."

I didn't care. I felt free for the first time since I hit puberty. No longer did I have to worry about the cheerleaders at school mocking my puppy fat, or being unattractive to the freshman class boys. I didn't have to worry about diabetes, heart disease, obesity. All my food guilt was gone.

When Beatrice placed the bowl of cheese fries on the table in front of me, I fell on it like a demon unchained. It was the most glorious meal I'd ever had, partly because calories didn't matter anymore, and partly because my sense of taste had heightened. It was like a mouth orgasm.

The tall milkshake glass had a deep ruby red

liquid in it, and a hard ball of ice cream floating on top.

It was simultaneously the funniest and most disturbing beverage I'd ever seen. Considering I'd recently seen a hipster with a lumberjack beard have a flaming sambuca shot mishap, well, let's just say, that my Type-O float was really something.

I tried a sip, and then another. I wish I could explain the taste of blood to someone who wasn't a vamp. It was like the very best wine, coffee, and chocolate fondue all rolled into one. I let out a little moan, and Walker's eyes widened. Whoops.

"That's really, really good."

"That's 'cause Beatrice does the best Type-O floats in North America." A deep voice said from over my shoulder. His voice was gravelly, somewhere between a rumble and a growl, and he had a thick southern accent. I turned and looked into the darkest blue eyes I'd ever seen. They were like the night sky right on dusk. My mouth seemed to unhinge, and a little Type-O float dribbled over my lip. The night blue eyes dropped to my lips, and then back to my eyes.

Walker cleared his throat. "Judge. What can I help you with?"

Once my eyes got passed his, I realized he was the man the townspeople called The Drifter. His shaggy black hair hung in waves to his shoulders and looked as if it had been hacked in a restroom mirror. His chest was broad, and the knit sweater wrapped around his shoulders like a present on Christmas morning. He made me salivate.

I gaped. "You're a judge?" That was almost harder to comprehend than the existence of Vampires.

"Just in name, Sugar. I just wanted to set the record straight. I've never seen this girl in my life. Though, I wouldn't mind seein' more of her now." He smirked at me, his pearly white teeth glistening in the fluorescent lights. The smile made something tingle.

"I have no suspects in this matter yet. I am following up all the evidence I've gathered and then I'll interview people."

Uh-huh. What evidence?

Judge nodded. "Well, if the little lady needs a hand with anything, anything at all, don't hesitate to ask. I am more than willin' to show Mika the perks of being a vampire, and help meet any needs she may have." His eyes twinkled with mischief, and I could understand why everyone automatically went to him as the primary suspect in my murder/rebirth. He just oozed bad-boy troublemaker out of his pores.

If only that didn't make me so damn hot.

"She'll be fine." Walker gave him a hard look, and my back arched up a little. Did I suddenly become unable to make my own decisions? Sure, I'd obviously made some bad ones because, hey, I was dead. But generally speaking, I was a good judge of character. I knew that Judge was trouble, but I didn't like being treated like a child.

"Luckily for everyone here, I have a voice of my own. Thanks for the offer Judge, I'll keep it in mind."

Judge grinned and touched two fingers to his forehead as he left. It was an old-world gesture, and it made me wonder what age Judge actually was. He didn't look more than twenty-five, but if we stopped aging, he could be centuries old, millennia even. I watched his ass as he left, and if there was ever a finer butt in the world, I had yet to see it. He must have been some kind of laborer when he was turned because his body was that lean musculature you could only get through hard, physical work. I sighed as he melted into the darkness beyond the streetlights

"If you are quite done, we are late to meet Alice, and I still want to take you out to where you woke up, see if you can remember anything."

Walker sounded pissed, but he could just eat me. I made my own damn decisions. I raised one eyebrow challengingly, as I slurped down the rest of my float. When Walker threw down a twenty, I again felt bad.

"Is there a way I can get at my money? I can't keep letting you pay for stuff."

"We'll figure it out late. It's no big deal." Walker held the door open for me, and we stepped out onto the brightly lit pavement. The light posts were the town's originals, ornate gas lamp style, and they emitted a warm golden glow. The night sky was so beautiful this far into the wilderness.

"Alice's practice is on the other side of the town square. We'll walk if you like." We crossed the road, although there was no traffic. Why bother when you could super speed everywhere.

"Have you made a decision about staying?"

I heaved out a sigh. Giving up my family, my life back home, it would be like dying all over again. "I'm not sure. What would I have to do, exactly?"

"Cut off all ties with your old life, change your identity, swear to uphold the values of the town. We have people that help you with the transition, of course. People who will work you up some new documents and help you adjust to our lifestyle. There are three months of compulsory therapy, as well. We'll set you up with a job within the town, so you can earn a living. You can go on trips and leave town, of course, this isn't a prison, but you have to have an escort for the first six months until you have the initial thirst under control. We learned that one the hard way." There was a sadness in his voice, and I sensed a story around that.

"How long has the town been here? I assume it didn't start out a vampire colony." Getting trades-people in would have been a nightmare.

"It was abandoned by humans about a hundred and fifty years ago after the gold boom was over. Five or so vampires bought it with a vision of a better life for us, one out of the shadows. So far, it has worked well. Every year we have one or two new vampires petition to join the town."

We walked the rest of the way in silence. I had a lot to think over, and I was getting hungry again. And not just for blood. I was going to have to ask Alice if this overwhelming need to rip off Walker's clothes and ravish him was something to do with being a vampire or my normal hormones. Let's face it, I probably would have had a hard time resisting him if I'd stumbled into town human.

"What happens when humans come through? Surely they must realize something is off?"

He nodded. "It's been known to happen, even though we are completely off the beaten track up here. We aren't on the road to anywhere, and we have no accommodation. So in most cases, they come into the gas station, fuel up and move on. Or they'll stop in at the diner and Bert will make them something absolutely abhorrent and they'll leave. This isn't an inviting town for the weary traveler."

It wasn't an inviting town for anyone with a normal heart rate and their mortality intact. There was probably a good chance you wouldn't get out alive.

CHAPTER THREE

"So, you'll need to feed every twelve to eighteen hours for the first fifty years, after which the thirst begins to subside, and you can drink less. Your body no longer produces its own blood, so a steady diet of blood, while your organs adjust, is essential. If you plan on losing any, for whatever reason, you'll need to either stock up beforehand, or replace it immediately. It is possible for vampires to die of exsanguination."

Alice had pulled out one of those medical mannequins and had pointed to all the differences my new vampire status had given me. For instance, not only could I run faster and live forever, my body was now less limited. I could jump higher and further, my strength was almost limitless, I could see like an owl in the dark, and my sense of smell was akin to a bloodhound. For all intents and purposes, I was now a superman, minus the lycra and the flying, much to my chagrin. During the discussion about my increased libido, Walker had excused himself on Sheriff business, promising to return for me later.

"Your new senses will be overwhelming for a while, so I suggest you adjust to coming out in the day slowly. A lot of the older vampires can walk around during the day without a problem, but I suggest you try coming out into the light a little at a time. Maybe try a minute or two earlier each day. Don't push it, you can do serious damage to yourself that will take decades to repair. You are lucky you only exposed yourself to the light for a few seconds earlier." She made a tsking noise while shining a light into my eyes. Artificial light didn't seem to burn my eyes like sunlight. "Also, your sex drive is going to be in hyperdrive for a few months, maybe even years. Sometimes even decades. I suggest you find yourself a bed partner or start a running tab over at the Stop'n'Shop for double D batteries. For vampires, our heightened predatory senses want us to hunt and obliterate our prey. When we deny that urge, we compensate by giving into another animalistic instinct. To mate, and mate a lot. But no humans. Ever. Biting and sex are now intrinsically linked. I don't have to elaborate on how that could go bad."

I just stared at her. None of my human doctors

ever prescribed getting laid. Well, that explained why I looked at Walker like he was a block of chocolate, and I was on the Paleo diet. My mind wandered to Judge. Now I know what he'd been offering, and why Walker was so uptight about it. Thinking about the hard lines of Judge's torso made parts of my own body clench in a way I didn't know was possible.

Alice packed me up with a little cooler full of blood bags and a pamphlet that was aptly named 'So You're a Vampire, Now What?' There were diagrams and everything. Though, why the town had a doctor was beyond me. If no one got sick, and I was an anomaly, then what did she do all day?

The doctor's office was a two-story building, the lower level built from stone, and the upper levels were vertical pine cladding. The whole town looked like someone had hewn it from the surrounding wilderness.

The town was centered around a central square, and it looked like someone had recreated a Monet painting. A whimsical bridge crossed a large pond, and there was an ornate rotunda sat off to one side. Large poplar trees spread their branches, and cement benches provided quiet little nooks for lovers and friends. The town had strung fairy lights through the trees and around the rotunda, and it looked magical.

"I see you are enjoying our little piece of paradise." I whipped around, my hand clasped to my chest. A lady in her late fifties, her dark hair streaked with grey, stood behind me smiling. She looked like a dark-haired, Helen Mirin. Her smile was warm and welcoming.

"You must be Mika. I am Catherine, one of the founders of the town. Welcome to Dark River." She had one of those faces that seemed familiar. Like she was your next-door neighbor as a child, or your kindergarten teacher or librarian or something. She just made you feel fuzzy.

"Thank you. It's been a bit of a whirlwind."

We continued walking across the square. "The situation of your turning is most regrettable. Have you thought about staying in town?"

I bit my lip, my fangs pressing sharply. "I'm still undecided. The town is beautiful though. You have done a wonderful job. Everyone is so nice."

She patted my arm fondly. "We are a close-knit group. I don't think anyone from Dark River could have done such an awful thing. It must have been an outsider who dropped you here because they knew we would care for you."

Like the unwanted baby drop bin at a fire station.

Don't think you can care for your undead offspring? Safely deposit it in the baby vamp drop drain under the sign!

I just smiled tightly. We reached the edge of the town square, and I saw Walker talking to a woman with really, really big hair. Like Jersey big.

"There's Walker. It's been nice meeting you, Catherine." The woman inclined her head and gave me a little finger wave.

I really wanted to try the superspeed thing, like the guy last night, and I thought this was a safe place to try it. Although I had no idea what I was doing, I figured it would be like learning to walk. I'd just instinctively know.

I concentrated on my feet and then ran as fast as I could across the empty road. I was across in a split second, my focus intent on Walker, but I had no idea how to stop. My feet were moving too fast for me to put on the brakes, and I plowed straight into the Sheriff, knocking us both down onto the pavement. His arms wrapped around my waist to stop my momentum, and we landed with a thud.

"Oh shit. I'm so sorry. I just wanted to try running like *The Flash*. Are you okay?" It all came out in one large run of words as I looked him over for injuries. As I realized he was okay, the predator noted our position, and the hardness of Walker's body beneath mine, and the hunger overwhelmed me. I dropped my face to his neck and inhaled the scent of his blood. It was like I had taken a back seat to my predator's baser urges, who just wanted to bite into Walker's neck and hump him into next week.

I vaguely heard someone saying my name over the steady rush of Walker's blood through his veins. Two strong hands pushed me away.

"Snap out of it, Mika!"

I reared back and noted the crowd of people around us. Blood rushed to my face. If Walker hadn't stopped me, I would have bitten and sexed him up in front of half the town. I scrambled off his body. I had nearly violated the town sheriff. No one in the crowd looked outraged though, they just looked at me with expressions of sympathy, and some with straight up pity. I wanted to run away.

"I'm sorry. I'm so sorry."

I shot to my feet and ran as fast as my new legs could carry me. Which turned out to be really fast. I stopped when the soles of my converses started to melt. The smell of the burned rubber was acrid in my nostrils.

I realized I was back at the WELCOME TO DARK RIVER sign. The reality of my new life crashed over me. If I couldn't control myself with Walker, how was I meant to control myself with my family? Alice had told me it would take decades for me to get my hunger under control. Was I going to go back to them, having not aged a day, and say, "Mom, Dad, I'm home!" But the thought of hurting them burned like acid in my gut. No matter what I did, they would feel pain. Physically or emotionally. I'd accepted all this so easily because I foolishly thought that I would be different. I would have better control than all the rest, and I could go home, see my family again. I'd been fooling myself.

Someone had done this to me, to them, and there was no going back. Rage burned up my body, and I screamed. I walked over to one of the towering pine trees and punched it as hard as I could. Someone had stolen my life without any thought of how much it would hurt the ones I loved. They would never have closure, always wondering if I would just wander back through the door, or stare at the phone every time it rang, hoping it was me. The unfairness of it all made me hit the tree trunk harder and harder until it cracked ominously and fell.

I sat down against the trunk of the tree and sobbed. Every sob seemed to tear loose a little piece of my heart.

"You'd make a killin' as a lumberjack." The deep gravelly voice that whispered out of the darkness was already familiar. He was the last person I wanted to see. I wanted to wallow in my self-pity without wanting to jump anyone's bones.

I just let out an inhuman growl. The sound made me cry more.

"Jesus, Sugar, don't cry. I'm a Southerner, I don't deal well with tears." Judge sat down next to me and patted my shoulder awkwardly.

I wrapped my arms around my knees and cried harder into my lap.

"It's not so bad. If you had to be turned anywhere, this isn't a bad place to end up. Trust me on this, Sugar. There are places far worse for a baby vamp to be than Dark River. The cities are littered with rival clans, some in the throes of all-out war. Toss in the Council Enforcers killing you for even a little slip, and the fact that you have to fend for yourself, and Dark River is a damn paradise in comparison. A little Stepford for my tastes, but I can understand what they were trying to achieve. Though, you are quite the fly in their idyllic little ointment. One of them must have broken the first and second commandments. Thou shall not drink a human dry and then desperately try to cover up your mistakes by making them a vamp. It would have almost been better if you'd stayed dead, for the town at least."

I stiffened at his words. His tone wasn't threatening, but his words sent a shiver down my spine. I edged away, and he laughed.

"C'mon. You can't think it was me? I don't have that kind of conscience. If I'd actually drained you dry, I would have buried you in the woods and hightailed it outta town. My moral code isn't that squeaky clean."

He had a point. "Why do you stay if you are so scathing of the system?"

Judge shrugged and slipped a cigarette from the packet in his pocket. "No system is perfect, but so far, this is the best the Vamps have achieved. I haven't drunk the Kool-aid yet, but I adhere to their rules, and they let me stay. Maybe I'll commit to the pledge, and get a cozy little job at the service station soon, or maybe I'll move on. I haven't decided."

Make that two of us. The smell of the tobacco made me want to gag. "That's disgusting. How can you stand the smell?"

"You get used to it after a while. Besides, it adds to my devil-may-care demeanor, don't ya think?" His hooded gaze and his one-sided smirk made me think all sorts of dirty thoughts. Thank God for cigarettes, or I probably would have tried to assault him like I had Walker on the pavement. We sat in the silence of the night, which actually wasn't very silent. Owls screeched in the darkness, and something skittered in the trees far above us. A wolf howled somewhere in the distance and was echoed by the howl of a second.

The blue and red flash signaled the police car pulling up on the shoulder of the road. Judge stood and tipped his imaginary hat. "Seems your white knight has arrived. I'll see you 'round."

With that, he disappeared back into the darkness.

My knuckles had already started to heal, and the only real evidence of my little outburst was the blood splattered on my t-shirt.

"I can hear you out there, Mika. You have no reason to be embarrassed. It happens to everyone." God, this sounded like my mother consoling me after I wet the bed when I was six. I stepped out of the surrounding woods just so he would stop.

I walked over to the storm drain where I woke up.

It was smaller than I remembered, and the thought of someone stuffing me in that cylindrical coffin made my cheese fries turn in my stomach.

"Last night's rain had washed away some of the physical evidence, and I couldn't pick up any scent except yours. That in itself means that we are dealing with someone of quite an age. Learning to mask your scent takes centuries of practice. We have a fang width measurement, but you'd already started healing by the time you got to town, so it's not as accurate as I would have liked. Also, the person who has done this has the ability to mind wipe, which again points to an elderly vamp. Most keep the ability a secret. We're a secretive bunch." He sighed and dragged his hand over his face. He seemed to do that a lot.

"I'm not going to lie to you, with evidence this sparse, it's going to be hard to catch the person who did this to you. I am praying that it was an outsider. I don't want to think that someone from the town could have done this. It hasn't happened in nearly two centuries."

I could hear the desperation in his voice, as he clung to the hope that it wasn't someone he knew, that he had breakfast with, that he'd chatted about ball scores over pints with.

"I wonder where my stuff has gone?" I knew I shouldn't cling to my backpack filled with clothes that needed a wash, and a worn pair of flip flops, but it felt like I had nothing left of my old life.

Walker shrugged. "I went over the area with a fine-tooth comb during the daylight, but I found nothing."

We searched the area together once more and then decided to call it a night. I felt emotionally raw, but somewhere in my emotional explosion, I had made a decision. I wouldn't risk my family and friends lives. If I were just declared missing, they would eventually move on. I needed to do what was best for all of us, and having their blood on my hands would haunt me for eternity. Literally.

I was silent on the ride back to town, lost in my own thoughts. I knew I'd have to make a decision this year, but I thought it would be about whether to join a sorority, or whether to do pre-med or pre-law.

"I've made my decision," I said into the silence of the police cruiser.

Walker didn't take his eyes off the road. "Yes?"

"I've decided I want to break from my old life and live in Dark River if you will have me. Even though, somewhere, one of them could possibly be my maker, I can't spend my life in fear. So, make me pledge allegiance, or recite *I'm A Little Teacup* naked, or whatever the process is, so I can start moving on from this shit storm."

I let the anger bubble up under my skin. All my life I had been the good girl, the peacemaker, and look where I ended up. My new life was going to be different. I was going to be different. I wasn't going to be obedient, I wasn't going to conform. I was going to be who I was supposed to be, the person I'd buried deep beneath social expectations. Because you only live once, well twice, and I wasn't going to spend eternity being a doormat.

CHAPTER FOUR

W hen we'd finally gotten back to town, Walker pulled up in front of a bakery. The lights inside the Immortal Cupcake Bakery were blazing, and as I stood on the footpath, I fell in love.

The bakery had split windows, the bottom half intricate leadlight designs in the shape of the sun rising over the ocean, and the top was normal glass. The other window had a panorama of golden horses running across a green meadow, and the detail took my breath away. They were works of art.

Once you stepped through the heavy oak door, with its ornate lion's head door knocker, you stepped into the heavenly aroma of freshly baked cookies. Straight in front of the door, were large glass cabinets filled with every delectable pastry you could think of. Cookies were stacked high in jars, perfectly frosted cupcakes sat like sculptures on sliding racks. Danishes and individual fruit pies sat side by side next to the world's most ornate chocolate cake. Fresh breadsticks were packed into wicker baskets, and crusty baguettes were filled with meat and salads and wrapped in decorative paper and tied with a string.

I'd just died and come to carb heaven. Walker gave me a little nudge, and I walked between the tables. I noticed an archway, and through it were floor to ceiling bookcases, jammed with everything from romance novels to leather-bound tomes. A gold railing ran across the top of the cases, a shiny mahogany ladder hooking over it.

"I'm really dead, aren't I? Because I'm pretty sure this place can't possibly exist outside of heaven."

"I don't know about that. My devil's food cake is positively sinful," someone laughed beside me. Wow, these people were really stealthy. I turned to look at a shortish woman, with curling red hair that stuck up at odd angles on her head. She looked Irish, with her shining blue eyes and ruddy skin. Maybe in her mid-twenties, but I knew she would be far older than that. Her teeth were slightly crooked, but her smile was wide and warm.

Walker leaned over and kissed the woman on the cheek. "Mika, I'd like you to meet Angeline. Owner, operator, and baking goddess of this little piece of temptation." There was genuine warmth in his tone, and I briefly wondered if he and Angeline were a couple. Jealousy surged within me before I realized how stupid that would be. This was a small town, and if Doc Alice was right, it was a small town full of people with overactive sex drives. Did I honestly think Walker had been sitting around waiting for me to die? Plus, there was something about Angeline that made me want to hug her. Maybe it was that she smelled of sugar and chocolate. But I wanted to be friends with her. I knew that instantly.

"I think I might love you," I blurted out. "This place is amazing." Angeline laughed, and it was warm and deep.

"And you haven't even tried my *mille-feuille* yet. Usually, the declarations of love come after that." They must have been good because Walker let out a little groan of appreciation. She plucked a cupcake out of the case. It had an impossibly high buttercream crown, complete with shiny silver sugar sprinkles. When she handed it to me, I could only stare.

"One for the road. Let me show you around." She walked through the archway. "Walker tells me that you are considering staying in Dark River, and as such, would need a job within the town. I just happen to need a projectionist/librarian for the shop. Now that I bake all the bread for Bert and Beatrice's diner, I don't have as much time as I did. I'm run off my feet." She stopped and eyed me still gazing reverently at the cupcake. "Don't just stare at it, take a bite, Sweetie. The real magic is in the first mouthful."

I did what I was told, peeling back the delicate foil

paper and taking a large bite. I let out a moan that resounded around the room. "Oh. My. Freaking. God. This tastes like unicorns vomited rainbows and carebears onto my tongue, and everyone is having a party. This is the best thing I have ever put in my mouth." I wasn't exaggerating. I took another slow bite, savoring the taste and then another. And another. Angeline and Walker waited patiently for me to finish eating. Walker looked amused and reached out to wipe pink icing off my nose.

"I'll do it."

Both Walker and Angeline looked confused. "Do what, Sweetpea?" Angeline, the baking goddess, asked.

"Whatever you want. Be your librarian/projectionist, sell you my kidneys, give you my firstborn, whatever you want. Just pay me in cupcakes." Angeline laughed and rubbed my back.

"That won't be necessary. I'll pay you a real wage. It'll be small, but you can have the apartment above the store for free. I lived there up until a few years ago, when I decided I wanted a little cabin out in the woods where I could enjoy nature."

Walker scoffed. "Little cabin, my butt. Your place has an industrial kitchen and a jacuzzi in nearly every room."

Angeline punched Walker's arm. "Who said I couldn't enjoy nature in a bubbling outdoor hot tub set at a perfect 104 degrees?"

As they bantered, I looked around the room. Apart from the books that lined the walls, there was a large white screen taking up the entire back wall, bracketed by deep red velvet curtains. A state of the art projector was fixed to the roof. Behind me was an open fire that smoldered low in the grate. I breathed a heavy sigh. I could be happy here.

"I'll do it. I can't thank you enough." I gave in to the urge and hugged her tightly. She wrapped her arms around my shoulders and hugged me back.

"No need to thank me. It's what we do here in Dark River," she said warmly. "Now, I was going to offer you the apartment, regardless of whether you took the job or not, so the townspeople have pulled together a few things to help you on your way into a new life. Just little things, clothes, shoes, some toiletries, and makeup. I took most of my kitchenware with me, so Bert and Beatrice gave you some of their old stuff, some old pots and pans. However, all my furniture is still up there, so you should be fine for now. If you want to change anything, go ahead. It's your home now." She pulled a set of keys out of her apron and handed them to me.

Tears welled in my eyes, and I worried I was going to break down right here in the shop. But I'd embarrassed myself enough for one day, so I blinked rapidly and just muttered a thank you. Angeline patted my arm gently. "Think nothing of it. Now go check out your new digs. Just go through the kitchen and up the backstairs. There's a back entrance as well, so you don't have to traipse through the shop all the time."

She shooed me away and went to serve a customer who had been waiting patiently. I didn't blame him. I would wait an eternity for one of Angeline's cupcakes.

At the back of the kitchen were internal stairs that led to the second story. A security door at the top made sure no one could just wander back from the store and into the apartment.

Now that I had met Angeline, I knew the apartment itself would be beautiful, but nothing prepared me for the enveloping warmth that washed over me when I stepped into the room and switched on the light. Polished timber floorboards gleamed under an ornate chandelier. The couch was a comfy dark leather, and when I ran my hand across the back, it was butter soft beneath my fingertips. A massive Persian rug, hopefully, a knockoff, designated the living space, in front of the hearth. Although there was a state of the art gas heater, the idea of sitting in front of a real log fire, drinking wine and reading a book had definite appeal. Two doors led off the living space, probably to the bedroom and bathroom, and straight in front of me was a large open plan kitchen. I'd been expecting an industrial kitchen, but in hindsight, that would have been ridiculous considering she had a commercial kitchen downstairs. Polished granite benchtops lined the walls, and an island bench with a dark wood top sat in the middle of the kitchen. The island was big enough that you could eat at it, doubling as a breakfast bar.

I headed back into the bedroom and found it basically bare except for an old wrought iron bed, and a solid chest of drawers. I imagined most of the decorative stuff that would have made this room feel homey went with Angeline when she moved. I looked forward to making the space mine eventually.

Walker was still standing near the door, and I saw there were several boxes next to him. "This is the stuff from the townspeople. Everyone donated what they could, and you should find some linen and things in there for tonight. There are some clothes and boots, we guessed the size, but enough until you get your first paycheck. Angeline said she'll pay you in advance, once you are all signed up and an official citizen of Dark River." The town's generosity was overwhelming. I opened the lid on one of the boxes, and I saw a beautiful quilt in purple and blue. I pulled it out and marveled at it. It was a work of art. It would have cost a fortune to buy in the store.

"That's from some of the quilting circle girls. Don't worry, they have dozens of them. Eternity can equal a lot of quilts. They sell a lot of them on eBay to pay for new supplies. Before you look further, I have two more gifts, and then I'll let you settle into your new place."

He pulled a black garment bag. "Ella over at

Baroque, which is the town boutique, said that if you decided you wanted to join, you should have something nice for the ceremony, so this is her welcome gift for you." I took the hanger from him and unzipped it to peek inside. It was a beautiful red lace dress, and I couldn't wait to get it out of the box.

"And this is a welcome gift from me." He handed me a cellphone box with a big white bow on top. "Just because we are in the middle of nowhere, doesn't mean you have to be out of touch with the world. My number is on the post-it note inside. Hopefully, I don't have to warn you not to do anything silly like calling your parents or going on your Facebook to change your status to 'dead'. Nothing traceable back to your old life."

I nodded a little glumly. That hard piece of plastic and glass made me depressed. Well, at least I could still play Candy Crush.

Walker stuck his hat back on his head, even though the sun had gone to bed hours ago. "Also, you might want to put some thought into what your new name might be. There is power in a name. We have to change them every eighty years or so, but you always remember your first." With a finger wave, he left, and I was alone.

I dragged the boxes further into the living room. I started unpacking them, giving myself no time to dwell on the past. What I would give for my iPod right now, some angry as sin prog-rock, and I'd forget all my troubles at least for a little while.

One whole box was from Bert and Beatrice at the diner. Slightly chipped, mismatched plates were wrapped in yesterday's newspaper. Unwrapping each individual piece was like Christmas morning. Did vampires even celebrate Christmas? Some pots and soda glasses came out next, and buried at the bottom of it was a bottle of red wine. Bless their sweet hearts. I poured myself a glass of wine into a soda glass and carried it into the kitchen where I stacked away all my new kitchenware. I realized there was an old 1960's style radio on top of the fridge, and I pulled it down. I turned the dial but got only static. Moving it steadily, I listened for the slight change in white noise that signaled a channel. Wow, I really didn't know how good I had it, with auto-scan tuning. Hell, with digital radio.

The only channel I got was a golden oldies station, with no DJ. That suited me just fine. With Joe Cocker telling me that I'd get by with a little help from my friends, I felt infinitely better. Soon the apartment started to take shape. I made the bed and put the clothes in the drawers. They were a strange mish-mash of clothing styles. Some looked straight from the puritan era, with long skirts and high necklines, but mostly it was a lot of old jeans and t-shirts, a few wool knit jumpers and a thick wool jacket.

I hadn't seen the bathroom yet, but when I walked

in, I was equally as in love with it as I was with the rest of the apartment. A clawfoot tub took pride of place straight in front of the door. Long brass taps affixed to the wall. Above it, a showerhead jutted out of exposed copper piping. A deep granite bowl on a pedestal was the sink. The toilet was the only new thing in the bathroom, everything else looked turn of the century.

I walked back into the bedroom and collapsed on the bed. I wiggled the phone out of my front pocket and stared at it. I knew my parent's numbers off by heart. We'd lived in the same house since I was born. I knew that phone number better than my own brother's birth date. My finger itched to dial just so I could hear their voices one more time.

I threw the phone away from me before temptation overwhelmed me. There was a knock at the door.

"Who is it?" I called out. I'd been to college, and watched slasher movies. The moral of those stories was always ask who's at the door, and hope the masked serial killer says, "It's a masked serial killer."

"Angeline. I brought you up some dinner, in case you are hungry."

The thought of food made my stomach rumble, and I hurried over to let Angeline in. She looked around the room.

"Looks like you are settling in alright. It's just a couple of baguettes leftover from today, but I thought you might want to stay in tonight." She was right.

After today's little exhibition on the pavement with Walker, I wasn't quite ready to face the townspeople at the diner.

I took the sandwiches she offered and put them in the fridge. Walker had already put my blood bags in there.

I looked over at Angeline, who'd sat down on the couch. I poured another soda glass of wine and handed it to her as I sat in the recliner.

"I have to choose a new name, but it's really hard. I couldn't name our family dog, let alone myself."

She nodded knowingly. "I always choose a name that I think will sound good when shouted out in climax. Angeline!"

Wine sprayed all over my shirt as I let out a snort of laughter. It did sound good when she shouted it out like that.

"Give it a go," Angeline suggested.

"Emma!" I let out a little giggle.

Angeline shook her head. "Nah, I don't think so. Too boring. You're a vampire now, a supernatural being with an almost immortal life span. Have fun with it, girl."

"Phoenix! Nope, too cliché."

"Oh I know, Vixen!" Her imitations of the male climax were getting deeper and more gruff. I had the giggles now.

"Well, that does sound good, but I think Vixen

might be a bit of a wild name to be saddled with for eighty years. How about Raine?"

She took a sip of her wine and thought it over. "I think it's perfect. Raine it is. The number crunchers will generate you a last name." She reached over and clinked our soda glasses.

"To Raine, and new beginnings."

To fresh starts.

CHAPTER FIVE

As it turns out, becoming a citizen of Dark River was a lot like a shotgun wedding.

I stood in the courthouse, in a red lace dress. Walker stood next to me, like a proud father giving me away.

The town council consisted of five old vamps. I mean, they didn't look old, one looked like he was twenty. But the weight of their collective age hung oppressively in the small room. I shifted from foot to foot nervously. This was like being called into the Dean's office, times five. Only Catherine smiled at me, the rest of the Council were pointedly neutral.

"Walker has informed us that you have decided to join us here permanently in Dark River. Has it been made clear to you what citizenship entails? Your duties and responsibilities?"

"Yes, it seems pretty straight forward. Start a new life, don't eat humans, don't turn humans. Got it."

The younger vamp laughed. "I do so enjoy having new blood come into our community. It gives everyone a new lease on life. We might try and stay up-to-date with all the new slang and outlooks, but sometimes we can become so horribly antiquated." He had a thick accent that sounded like old English. Or maybe he was just speaking proper English. Both sounded foreign to my ear.

"And do you accept these responsibilities?" Another woman asked. Her face looked around my age, but her eyes seemed ancient in a way that only people who have seen a lot of pain and misery can.

I swallowed hard. This was it. After this, there would be no going back to being Mika McKellen.

"Yes."

Catherine smiled. "Excellent, from this day forth, you will be known as," she looked down at a sheet of paper in front of her, "Raine Baxter, citizen of Dark River, Alberta." This time they all smiled, and the effect was almost as terrifying as their silence. They slid a manila envelope across to me. "There is your new identification, including a social security number, driver's license, and anything else you may need. Angeline tells me that you've accepted the job at The Immortal Cupcake, and rented out the apartment above the store. Is everything to your liking?"

I thought about my first day of work yesterday.

Turns out, everyone wanted to come in and check out some books. Or check out me. I'd been so busy that the day flew by. I'd barely had time to suck down a blood bag and maul a cupcake on my lunch break. Every night, well morning, at three A.M, a movie would play on the overhead projector. I'd loved the movie catalog. There had been everything from today's blockbusters, to the classics of the golden era.

Last night had been Casablanca night, and each ticket came with a complimentary themed cupcake. In this case, it was a coconut and rum cupcake with pineapple icing, based on the Casablanca cocktail. I'd eaten four.

Back in the present, I smiled and nodded to the group. "Everyone has been amazing. Thank you."

A man who actually looked ancient nodded back sternly. Actually, dressed in a black hooded cloak, he looked a little like the Grim Reaper. "Walker tells us that he hasn't made much progress with your murder case. I hope they catch whoever did this. Although we welcome you to our town, we wish the circumstances weren't so unfortunate."

Yeah, you and me both buddy.

Outwardly, I just thanked him for his kind words.

We headed over to Bert and Beatrice's after the ceremony was over. I'd signed all of the documents, made all the pledges, vowed to follow the rules on pain of death, blah blah blah.

When I stepped into the diner, I stopped dead.

The place had been transformed. There were Happy Birthday banners and people wearing party hats.

"We might have to go to Angeline's place. I think they are having a party here," I whispered over my shoulder to Walker. When he didn't say anything, I turned to look at him. He was grinning widely.

"It's your party. Happy Rebirthday, Raine Baxter." He laughed at my expression. I could feel the stunned mullet look on my face. Everyone was looking at me intently, and then Beatrice pushed out of the kitchen, followed by Angeline, who carried a huge stand of her cupcakes.

"There she is, the girl of the hour! Sit down Lass, this is your big day." Beatrice pushed me toward a table that had a balloon patterned tablecloth and a huge pink hat. She snapped the party hat on my head with enough force to sting my chin. Angeline put the tower of cupcakes on the counter and came over to hug me. Most of the faces seemed familiar now. There were only a few hundred people in the town.

"Wow." I was bewildered, to say the least. There must have been fifty people jammed into the diner. Even Judge was there, tucked in the far back corner. He tipped his imaginary hat to me, and I gave him a wan smile.

Walker's strong, tan hand came down onto my shoulder and squeezed. "I know this is a hard day for you, giving up everything you were. But we wanted you to know that you aren't alone and that we are all here for you. We've all stood where you are today, and know how hard it is. So, we wanted to celebrate, and there's no better way than with a party at the diner."

I wanted to cry. So I did. Grief and relief warred within me. I dropped my face into my hands and sobbed. This may have been my birthday, but it was also the funeral of Mika McKellen. I had to mourn the girl I could have been.

Walker pulled me into his arms and patted my back until my tears subsided. I took a few deep breaths until I was no longer letting out hiccupy sobs. "I'm sorry," I told the room.

"Tsch, love, it's fine. It's your party, and you can cry if you want to, isn't that how the song goes? But enough of that. You have a century to grieve for your old life. Today should be a celebration. Unless you plan on being one of those moody vampires the younger ones are always quackin' on about? Edward someone?" Beatrice said, pushing my hair back from my face.

I laughed, then screwed up my nose. No *Twilight* references, ever.

Someone put the jukebox on, and music spread through the room. Bert, who didn't seem to say much but followed orders well, started bringing out trays of sandwiches, cheese fries, mini burgers and savory pastries from the kitchen and placed them along the counter. Everyone came over to offer their congratulations.

Ella, who had given me the dress, came over and told me how beautiful I looked. I couldn't thank her enough for her kindness. "Don't worry about it. You just come over if you want to buy yourself some clothes. A girl has to have her own style, I think. We'll flick through the catalogs and order in any style you like. I'll start you a tab until you get paid." We talked a bit more, and I learned that she'd been a vamp for over a hundred years.

The woman with big hair that I'd seen Walker talking to the day I'd violated him on the footpath came over and introduced herself as Cresta. She handed me an envelope with a gift voucher. "Sometimes, it's nice to reinvent yourself. Come around any time, and I'll give you a makeover."

It sounded fun, though Doc Alice had told me that my hair wouldn't regrow at the same rate, and neither would my fingernails.

"That sounds great. I'll definitely take you up on that."

The rest of the night passed in a blur of names and faces, laughter and good food. Someone cracked the champagne, and although the alcohol wouldn't affect me, it didn't really feel like a celebration without it. The sun was just lightening the horizon when Judge strolled up to stand next to me. Everyone seemed to have forgotten that they'd accused him of my murder less than three days ago, but thus was the nature of small towns.

"Well, Sugar, this has been quite the shindig. Seems the town has embraced you with open arms." He was standing close to me, and I breathed in his spicy scent. Almost instantly, my body tightened and my fangs elongated. My body craved, and it wanted Judge more than its next bag of blood.

"I was surprised you came," I purred. I was actually shocked at myself. I had never been a sex kitten, but the way my voice had dropped and my lashes fluttered, I was really turning it up.

"Well, I couldn't miss the birthday of my favorite citizen of Dark River, could I?" His voice was low, and heat radiated from his innocuous words.

I wanted him, wanted him like a cheeseburger at one a.m. after a big night of tequila shots. I looked over my shoulder at Walker, who was laughing at something Angeline was saying. The light hit his face just right, making his hair shine and his eyes sparkle. He looked so pure and earnest. Judge, on the other hand, made my body combust, and I was hungry. His eyes were hooded, and he stepped closer, so I could feel the energy around his body seep into mine.

"Sugar, if you don't stop starin' at me like that, one of two things will happen. One, I'll put my hands up under that pretty dress of yours, push you against the wall and make love to you right here in front of the town." I sucked in a gasp, and all the heat from my body dropped to my nether regions.

"Two, the Sheriff over there will notice that you

are eye-fuckin' me with enough heat to cook a hash-brown, and one or both of us will end up in the lockup tonight for indecency, or whatever else he can cook up to make sure I don't climb on top of all those sweet curves and play with your body like it's a wonderland."

My mind fritzed. Like when your computer just freezes, and no matter what you do, you just can't get it working again. All I could picture was Judge's naked chest pressed against mine, his mouth nibbling at my tender flesh, my teeth piercing the throbbing pulse point in his neck. Judge let out a groan.

"Dear lord, you smell like Christmas right now. Sugar, please, please tell me you want me to come home with you tonight, because otherwise, I might just explode." He actually sounded like he was in pain, and he shifted uncomfortably from foot to foot.

I looked down, and I could see the jean-clad reason he was uncomfortable. Woah.

I had a little moment of panic. This wasn't what I did. I didn't go home with guys I barely knew. I stuck to those cosmopolitan ordained rules; four dates before you release the goodies. Mika McKellen was no slut. I was a good girl through and through.

But I wasn't Mika anymore. I didn't have to stick by the rules to protect my image, to make my parents proud.

Raine could have her beefcake and eat it too.

"Do you know where my apartment is?" My

whisper was barely audible. I was in a room full of vamps with supernatural hearing. A normal whisper would have been like yelling across the room.

Judge nodded.

"Meet me there, after this is all over?"

Judge nodded again and bent to kiss my hand. His lips were softer than I imagined, and hotter, and the brief touch made my heart race. He gave me another hot look, turned and left the party. Walker and Angeline turned to watch him go, Walker looking suspicious. Angeline looked at my rosy cheeks and waggled her eyebrows. That made me blush harder. I needed a cupcake.

I launched my face into the buttercream with abandon, and Doc Alice came to stand next to me. "Well, I'll be. I was sure you were going to go after the good Sheriff, but watching that little exchange with the drifter, I can see why you'd be attracted to the bad boys. Now drink this." She handed me a bag of Type O, which she must have had on her body somewhere. What was she, a walking blood bank? I obediently downed the blood, and Doc Alice gave a little nod. "Now I don't have to worry that you'll get too carried away and get exsanguination. Now go, say your goodbyes, and chase down that hunk 'o' vampire. If I were a little younger, I'd probably race you." She laughed and walked away.

Although I didn't race out the door like I wanted to, I did start the rounds of goodbyes, saying thank you to all my new friends. They'd made the effort to come and support me today, I wasn't just going to run out because I now shared my body with an extremely horny predator. I left Walker and Angeline 'til last, hoping that Judge's exit had faded from their mind. Still, my cheeks flushed when I said goodbye. I hugged them both.

"Thanks for this, guys. Thanks for everything. Today would have been one of the most miserable in my existence if it wasn't for you two. But now I'm pooped. I think I'll just go home to bed."

"Well, I hope you have a good *sleep*," Angeline grinned. "I'll see you at five."

Walker was frowning, and he kept opening his mouth then snapping it shut. Finally, he sighed. "Be safe." Was that a touch of jealousy on his face, or was it wishful thinking on my behalf?

I didn't think I had enough blood in my body to blush this hard, but every inch of flesh from my feet to the roots of my hair went pink. I just nodded, mumbled my goodbyes and escaped out of there as fast as I could.

I whisked to my back door and barely got my key in the door before I felt Judge. He was a step or two behind me, but the energy changed when he was around. I looked over my shoulder and smiled. I felt the predator lift her head, felt the wild lust spread through my limbs, making me tingle. Judge growled and stepped into my body, spinning me and pinning me against the door. His lips were on mine.

His tongue pushed into my mouth, and I moaned as he ran it over my fangs. He grabbed my ass and lifted me off the ground, and I wrapped my legs around his trim hips. He held me effortlessly with one arm and finished unlocking the door with the other. We only made it a few steps into the room, before Judge was pushing me back up against the wall. He unzipped the back of my dress until I stood there in my cotton bra and panties. Not exactly the sexiest lingerie, but at this point, I was beyond caring.

I threaded my fingers through his hair, pulling his head back slightly so I could bite his lower lip. He groaned loudly, and pulled back, making my fangs cut his lip. When the taste of his blood hit my tongue, something came over me, something I couldn't control, and didn't really want to control.

We were on the couch in a blink of an eye, and I rolled on top of him. I tore at his clothes like an animal, needing to feel his skin beneath my fingers. Judge was just as wild, tearing my bra off so his mouth could find the aching peaks of my breasts. I pressed my body close, so he could draw me deeper, and I felt the slight prick of his fangs piercing my breast. When he started to draw my blood, my tight nipple still in his mouth, I lost all coherency. I writhed against his erection, still annoyingly covered by his jeans. I rubbed my aching flesh against him, the delicious friction building and building until I cried out, my breaths coming in pants.

I'd had orgasms before, I was no wilting virgin, but that was something else entirely. It was a wonder I didn't burst a blood vessel in my eye, it was that intense. All I could mutter was a gasping, "Wow."

Judge pulled away, a self-assured grin on his face. "Oh darlin', you ain't seen nothing yet."

He flipped me on my back so quickly the breath was knocked from my lungs. Or perhaps it was because he had shucked his clothes in record speed and was standing in front of me in all his naked glory. Because that man was definitely glorious. There wasn't an ounce of fat on his body, but he wasn't muscle-bound. He was sleek edges, and his long corded thighs made me want to weep at the beauty of them. I eyed him greedily, and he stood there and let my eyes wander. And the guy was impressively endowed. He wasn't going to give Seabiscuit a run for his money, but I still wet my lips at the sight.

He prowled forward and knelt beside me on the couch. He reached for my panties and peeled them off gently like he was unwrapping a delicate present. His gaze traveled down my naked body, and his eyes seared my skin where they landed. I wasn't even self-conscious, because there was so much desire in his expression that I felt like the sexiest woman on the planet.

"Mmm, beautiful." His voice was now only a low

rumble, filled with lust. He grabbed my hips and pulled me onto the floor with him.

Pulling me onto his lap, my wetness coated his hard cock, and his eyes rolled back in his head as he moaned.

"Has anyone taught you to feed from a person, darlin'?"

I shook my head as I kissed my way across his jaw and bit his chin gently. His moans were a deep rumble, almost a purr. "I'll teach you. Find that spot, you'll know it naturally." He tilted his head to the side, giving me better access to the delicate flesh of his throat. My heart started to thump in time with the beating of his pulse. "Suck it into your mouth, and then bite down gently. Your itty bitty fangs will do all the hard work. Once you've pierced the skin, wrap your lips around it and suck. I'll tell you when to stop. I got you."

I did as he said, sucking his pulse point into my mouth. I felt it beat against my tongue, and my fangs slid into his skin of their own accord. Sucking hard, I dragged the first mouthful of blood and moaned. It was indescribable.

As I continued to draw, Judge lifted my hips and slid his shaft into my aching body. It felt so good I almost let go of the suction on his neck. His own moan vibrated against my mouth, and he started to move, his body pumping into me in time with my pulls against his vein.

One of his hands captured my wrist, and I felt his fangs puncture the skin there. His own long draws as he sucked my wrist matched my own, and soon we were a perfect dance of pushing and pulling, sucking and fucking. I was no longer Mika. I was no longer anyone but this hedonistic creature who desired it all and took what she needed.

I felt my orgasm creep up, building, filling me up. Judge released my wrist and stuck his finger in my mouth, releasing the suction from his neck. I mewled at the loss, but his hand threaded in my hair, keeping me from launching back against his neck, back to the delicious nectar of his blood.

"Lick the wound." His voice was guttural, barely coherent, but I did what he said. The bleeding stopped instantly. He pulled my face to his mouth and his tongue thrust in and out of my mouth in time with his cock. He tasted of blood and sex.

He fucked me faster and harder, our bodies a tangle of fevered kiss and roaming hands. My orgasm crashed over me like a baseball bat, colors flashing behind my eyes as my body stiffened with wave after wave of pleasure. Judge's yell quickly followed, burying himself deep in my body as his muscles spasmed.

I collapsed against him, my body wrung dry. He leaned back against the couch, snaking his arms around my waist to hold me loosely against him.

"Holy fucking shit," I panted out. My lungs

heaved for breath as if I had just run a marathon. I went to roll off him, but he held me firm against him. I laid my head against his shoulder, and he nuzzled my hair.

"Is sex always going to be like that?"

One of his hands dropped to my ass, and he gave it a love tap. "It will be with me, Rainy Day. Every. Damn. Time."

I could hear the smugness in his voice, and it made me smile. "I'm happy to test that theory."

He stood up, and I twined my legs around his waist and felt him growing hard inside me again. He moved us to the bed. I nuzzled his neck again, dying to taste him on my tongue.

"Nuh, uh, Sugar. No more of that or neither of us will be able to get outta bed tomorrow. I'm gonna make love to your delicious body all night, human-style." With that, he dropped us both on the bed, and we made love "human style" until we both passed out from exhaustion.

I WASN'T SURPRISED to wake up the next evening and find Judge gone from his side of the bed. I could smell his scent on the sheets, but the bed was cold. Judge was a drifter, and if that didn't scream commitment issues, then nothing did. He was never going to get up and cook me breakfast. A slow grin spread across my face. I didn't even care. I was blissfully sore from head to toe, and I felt fulfilled in a way I never had before.

I'd had a few boyfriends in college. Everyone from football scholarship jocks to the art majors. Some were even great in bed. But I had never, in my life, imagined that sex could be like that. If normal people compared the big O to fireworks, then what I'd experienced last night was an atom bomb. Every cell in my body rushed with pleasure.

I looked at the clock and groaned. I had to get up and go to work. I stood stiffly and shuffled to the shower.

CHAPTER SIX

W hen I finally walked gingerly down the back stairs into the kitchen of the bakery, I was greeted by the smiling face of Angeline.

"Well, someone looks like they had a good night." I just grinned smugly back. I'd had an amazing night. But a lady never kissed and told.

Angeline handed me a croissant, crisp and flaky golden pastry falling across my boobs as I nibbled it delicately.

"Okay, get out of here. Ella's expecting you."

I blinked a few times.

"Huh?"

"I'm giving you the day off. Think of it as a belated turning present. A makeover is just what every girl needs at such an important turning point in her life. Now, skedaddle!"

I wandered across the square to the boutique,

greeting the vaguely familiar townspeople as I passed. The lights of the boutique lit up the mannequins in the front window, all dressed in the most recent styles. A little brass bell dingled over the door when I walked in.

"Hello?"

I could hear Ella moving around at the back of the store. "I'll be with you in a minute, Raine." I looked around the store to see who she was talking to before I remembered that I was Raine. It was going to take some adjustment. I still thought of myself as Mika. Now I knew how my pet dog Buddy had felt when we had gotten him from the pound at the age of six or so. We'd call him, and he'd look at us like we were strange. Obviously, he'd had an entirely different name for all of his life. But he eventually learned, with the help of dog treats and belly rubs.

Maybe I could get Judge to rub my belly while yelling out my name.

Ella appeared from between the racks. "Heya Raine. How're things?" She bustled around, straightening items on clothes hangers, putting them in order of size and color. She was a constant hive of activity.

"Angeline said you were expecting me." I trailed around after her as she moved through the shop.

"Oh, yeah. We decided after you left last night, that you might need a day to find Raine in the ashes of Mika. I know my own turning was difficult, and I found it hard to reconcile myself with who I was now.

I wasn't the slave girl from Athens anymore. I was a powerful predator. This was a long time ago, and well before I came to the town. Back then, you could keep your name for the first hundred, two hundred years."

Holy crap. Ella looked twenty if she was a day. She had long, dark, curly hair that hung down her back in ringlets and deep brown eyes. Her skin was a golden bronze, and now that she'd told me, I could see her Greek ancestry.

She led me to an antique chaise lounge. She looked me up and down intently, staring at me as if she was trying to judge the very nature of my soul.

"Okay, get undressed."

"Excuse me?" Apparently, I'd woken up in the twilight zone. Or a high-class brothel, if all this velvet was anything to go by.

"Not here, silly. In the change room. I think I've got a grasp on a style that will suit the new you. I'll hand you some outfits, and you tell me which ones you really like. And I mean *really* like. There is no room for politeness in a wardrobe makeover." She grabbed my hand and pulled me out of the chair with ease that belied her small frame. She shoved me towards a dressing room with heavy velvet curtains and was out amongst the racks before the curtain had closed behind me. I sighed and slipped out of my jeans and t-shirt. If you can't beat them, join them.

Outfit after outfit snaked its way through the curtain and I obediently tried on every single one.

There seemed to be something from every era. Long flowing dresses in the softest chiffon, with beaded empire waists. A pencil skirt with a pretty peach-colored blouse, then a bohemian style skirt and peasant blouse, followed by a floral dress with a full skirt and pretty purple petticoats. I tried them all on and paraded myself out of the dressing room at the end of every outfit change.

Ella didn't say much, just eyeing me like I was a masterpiece that wasn't quite right and then disappearing back amongst the racks of clothes. I was starting to get weary, as the next outfit popped through the opening. A pair of black jeans, a tank with tiny cherries all over it and a neckline that plunged dangerously low, and a short black leather jacket with intricate gold buckles. I knew, before I even put it on, that this was it. I slipped into the jeans that molded to my body like a second skin, and the tank scooped deep to showcase the tops of my breasts.

I never would have worn this back home. Back then, I followed the trends, the ugly pastels, the blinding neon of the early '00s, pretty feminine sundresses in the summer, and blue jeans and sweaters in the winter. I was a truly All-American girl.

This girl looked like a rock goddess. She didn't take any crap, she drank what she wanted to drink, ate what she wanted to eat, and screwed who she wanted to screw. She – no I – was unapologetically me. I walked out of the dressing room into Ella's waiting gaze.

"Spin." I turned on my toes like a ballerina. When I'd finished my three-sixty twirl, Ella was nodding. "This is it. How do you feel?"

I grinned. "Strong, kickass, and if I do say so, pretty goddamn sexy."

"Perfect!" She rushed away and reappeared with a pair of black combat boots. They had a series of tiny gold studs in swirling patterns. The insides were lined with some kind of faux fur. "These will finish it off just nice. I love it when fashion and practicality collide." I slipped on the boots and the jacket and gazed at my reflection in the mirror. I looked hot, but not just sexy hot, I looked mysterious and confident.

"Come back in when you can tolerate the light a bit more, and I'll get you the cutest pair of Ray-Bans with specialty lenses."

She bagged up all my old clothes and sent me out the door. "Head on over to Cresta's. She's expecting you. I'll put your new purchases on your tab. You ever see anything you like in the magazines, let me know, and I'll get them in." The woman hustled me to the door and then back onto the street. She was like a tiny whirlwind.

Cresta's Beauty Solutions was two doors down from the boutique. I could smell the coffee brewing from the front of the boutique.

Warm air rushed against my face as I pushed

open the heavy wooden door. The salon was in a narrow building. A long leather couch ran along one wall, and an old scarred oak desk sat in front of the door, a laptop propped open on its top. At the back was a single partition wall with a huge gilt mirror, that took up most of the wall space. A leather hairdresser's stool on wheels sat beside a tall, scarred wooden stool in front of the mirror. Cresta stumbled around the partition wall, yawning.

"Raine! It's good to see you. Wow, I see you've been to Ella's place. You look smokin' chicky!" I didn't know if she was naturally loud, or if my new, improved hearing was just ratcheting everything up a notch.

I slid the gift voucher out of my pocket and onto the desk. She just pulled me over to the leather chair. "I tell you, seventy years I've been running this store, and I still hate having to start so early. I swear, my brain doesn't even kick into gear until midnight. Want a coffee? I'll make you a latte." She went back behind the partition, and she continued to talk without even pausing. "I bought one of those state-of-the-art coffee makers last year, and I swear, I am in love. It does everything short of making me scrambled eggs in the morning. The problem is, now I drink way too much caffeine. I must have ten cups a day. Oh well, it isn't like it's going to give me high blood pressure, right?"

I didn't know if she wanted an answer to that or not, so I just hummed agreeably. Given the rate she could burn through words, she could probably lay off the caffeine.

I started to tune her out, not because I wanted to be rude, but because my brain just couldn't process the amount of words pouring out of her mouth. Have you ever had one of those moments when you are looking at someone's mouth, watching them speak, and still have absolutely no idea what they are saying? I had that problem a lot when I dated a biology major about a year ago.

Apparently, Cresta didn't require any answers to whatever she was saying, because she returned to my side of the partition with a travel mug. It had a picture of a sleeping kitten on the side. I took a sip and sighed. Apparently, drinking a dozen coffees a day didn't make you a great barista. She must have put a triple shot in it because I swear I could hear the blood hum in my ears.

Cresta stared at me intently, cocking her head from one side to the other.

"Okay. I've got it. You trust me, don't you Raine?"

I narrowed my eyes. Why do people even ask that? It always made me instantly suspicious that something terrible was going to happen.

Seeing my hesitancy, Cresta gave me her most winning smile. "I promise, I'm not going to shave your head ala, Britney. It takes us a decade to grow back an inch of hair, so I don't do many cuts. Ten years is a long time to have a bad haircut, you know? But I'm going to try something different, something that will compliment your hot new look. If you hate it, we can fix it straight away. I swear on my coffee machine." She put her hand over her heart, and I laughed.

"Okay, okay. I trust your vision. Besides, you only live once, right?" That joke was never going to get old.

Cresta looked like a kid let loose with a can of paint and a blank wall. She buzzed around with single-minded intensity. She pulled a string, and a velvet curtain fell across the mirror.

"No peeking until the end," she tutted before thrusting a magazine into my hands. She flitted off around the partition. There was a lot of rustles and clangs, and I swear I heard her cackle.

By the time she appeared, I was fully immersed in the scandal of a starlet going off the rails and cheating on her superstar boyfriend with the producer of her last film. I know it was trash, and I was perpetuating a culture of voyeurism and stupidity, etc. But it was either that or staring at the velvet curtain. Cresta was strangely silent when she was working. Like an artist working on their masterpiece, she was completely focused. And super fast. I could only catch blurred glances of her hands moving in my peripheral vision.

All too soon, she stuck me under a thing that kind of looked like my Mom's air fryer. It felt a little like that too. I had more foil in my hair than crazy Earl back home, who quite frequently wore tinfoil hats that made him look like a giant Hershey's kiss. Thinking of Earl made me homesick.

I closed my eyes and blanked my mind. I wasn't going to cry in the salon.

I must have dozed off under the dryer because when I woke up to the sound of an egg timer chiming, I smelled like singed carpet.

"Hey, Sleepyhead! I think you're all done. Oh, I can hardly wait. You are going to look like a goddess. I love makeovers!"

She was grinning as she unwrapped the foil from my hair like it was Christmas. I liked Cresta. She sparkled like a diamond, and her enthusiasm was infectious. I'd never be as extroverted as Cresta's little finger. We were different people. While I wasn't exactly a wallflower, I was a more relaxed type of outgoing. I loved people but didn't need to be the center of attention. I couldn't see that changing, despite the makeover.

"How'd you end up in Dark River?"

Cresta made the perfect hair stylist. You just wanted to talk to her, even if you did get overwhelmed with words. Silence just didn't seem natural with her.

"Oh that's a long story, you don't want to hear that ancient history. And quite boring, actually. Not nearly as intriguing as your own turning." She waved a hand, but I could hear the eagerness in her voice. She wanted to tell me but was being polite.

"I would love to hear it if you want to tell it." I always found good manners was a bit of a dance. There were certain steps, little white lies if you will, that you had to tell in order to maintain your manners. I found out the hard way when I told my mother's best friend she looked like a poodle after a really bad perm. In five-year-old me's defense, it was a truly horrendous perm.

"Oh, well if you want to hear it, Chicky."

Turns out, Cresta was a ladies maid in England when she was turned in the sixteen hundreds. A guest of the household was a vampire, although the master of the house had no idea. When the vampire drank too deep, he had a fit of remorse and turned her. Her sire was one of those who had the ability to wipe memories. Apparently, Cresta had inherited that ability too. I filed that little tidbit away.

So, Cresta had traveled with her 'family' for several centuries, until they got too big. Some of her brothers and sisters branched off and made their own families, and continued to travel around the globe, eating, drinking, and partying like they were going to live forever. But Cresta was sick of the constant need to be on the road, and when she'd heard about Dark River, she'd moved here. She opened a salon a couple of years later and had been here for the last century.

I remembered what Walker had said, about my maker being able to wipe memories, and stiffened. Could Cresta have been my maker? It would explain her generosity, and it would be a tale similar to her own making. It all fit, but no matter how hard I tried, I couldn't see the woman buzzing around me, plucking me off the side of the road and draining me dry. She seemed happy here. I didn't think she would do anything to jeopardize it. I would still tell Walker my suspicions, even if my gut said no.

I found myself telling Cresta about my own life before I'd come to Canada. About my folks, and my brothers. I told her about my wild college freshman year, and how I'd tried to break out of my self-imposed good girl persona but failed miserably, always being the friend holding up my roommate's hair as she threw up, instead of making out in darkened corners. I told her about doing everything I was expected to do; maintain good grades, join campus societies that would look good on my resume, date good looking pre-med students, volunteering to help with anything that was asked. I told her how it all seemed like such a waste now. My only true act of rebellion had been this trip to Canada instead of choosing a Major. And look how that ended.

Cresta made all the appropriate noises, moving from torturing my hair into submission with a curling wand to doing my makeup. She honestly sounded as if she couldn't hear enough about my old life. Asking me questions about past boyfriends, and what college was like, what the hell Twitter was. It was like she was soaking in my life, trying to live vicariously through me.

It was cathartic. Now someone else knew about my old life, I could let it go. That my memories wouldn't die if something happened to me. That there would be someone else out there, who would know all of Mika McKellen's hopes and fears.

"Alright, Chicky. I'm done. Now if you hate it, we can change it. No problems. But I have to say you look fantastic. The best makeover I've done in a century." She beamed down at me, her face alight with pleasure. All I felt were nerves raking down my gut. I hoped I loved it. I didn't want to break Cresta's heart after she'd been so nice to me.

"I'm sure I'll love it. Let's see!"

Cresta pulled the cord to raise the curtain, an agonizing inch at a time. My jaw dropped, and I blinked.

I hardly recognized the person in the mirror. I know that sounds cliché, but she was so far removed from my old look, with my dirty blond hair and pale blue eyes. Staring back at me was a person that could be only described as a bombshell.

Cresta had dyed my hair an ombre red, starting out cherry red and then gradually darkening to a deep blood red. The cherry red of my hair was mirrored in my lipstick, and she'd given me dark smokey eyes that made the blue of my irises turn almost icy. My makeup had contoured my face, highlighting my cheekbones like never before. I looked svelte and pouty, sexy in a way that wasn't overdone. I looked exactly how I'd always dreamed I could, but never been game enough to try.

"It's...wow!"

Cresta squealed and clapped her hands together with delight. She grabbed my jacket and put it on.

"I'm closing the salon early. I want to be there when Angeline sees you. I'm texting Ella to meet us at the Immortal Cupcake. They are just going to die when they see you!" She rushed out the back, texting furiously, and returned with her own jacket.

I felt like I'd fallen down a rabbit hole and ended up with three fairy godmothers. Eat your heart out, Cinderella.

The short trip across the square was a surreal experience. People stopped and complimented me on how beautiful I was. I'd been called cute, pretty and other variations of lukewarm compliments that you give people who were not unattractive but not stunning. No one had ever used the word beautiful though. My cheeks flushed red, but deep down, I was sucking up the praise like a neglected puppy.

The Immortal Cupcake was having its lunch rush, and when I walked in, everyone stopped silent, and I was suddenly the center of attention. I kind of wanted to hide behind Cresta until everyone returned to what they were doing.

Angeline was grinning from ear to ear. "You look so amazing! Do you like it?"

"I love it."

I blushed from head to toe when I noticed Walker off to the side, staring with his eyebrows raised and his mouth slightly agape. Next to him was another extremely attractive stranger who was staring at me with overt appreciation. I stared back. He had long black hair, black almond-shaped eyes, and deep olive skin. His strong, straight nose and high cheekbones marked him as a native American. Or Aboriginal Canadian? Adjusting to the fact that I was now Canadian was more difficult than adjusting to being a vampire. Whatever he was, he was fine, with a capital F.

What was it about this town? Did they only let in the good looking ones? I thought about Bert at the diner. Maybe not. Fortunately, everyone was talking again, thank God.

I cocked my head to the side. In the hubbub of the cafe, something seemed different. It took me a while to work it out. Amongst all the slow thumps of the vampires' pulses was a faster beating heart. It was beating overtime, even too fast for a human. My eyes shot to the stranger, and my fangs extended.

The stranger curled his upper lip. "Don't look at me like I'm a hamburger, Deathdealer. You're hot, but I'm not looking to be anyone's dinner."

I whacked a hand over my mouth. Walker punched the stranger's arm.

"Don't talk to her like that, Brody. She's new. Not even a week old."

The stranger, Brody, shrugged and grinned. Not quite an apology, but not his earlier snarl either. Walker just shook his head.

"Raine, meet Brody. The best tracker in this part of Canada."

"In any part of Canada," Brody corrected, a smug grin lighting up his face.

Walker rolled his eyes. "He's also a shapeshifter, which is cheating, in my opinion."

"You're just put out because I tracked down that mountain lion last year before you. You've got skills, Sheriff, but no one can out-hunt a shifter." He elbowed Walker good-naturedly, and I could sense the friendship between the two.

I stuck out my hand. "It's a pleasure to meet you."

Brody shook it, and I pulled away with a gasp. His skin was so hot, it was like he was running a fever. I looked at him with wide eyes.

"First time touching something that's alive since your turning?"

I nodded. I was still alive, wasn't I? I had a heart-beat, so that made me alive, despite what Brody was insinuating.

Walker filled in the gaps, just like he always did. "Because our hearts beat slower, our core temperature is lower, so our skin is cooler. You haven't noticed yet because everyone here has the same body temperature as you. Brody also runs a little hotter than the normal human as well, which is why he seems especially hot."

"That's what the ladies tell me." Brody winked.

Walker shook his head. "Brody is here to see if he can't track down your pack or anything that belonged to you. Maybe he can get a scent of it where I failed."

It looked like it physically hurt for him to say that in front of his friend, and judging by the shit-eating grin on Brody's face, it was going to be an admission that he wouldn't soon forget.

Brody stepped forward. "May I?" His face was all business now. I nodded, although I had no idea what he was asking permission to do.

He leaned forward and stuck his face where my neck touched my shoulder and breathed in deeply. The touch of his skin almost burned, and my blood stirred at his proximity. I held myself tightly in check, even though every instinct I had wanted to throw him on a table and taste him. He pulled back and sneezed.

Nothing breaks a girl out of a lust cycle than realizing a guy is allergic to you.

"Just got the hair-do, hey? I can't pick up anything there. All I can smell is the ammonia." He sneezed again. He dropped to his knees in front of me, and I looked down in shock. He was a tall guy and kneeling in front of me, his head sat just under my breasts.

The predator in me was back, and heat was rushing south, pooling somewhere low and totally inappropriate. Brody looked up at me, lust flashing in his gaze for a second before it was back to pure business.

"May I?" I nodded and held my breath as he lifted my shirt and nuzzled the skin of my stomach, taking in a long, loud draw of air. I swallowed compulsively, trying to keep my lust in check, but failing miserably. My vamp was aroused, and she craved the shapeshifter's blood, or body, whatever she could get. My fangs ached almost as much as other parts of my body right now. Brody let out a little growl as his nose twitched. He stood quickly, stepping away from me in the process. He gave me one long, hot look and then turned to Walker.

"I've got it. I'll head out now and let you know if I find anything in a couple of days." Brody nodded to me, and the group of women behind me, and was out of the room. As soon as he was across the road and into the square, the air blurred. Where the handsome Brody had once stood, there was now a small, silver fox. It darted quickly into the darkness.

"That guy really lights my fire," someone said from behind me. I couldn't have agreed more.

CHAPTER SEVEN

I felt like I'd shed my skin, emerged from my cocoon, risen again. Whatever cliché you wanted to use, I sloughed off who I was, and settled into my new life and my new persona. I was now everything that I wished I could be, and it felt liberating. I made friends but didn't agree with everything they said just to ensure their friendship. I said what I thought, ate what I liked, and put myself first every time. There were no strings on me. I was free.

For the next three days, I went about my new life with unabashed abandon. I got my first real paycheck, and after paying my rent and all the tabs the town had given me, I blew the rest on designer sunglasses, vinyl records from eBay, beer, and cupcakes.

I didn't have to worry about making good grades, going to bed early so I could make my early classes, paying off my college debts. I never had to worry about walking alone at night or eating a balanced diet. Maybe as I settled into my life, worries would probably emerge, but for now, I was like a teenager who had just realized that I could stay up as long as I liked. Liberation from earthly turmoil felt great.

Judge had returned to town two days after my makeover, looking stressed and pale, but not wanting to talk about it. Instead, we'd made love until the sun had set in the sky. We'd talked about nonsensical things, nothing serious, and he'd stood and dressed, kissing me on the forehead and left without another word.

The old me would have fretted about this. I'd be plagued for days about what it meant. Didn't he like me? Was I bad in bed? Was he getting tired of me? Was I too fat? Too thin? Was he just using me?

But you know what? These days I didn't even care. So what if he was using me? I was definitely using him, for his body and his blood. So what if I was too thin or fat? There was nothing I could do about it now, I was this way forever. I'd embraced myself in a way that I never thought possible.

Everything was going well, so when Walker had walked into the library of the Immortal Cupcake looking grim, my stomach dropped.

I clenched my jaw and continued to put away books. I wasn't ready for my new found carefree lifestyle to be over.

Walker cleared his throat. "Raine, could I have a moment?"

I took a deep breath and let the tension flow from my body. I didn't think that he would just go away if I ignored him for long enough.

"Sure, Walker. What's up? Coming to arrest me for jaywalking? Because I swear, I thought it was a crosswalk. Maybe I was woozy from blood loss."

"I think I can let it slide this once." He gave me a strained smile. "Can we sit?" I moved over to the old chesterfield couches and sank into the leather, letting it embrace me like a hug.

"Mika McKellan has been formally declared missing. The fax came through to the station today."

I tried to stay detached, but it was like a sucker-punch. My parents would be beside themselves with worry. Family would fly in from all over because that's what the McKellen's did in a crisis. Aunt Rose would come and cook a dozen casseroles and pot roasts. Uncle Stew would probably go down to KwikCopy and order a dozen fliers and get his six sons to post every pole in my old town as if anyone there would know where I'd disappeared too. Maybe some of my cousins would fly to Canada to try and track me down. Everyone would be frantic, praying at church for my safe return, because that's the kind of Catholics we were. We ignored church except for weddings, funerals, and times of crisis.

They were crying and praying, and I was in the

middle of nowhere, with the audacity to enjoy my new life.

I closed in on myself, frantically trying to prevent the wall around my heart from cracking. The one that I told myself would come down by itself as time went by, and I forgot about this initial pain.

The bell over the door tinkled, and Brody swaggered in. I swallowed back my tears; for some reason, I didn't want Brody to see me cry. He'd never met Mika, he'd only known the flame-haired Raine. I wanted to maintain that image for him for some strange reason. I gave him a bright, fake smile.

He gave me a long look, and strode over, dodging the other inhabitants of the cafe with preternatural ease. He lifted me out of the chesterfield, wrapped me in his arms in a hug that encompassed all of me, and sat down, pulling me onto his lap, his arms never loosening. Pressed against this stranger's chest, I let the tears fall again.

He stroked my hair and whispered things in his native language that I didn't understand but were reassuring nevertheless.

"The smell of your sadness burns my nose. It is okay to let it out, let your sadness be free, it is the only way to heal," he whispered against my hair. My legs were curled up against my chest, creating a protective ball around my heart.

I seemed to spend a lot of time crying into the chests of random men. A wave of embarrassment flooded me and snapped me out of my pity party of one.

I wiggled off Brody's lap, and he let me go. I sat next to him on the couch, and he slung an arm across the backrest.

"So, what do I do now?" My voice was chopping from the sniffing.

"Nothing. Just go about your life as normal. You look so different from the girl who first stepped through the doors of Bert and Beatrice's, that if the authorities walked right past you, I doubt they'd make the connection."

"I found your things buried in a national park almost two hundred miles away."

My head whipped towards Brody. "Did it tell you anything? Was all my stuff there? Did you bring it back with you?" He shook his head as I fired questions at him.

"I found no concrete evidence. I'm sorry, Raine, but I thought it was best to leave it all there. If the authorities find it there, they'll have no reason to come to Dark River. Someone had buried it, but I placed it back on the surface. Maybe a hiker will find it one day, but it's pretty deep in the woods. Give your family some kind of closure."

So they'd think I was dead and buried in a forest somewhere. Sadness ran like acid in my veins. Brody squeezed me to his side.

"I got you this though." He reached into the

inside pocket of his fleece-lined jacket and pulled out my camera bag.

The tears, this time, were happy ones. My Dad had bought me the camera as a graduation gift after my senior year of high school. It was a proper professional DSLR camera, and I'd loved it. I'd filled up memory card after memory card with photos, of my family and friends, of college and my home town. I flipped it open, and there, tucked securely in a zippered pocket, was all my memory cards. I'd never deleted a photo. It was a catalog of my life.

I launched myself at Brody, wrapping my arms around his neck. "Thank you, thank you, thank you." This had been beyond thoughtful. He'd given me something small, a little bit of my old life that I could look back on, but it felt huge.

He patted my back hard and let out a little grunt. "Not so tight. Some of us still need to breathe." I jumped back, but I couldn't wipe the grin from my face.

"This was really nice of you. I owe you one."

Brody grinned. "Let's just hope that no hunters saw a wolf trotting around the woods with a camera around his neck, or we'll have those Twilight nuts around these woods searching for Caleb, or Jacob or whatever the hell that kid's name was."

The image made me laugh out loud.

Walker squeezed my shoulder and left to talk to Angeline. I was starting to think that Walker had a serious thing for Angeline. I didn't want to examine the burning feeling in my chest that came on the heels of that thought.

Brody put his feet up on the coffee table. "What's the movie and cupcake theme tonight? I may as well kick back here for a couple of hours and head home when you lot migrate indoors for the day."

I stood and looked at the schedule. A small laugh bubbled up in my throat, and by the time it broke free of my lips, it was a full-blown guffaw.

"An American Werewolf in London."

He groaned. "You're kidding, right?"

All I could do was laugh harder.

AT ANGELINE'S NOD, I covered the snoring Brody with the mohair blanket from the back of the leather couch. The dawn was just painting the horizon. So much for his big plans to head home at daylight.

The last of the customers had headed home, full of lattes and pastry, and Angeline was switching off the lights.

"I'll see you this afternoon, Raine," she called as she hurried out the door. I waved and finished putting the chairs away out the back. I liked the calmness of the early morning. Unless Judge was here, the time before sleep could be torturous. Better to wear myself out until I fall into a dreamless nothingness.

By the time the store was back to its well-ordered

state, the bright morning sun was over the horizon and shining through the stained glass, painting the room in glorious technicolor. I was trying to stand in the sunlight for a few minutes at a time, gradually extending the duration. The sun dawned bright and happy, it was going to be a nice, sunny day in the mountains. I missed the sun. My eyes began to sting, so I turned and walked up the stairs to my apartment. Time for a bag of O neg and then snuggling up under the comforter.

Pushing my key into the door, lethargy weighed down my limbs. I wanted to skip the blood and just head to bed, but Doc Alice had been very specific about my daily intake requirements. I trudged into the darkened kitchen and over to the fridge. Seeing row after row of neatly bagged blood was no longer disconcerting. I guess I was adapting.

I'd just turned back towards the bedroom when the kitchen blinds were wrenched open, the bright sun searing my eyes.

I screamed and dropped the blood on the floor. Everything went white as the light burned my retinas. Someone was behind me, holding me to the light.

"If you know what is good for you, you'll find a way to get the Sheriff to drop his investigations." A voice growled, deep and unrecognizable. I tried to slam my eyelids shut, but I couldn't physically make them move. "You've got it good. I made you, and I can break you just as easily."

With that, my attacker let me go, and I dropped to the floor. I curled into a ball, trying to protect my eyes. It had only been fifteen seconds at the most, but every second had been like someone spearing electric shocks into my eyeballs.

Tears streamed down my face, and I heard a thump as someone burst through my front door.

"Raine? RAINE!" Brody was at my side in seconds. Noticing the Venetians, he closed the blind with a metallic screech. He wrapped me in his arms, and I buried my face against his chest. "What happened?" he checked me over for injuries, probably because of the amount of blood on the floor.

"Someone was here. My eyes." Tears streamed out of my eyes, desperately trying to heal the burns.

Brody was up, and I could hear him prowling around the apartment.

He picked me up in his arms like a child. "Whoever it was is gone. Let me put you into bed and then I'll call Walker." His voice was low and soothing, his arms holding me tightly to his chest.

He placed me on top of my comforter and put my throw rug over my legs. I heard him creep out of the room, dialing Walker's number as he left.

My sense of hearing seemed to make up for my lack of sight because no matter how low he whispered, I could still hear their conversation.

"Walker, it's Brody. Someone attacked Raine in her apartment." I could hear him pacing agitatedly. "I don't know. There is no other scent here than Raine's. What does it matter what I was doing at her apartment, man? Look, just get over here."

He snuck back into my room, and I felt the bed sink at the foot. He squeezed my ankle reassuringly. My eyes had stopped watering, but I still couldn't open them. I heard the front door slam open again, impossibly quickly.

Two sets of steps charged into my room.

Soft hands touched my face. "Raine, it's Doc Alice. How long did you look into the light for?"

"Only about fifteen seconds, but I couldn't close my eyes. I tried. It's like my body no longer obeyed me."

"Her maker," Walker whispered, horrified.

Doc Alice pried open one lid, and I whimpered. Even the small amount of light in the darkened room made my eyes ache. "They are pretty badly burned. I'm going to bandage her eyes for at least twenty-four hours, give them time to properly heal before we expose them to any type of light. Someone will need to stay with her."

"I'll call Angeline."

I shook my head. "Angeline has a business to run, and she'll be down a staff member as it is. I'll be fine by myself." I didn't feel quite so tough, but I didn't want to be a burden.

"I'll stay then," Walker said firmly. I shook my

head again, about to protest when Brody spoke from somewhere near the door.

"You need to find the scumbag that did this. I'll stay and watch her. I was only going to go fishing today anyway. Much better to spend it in the company of a beautiful woman who can't see me leering at her." I could picture his smug grin, and a smile tugged at the corners of my mouth.

"It's fine with me if I get hungry, I can just take a bite out of Mr. Big Shifter over there." My voice sounds shaky despite my words.

Walker humphed, and I could imagine him shooting a warning look at Brody, reminding him to mind his manners.

Doc Alice bandaged up my head and handed me a blood bag.

"You'll have to up your blood intake while you heal. Double your usual amount." She gave me a few more instructions and then took her leave. Walker sat down on the edge of the bed.

"So, tell me what happened. Don't leave any little detail out, no matter how inconsequential it seems. Don't just tell me what you saw, try and remember with your other senses as well."

I recounted everything, wracking my brain for any hints. Did I feel someone in the room, hear their heartbeat? Could I smell their cologne? Hell, I couldn't even tell Walker if it was a man or a woman. The growl had been animalistic, almost a whine. Their arms had been like steel bands, but every vamp had super strength. I had felt a tingle down my spine, but I'd written it off as fatigue. Other than that, there was no indication there had been anyone else in my apartment.

I felt sick that someone had invaded my new safe haven. Did this confirm that my murderer had been a local? Someone who'd attended the movie night, or maybe checked out a book from the library? Had they attended my rebirthday party, smiling and happy, eating cake while the whole time knowing that they were the reason my old life was over?

I could hear his knuckles cracking when I told him about my attacker threatening to break me.

Once he'd finished questioning me, Walker proceeded to prowl around my apartment with Brody. Brody was grumbling that he couldn't pick up a scent again, just like with my pack.

"Obviously, it's a vamp who can block their scent and wipe memories. How many of those can there possibly be in this one-horse town?" His voice was stormy. I didn't know why he was angry; I was the one who was temporarily blind and in incredible pain.

"There is no one who fits that description in this town," Walker growled out. "None of my list of possible suspects has this ability. It's blown my investigation to hell."

"People lie, Walker Walton. Why don't you earn that Sheriff's badge and track this asshole down? I'd like to tear him to shreds. Raine doesn't deserve to live in fear, she's been through enough already."

"You don't think I know that?" Walker whisper/shouted. "I want this guy brought to justice, even more than you do." I heard him stomp in the direction of the door. "Look after her." The 'or else' was implied.

Brody walked into the bedroom and laid down on the bed next to me. "Sleep. I'll be right here if you need me."

As if he could feel my panic, lost in the darkness of my mind, he reached out and wrapped my hand in his. The warmth of his touch let me drift off into a healing,, dreamless sleep.

CHAPTER EIGHT

W ord of the attack spread like wildfire, and gossip about my turning was once again front and center in everyone's mind. I barely slept, despite the comforting presence of Brody in the bed next to me. Or maybe because of Brody in the bed next to me. His heart rate was slower in sleep, but warmth radiated from his body like a furnace. And he smelled delicious, like pine and earth and man.

I was sitting on the couch, eating a sandwich, and listening to what Brody called the world's best "Pirate Bluegrass Band" playing from my new stereo. The guy was smokin' hot, but his taste in music left a lot to be desired.

Angeline sounded like she was getting a bumper day of sales in the cafe as people came in to see if I was okay, and gawk. Unfortunately, they were going to be disappointed. I had no intention of leaving my apartment for the next two days.

The steady hum of voices, coupled with the bell over the door ringing nearly non-stop, was soothing to my raw nerves.

So when the noise below went silent, I knew something was happening. Actually, I had a fair idea about what had happened, and I wasn't surprised when there was a knock at my door. Brody, however, was up over the back of the couch and at the door in seconds. He ripped the door open and growled.

"Who the fuck are you?" Brody sounded menacing, but I was secretly glad that it wasn't my attacker. Obviously, Brody had never been a woman in the big city. Never open the door to someone you didn't know, that was rule #1, #2 and #3.

"Depends who's askin', Shifter. I'm here to see Raine." I could hear a scuffle as Judge pushed past Brody and then Brody's deep rumbling growl.

"It's okay, Brody. Judge is a friend."

Brody muttered something I couldn't quite hear. I could feel the vibrations of Judge's rolling gait walking towards me. "Oh Rainy Day, what have you got yourself into now?" He laid a hand on my knee, and I could hear genuine affection in his voice.

"Oh, you know, the usual. Wild orgies, and being attacked by psychopathic makers. Did you get some death stares from downstairs? The silence was deafening, even up here." Judge sat next to me on the couch, making Brody growl again. I could hear his heartbeat move until it was just opposite me. Standing sentinel probably.

Judge chuckled. "I see you got yourself a pet as well. You have had a busy couple of days."

Brody's heart beat faster, and I could almost hear his blood boiling.

"Don't be rude, Judge. Brody has been great, looking after me when he didn't have to. If you are going to be a jerk to him, you can leave and come back when you learn some manners."

Judge rubbed my thigh, leaving behind a delicious heat in its wake. "I'm sorry. I apologize for my rudeness. I was just worried about my girl."

I scoffed. Now I understood what was going on here. The last thing I wanted, or needed, was some macho bullshit.

"You're still being a prick. We both know I'm not 'your' girl. I'm my own girl, so you can just lay off the territorial bullshit, both of you."

Judge just laughed. "Got me. I just came to see how you were doing, Sugar. Beatrice sent me over some dinner for you. Lasagna, if my nose isn't lyin'. I'll leave it in the kitchen. You just let me know if you need anything, anything at all. I'm always here to meet all your needs," he purred. I'd roll my eyes at him if he could see it. Instead, I just gave an exasperated sigh and shook my head.

"Thanks, Judge. I'll let you know. Thank Beatrice and Bert for the food."

Two hands pressed against the couch either side of my head. I could feel his warm breath on my face, and then he kissed me. Softly, but with so much heat that it could have set my panties on fire. "I'm doing my own digging into your maker. I'm close to something. Stay safe," he whispered against my lips.

This was the Judge I knew, the one without all the bravado, the intense, passionate man with a wit so sharp, he could tear a person to shreds with it.

I nodded and squeezed his forearms. I knew he cared, despite his teasing. But he was a wild one, and I didn't fool myself into thinking that we were anything but passionate passing acquaintances. He kissed my forehead and was gone. He had his own energy, and you could feel the emptiness in the room when he left.

Brody huffed. "So that's the drifter. People are saying he did it, you know."

I nodded. Popular opinion had him pegged as the culprit since day one. But I knew different. Judge was harsh, but he respected life in his own way.

"It's not him. His scent is strong, like cayenne pepper and bullshit," he huffed. I could tell it seriously peeved Brody to admit my attacker wasn't Judge.

"I know. How about we slice up some of this lasagna and have a beer. We can even watch the baseball," I cajoled. I didn't want to be stuck in the apartment with a pissed-off guy who could turn into a grizzly with a thought.

He sighed. "Fine, but only because Beatrice's lasagna is known to be the best in five hundred miles by those in the know."

He wasn't wrong. Beatrice was a miracle worker with ground beef and bechamel. Although I couldn't see the baseball, I found that I appreciated the commentators and the sounds of the game. The crack of a home run, and the cheers of the crowd. Brody filled in the blanks, yelling at the ump, and encouraging the players. I think I enjoyed the baseball game more now that I was blind.

We listened to the news, one morose story after another. Canadian soldiers killed in a roadside bombing, an earthquake in Japan, an American tourist missing in Alberta.

I sat up straighter when I realized the news anchor was talking about me.

"Mika McKellan was last seen by her friends in Vancouver over a week ago. McKellen, a college student at UWS, is believed to be hitchhiking her way across Alberta, up towards the Yukon. Anyone with information on her whereabouts is urged to contact the police hotline."

My body went rigid, and Brody pulled me against his side.

"Just breathe."

I let myself melt into his warm side and slowly breathed. I knew this was inevitable. It was better than going home and murdering my family. It was for the best. I repeated it over and over. It's for the best, it's for the best.

Eventually, the news finished, and Gordon Ramsey's *Hell's Kitchen* came on. There's only so long you can listen to Gordon Ramsey berate someone before you smile. And then feel bad for finding it entertaining. Either way, it distracted me from my meltdown. I'd cried in Brody's arms enough for one lifetime.

"Tell me about being a shifter? I don't know much about this world." Brody switched off the TV, and my ears were bruised by the amount of f-bombs Ramsey dropped.

"It's a freedom that can't be explained. What would you like to know?"

I wanted to know everything. "Can you shift into anything?"

"Only mammals."

"So no flying? That has to be disappointing. Weirdest thing you've ever shifted into?"

I could feel his chuckle deep in his chest. "An elephant. I could do things with my trunk that you couldn't even dream of."

I grimaced. "That's disgusting. Pervert." I slapped him on the chest. It was hard and broad, and I tried to ignore the feel of it beneath my hand. I didn't need pity sex, and quite frankly, if we were going for a home run, I'd definitely want to see the goods.

Little by little, I got Brody's story. He'd grown up among his tribe, who still live reasonably traditionally, off the grid. He went away to college, because he wanted to, but came back when he realized he couldn't be himself amongst humans. His family had a long history of shapeshifting, passed down by his forebearers, with legends to match. He didn't go into detail about the legends, much to my disappointment, but I could understand the need to keep something to yourself in a world where information is disseminated and distorted almost instantly.

"Have you guys always known the town was here?" If I were a pack of Shifters, I'd be pretty pissed if a bunch of vampires set up shop in my neighborhood.

"Your Council introduced themselves and formally asked permission. I'm pretty sure it impressed the tribe elders, although we'd never had a very good relationship with the Deathdealers. At least until Walker became Sheriff. The guy is so damn personable that my own mother falls all over herself to feed him when he visits, and my sisters basically beg to have his babies." There was good-natured disgust in his tone.

"Why do you call vampires 'death dealers'? I mean, I like the term, makes me want to dress in faux leather and buy some big swords, but it does sound rather ominous. Let's face it, the majority of this town look about as ominous as bunnies."

"Every single person in this town is deadly, and it would be best not to forget that. Especially you. We call them Deathdealers because there was a black period in history where vampires overran the country, and the husks of whole families blew in the wind like tumbleweeds. It was a long time ago, and the Vampire Nation gave the supe world a semblance of control over the vamps, but it was a lesson hard learned. Just because you can train a tiger to be a house cat, doesn't mean one day it isn't going to turn around and tear you limb from limb."

I chewed my lower lip. I didn't want to think that I had the ability to kill a family; mothers and children, innocents and guilty alike, but deep down, there was a hunger for blood that never eased. Even when I drank bagged blood, it was still there, curled and waiting. If I gave into that urge, it would be easy to decimate a family, or a town, until I was satiated.

We fell into silence, as my mind turned over everything. I made a promise to myself to search more into vampire history, my history now, I guess. At least find out more about the Vampire Nation; even Walker talked about them like they were a cross between the Russian Mafia and the Boogie Man.

"So, what's going on with you and Mr. Smarmy?"

My head whipped around, even though he couldn't see my incredulous look. "You mean Judge? Nothing, really. We have a mutually satisfying arrangement."

I cringed. Mika would have been horrified that I just referred to sex as a mutually satisfying arrangement. But I was determined that Raine was going to do what she wanted, regardless of what people thought. If I wanted to have sex with a good looking guy with a southern drawl that made my panties wet and kisses that set me on fire, then that's what I'd damn well do.

"Fair enough. But you could do better." When he turned and kissed me, I was so surprised that I just sat there with my mouth open for a full ten seconds while my mind caught up with my body. Then I was kissing him back. His lips burned mine, and when he ran his tongue along my bottom lip, I stopped breathing. He gently nipped my lower lip and stood.

"I'm going to go take a shower. I'll take the couch tonight."

I gaped until I heard the shower turn on. I stumbled to the bedroom, kicking my toe on the coffee table and the door jamb. I flopped down on my bed and willed my body back to a normal temperature.

CHAPTER NINE

The first thing I saw when Doc Alice took off my bandages was Walker's disgruntled face. He was pissed because he still had no leads. Nothing about my original murder, it was still weird calling it that, or anything on my attack the day before yesterday.

The second thing I saw was Brody's smiling face. "Hey there, Blue Eyes. It's good to see you." He winked and laughed at his bad pun. I groaned and threw a throw pillow at him. It whacked him in the forehead. It was good to be able to see again. My day and a bit of forced blindness was grueling. I empathized with the blind; it had been a struggle just to get around my apartment. To have to navigate the scary world without my sight filled me with horror. I would be making a hefty donation to the Seeing Eye Dog Foundation. The whole ordeal had made me respect my old neighbor Tex, even more. He'd been blind since birth but was still the coolest guy I knew. I mean, known.

"Extra blood for the next couple of days, and avoid dawn and dusk for a few weeks." Anger welled up in me. My attacker, my maker, had made me helpless. It wasn't something I ever wanted to feel again.

As if to reiterate her point, Doc Alice handed me a bag of blood. The woman was like a walking blood bank. She gave them out like suckers at the end of a doctor's appointment.

"Take it easy at work. No staring into the lens of the projector." I just rolled my eyes. Like I did that for fun.

I was actually a little sad to see the bandages go. It meant that Brody would go too, and I had gotten used to having him around.

Doc Alice left in her usual whirl of brightly colored kaftan, leather doctors bag in hand.

Walker looked at me, worriedly. His face looked pinched, and I felt bad. I had a good life here. I liked the town and the people. Well, except for the daylight wielding nutjob sucking dry unsuspecting tourists, of course.

"Maybe we should drop the investigation. I don't want to live in fear for the rest of my life. I think whoever he or she is would just go back underground if we stop looking. I just want to get on with my life," I whispered.

Walker shook his head. "That's not how this works, Raine. This person has killed once and attacked you in your home. If we do nothing, who's to say that they won't do that to another person, and another? At what point do we say, no more? Wouldn't you like to save someone else your pain?" Damn him, he knew I would.

"I want this whacko caught too, but I don't like the fact that Raine will be a sitting duck, waiting for his retribution. I won't be just downstairs next time," Brody growled, his face intense. The fact he cared so much made me feel a little fuzzy on the inside. But he was right; the idea that I would be up here by myself all day filled me with terror, even though I tried not to show it. Walker had enough to worry about, and Brody couldn't babysit me forever. I needed to stand on my own two feet. I wasn't going to be the kind of girl who needed saving, a perpetual damsel in distress, for the rest of eternity.

"Maybe Judge could move in...."

"No!" Both men shouted. Geez, what was their problem?

"We both know he isn't my maker, so why not?"

Walker frowned and Brody ground his jaw. A look passed between them, one of blatant disapproval. The same look Walker was giving Brody less than forty-eight hours earlier. Apparently, they were now united in their disapproval.

There was some macho mind-meld going on

because Walker nodded. "I don't trust him. He might not be your maker or your attacker, but he's still shifty as hell. I can't find any information on the guy anywhere. Not his maker, his age, his abilities. Nothing."

I raised my eyebrows at Brody. "And what's your problem?"

"I just think you can do better," he grunted.

"Better like you?" I prodded. Walker shot Brody the stink eye. I'd bet my favorite new Ray-Bans that Ella had dropped over earlier, that Walker was going to chew him a new one later. But Brody just raised his chin.

"Yeah, like me. You're smart, beautiful, and kind. You deserve better than some dude treating you like a toy that he can pick up and put down whenever he wants."

I blinked. And then blinked again. Well, I didn't see that coming. Blood rushed to my cheeks, and Walker's face got even stormier. He grabbed Brody by the t-shirt and hauled him out of my apartment.

"I'll see you after your shift at Angeline's. Lock the door!" he yelled over his shoulder as he barrelled Brody down the stairs.

Well, holy crap on toast. Brody wanted to be my boyfriend. Why didn't hot guys with abs like a washboard want to be my boyfriend when I was a human? Apparently being a vampire was like being married, but times ten. Now I wanted to be free and easy with my sex life, someone wanted to make an honest woman of me.

I'd ponder that quandary later. I walked to the shower. It was going to be fantastic to wash my hair and head down to work. I was getting cabin fever, and not the hot kind with pirates and saucy wenches.

IN THE END, work was pretty quiet. Well, maybe quiet wasn't the right word for it. I think nearly every person in Dark River turned up in the cafe to say hello and see how I was feeling; it's just that no one was borrowing books. Though Angeline was making a killing with her sunshine cupcakes, a lemon cupcake with cream cheese frosting and a bright yellow fondant sun on top in honor of my return to work after being nearly blinded by, yep you guessed it, the sun. Angeline had a warped sense of humor at times, but it was one of the reasons I liked her.

The problem was that everyone asked the same questions. Did I know who it was? Did I have any suspicions? Was I permanently blind in one eye? Apparently, that last rumor had spread quite prolifically.

In the end, Angeline had sent me to the diner, just to get rid of the crush of loiterers in the store. At one point she yelled that she ran a bakery, not a circus sideshow. I wasn't offended; I was starting to feel like a freak.

I walked into the diner and sat at the long counter. Beatrice took one look at me and yelled through the hutch, "One extra-large order of cheesy fries, extra bacon." Beatrice was a goddess in a gingham apron.

"How are you doing, Lass?"

Beatrice seemed like someone's mother. She just had that maternal vibe about her, like a mother hen. From here, the question I'd answered a million times today didn't seem so intrusive or tedious.

"I'm doing better, thanks, Beatrice. And thanks for the lasagna. I don't know what your secret is, but it's the best lasagna I've ever had."

Beatrice preened. "You're welcome, dear. Anything I can do to help." Another townsperson waved to her down the end of the counter, and she bustled off.

Someone came and stood beside me at the counter, and I realized it was Catherine and another one of the Council members.

"Raine! I heard about the attack. Walker assured me that you were okay, but I'm glad I can see it for myself." Catherine frowned and gave me the once over as if both Walker and Doc Alice had been lying to her. I hadn't seen Catherine, or the other Council member, the really ancient one, I think his name was Tomas although he'd always be Grim to me, since my citizenship ceremony. The Council members didn't seem to hobnob much with the other townspeople.

I guess being a Council member was kind of like being minor royalty.

"Thank you, Ma'am, Sir, but as you can see, I am fine. Nothing my super healing can't fix." I smiled at Tomas, and the old guy smiled back. It looked like someone stretching skin across a skeleton and totally gave me the jeebies, but I kept that to myself.

Catherine was nodding and patted my arm in a motherly fashion. "Don't you worry, Walker will make sure this madman is caught. I've already told him that he has all the resources of the Council at his disposal. If there is anything you need, don't hesitate to ask."

"Thank you, Ma'am."

With one last nod, they left.

Beatrice placed a huge plate piled high with cheese fries and what looked like half a side of bacon, in front of me. She also gave me one of Bert's famous type-o floats. I picked up a fry, the cheese stringing off it, and a piece of bacon got caught in its gooey web. I took a bite and moaned. Heaven. Exactly what I needed.

Beatrice was grinning. I had a theory that she was trying to discover if I could die of a heart attack, even as a vampire.

"Beatrice, can I ask you a question?"

She started refilling ketchup bottles on the coun- tertop. "Sure, Lass. Anything."

"What do you think about Judge? He seems to

spend a lot of time here." Beatrice clucked her tongue.

"That boy, he's a complex one. He's never said it, but I think he has quite the violent past. Not that you would ever know from his behavior, hasn't so much as lifted a finger against anyone in town, even when you turned up, and all the busybodies started pointing the finger in his direction. Nae, you see it in the way he's always tense, always coiled to strike. I've yet to see that lad relax."

I hadn't either, except when we were lying alone after sex. Then he always seemed so carefree and at ease. At least, until it was time to get up and face the world. At those times, you could almost sense him putting on his armor.

"After I rented him the room above the diner, he can't help me enough. Always pays his rent on time, though I have no idea where he's getting the money from. He gets a bad rap, but I think he's a good boy. But don't go getting your heart set on him, Lass. I know his type. It'd be easier to pin down a cloud. His type need to wander; they have an itch in their soul that needs to be scratched."

I thanked her and stuffed another fry in my mouth. Judge was an enigma.

Who would think that as a newly turned vampire, who was currently declared missing, presumed dead, and had a maniac making nefarious threats after sneaking into my apartment, that the most pressing thing on my mind would be boy trouble? I seriously needed to get my priorities straight. Or maybe I needed that therapy.

I finished my dinner in blissful peace and walked back across the square to the cafe. Angeline was closing up early, so no classic movie night. She said it was because she was exhausted, and that was a possibility. She had been run ragged for the last couple of days without me. But I couldn't help but think that she was doing it so I wouldn't have to run the late session and be exposed to the early morning light, and the chance of someone sneaking up to the apartment again.

She confirmed this by insisting she walked me upstairs after I grabbed a book on vampire history, that was ironically misnamed, *A Statistical Study on the Migration Patterns of the Little Brown Bat.* I almost fell asleep reading the title, but I guess it did its job. The casual viewer wouldn't pick it up, expecting to find vampire kinds greatest secrets.

Once Angeline had assuaged herself that the apartment was intruder free, she left me with a box of four sunshine cupcakes and my book.

I scarfed down one cupcake and sat on the couch. I skipped to the part about the Vampire Nation. I'd go over the history at a later date.

THE VAMPIRE NATION *was set up after vampire*

numbers reached near plague levels within the Americas. Many vampire families had turned rabid and wild, and remaining families chose to band together to protect humankind and the race's food source. The first order of business for the newly created alliance was to create a specialist branch of vampires (see ENFORCERS) to hunt down rogue and rabid individuals and families that threatened the entire species. The Enforcers have the ability to summarily execute rogues when issued with Kill Orders (see KILL ORDERS). The Vampire Nation has evolved and changed over the centuries, and are now elected rather than being familial in representation. However, the laws remain as stringent and deadly as those in centuries passed. Such laws are necessary to protect the vampire species as a whole.

WELL, they sounded scary. No wonder everyone freaked out at the mere mention of their name. Not for the first time, I was glad that I'd chosen to stay in Dark River. All this talk of families and enforcers made me think of reruns of The Sopranos. I placed the book on the coffee table. If I read any more of that tonight, I'd be having nightmares about waking up next to decapitated horse heads. I laid my head back on the couch and let my eyes close. Maybe I'd have a ten-minute nap and then read some more.

I WOKE up to my cat sleeping on my chest. I scratched the scruff of its ginger fur before I realized I didn't have a cat. I pulled my hand away, and it opened its eyes slowly. Then, I'm pretty sure it grinned and winked at me.

I screamed and threw it off my chest. What the goddamn hell was going on? The air twisted and shimmered in the middle of my living room, and where a ginger cat had once stood, was now a naked Brody. I spun around and faced the wall

"Argh, you're naked. Put some damn clothes on."

I heard his deep laugh, and my whole body blushed. "Aw, I know you don't mean that, but if it will make you feel better." I heard the distinct sound of a zipper and decided it was safe to look.

"What are you doing here? You scared the hell out of me. I thought you'd gone back to your place." It all fell out in one embarrassing jumble, as I looked everywhere but in his eyes. He still wasn't wearing a shirt, and my eyes involuntarily followed the V of his obliques to where there was a very impressive D if you catch my drift.

His grin was so wide that it showed almost every single one of his pearly white teeth. "I couldn't sleep knowing you were here, alone and unprotected. So I came to guard your body."

"As a house cat?" I screeched. "What the hell were you going to do as a house cat? Scratch them until they bled out?"

Brody sniffed, apparently I'd put a dent in his kitty cat pride. "It's a short transformation between a house cat and a tiger. I thought you'd react better to a tabby than a fully grown tiger in your living room."

He had a point. I probably would have had a coronary on the spot if a tiger had been lying on my living room rug. Now, I just felt like a jerk.

"Look, I'm sorry. Your help is appreciated, thank you. You're right, a tiger would have scared me."

Brody shrugged. "Wanna see it anyway? It's pretty impressive."

I shook my head vehemently. My heart was already racing a million miles an hour, well for a vamp, so I didn't think I could take much more of a fright. "Maybe some other time." I tried to draw my eyes back to his face, completely against their will and my more amorous judgment. My fangs punched out, and I groaned with embarrassment. I was like a teenage boy, every lustful thought and out they popped.

"Unless you want to be my midnight snack, you better put a shirt on," I mumbled around my fangs. They really did make it hard to talk, unless you practiced. No wonder Dracula had a dumb accent, it was like a lisp, only more painful. I deep breathed and worked on getting them retracted. Angeline had been helping me practice this on my lunch breaks. I looked up and noticed that Brody was still shirtless. "I'm serious, Brody. I have really poor impulse control."

He cocked his head, his gaze intense. "Well, stop denying yourself."

My fangs popped out again as I processed what he said slowly. I think I must have heard it wrong.

"Pardon me?" I was drifting toward him, though I don't think I took a physical step. A haze had come down on my brain, and the haze was a mixture of hunger and lust.

"I want you to bite me."

I looked in his eyes, hard, to make sure he wasn't joking, and that he was in his right mind.

"I can't. I've never, you know, with anyone who wasn't a vamp. What if I hurt you?" Or drained him dry. All I could hear was the steady thump, thump, thump of his heart, and even now my tenuous control was slipping.

"I trust you. Besides, I'm not completely defenseless. If you get carried away, I can stop it." He stared down at me. Somehow I was only inches from his face.

"Are you sure?" I whispered. He nodded, and that was enough.

It took cast-iron resolve to not just launch myself at him bodily. Instead, I eased him back on the couch and straddled his hips. I twisted his hair in my fingers and slid his head to the side. I poised my mouth over his throat, and sucked gently, raising the blood to the surface. As my teeth punctured through the thin skin of his neck, I came. It was embarrassing and unexpected, but I didn't care. My lips suctioned against his skin, and I drew his sweet blood into my mouth with every thump of his heart.

Little moans of pleasure tickled deep in my throat. This was incredible. If bagged blood was like a frozen dinner, then blood from the neck of another vamp was like your Mom's home cooking. But this, this was something else. Drinking from Brody was like dining in the world's finest restaurant. His blood was hot and sweet, with a hint of magic that buzzed on my tongue.

I could hear Brody moan, and he was grinding against me. I was so blissed out by the taste of him that I was hardly aware of my body. I could feel his hands roaming over me, touching my breasts and my ass, pulling me down harder into his lap, but these sensations were secondary for the ecstasy that was happening in my mouth, in my body as his blood ran through my veins.

His heart thumped faster and faster, and then he let out a grunt as his body spasmed. A little voice in my head told me it was time to stop, and I pushed the thought to the front of my brain. With every ounce of resolve I knew I had, and some serious control that came as a surprise, I loosened my grip on his neck and let him go. I sealed the wound with my tongue and rocked away. My body felt languid and full. The hunger in me was sated for the first time in weeks. I collapsed against Brody's chest.

"Are you okay?" I mumbled.

"Tired, and woozy, but okay. You?"

"I don't think I've ever been better than I am right now. I feel like the bloodlust is gone."

Brody stood up and wobbled on his feet. I put out a steadying hand. I felt lethargic and buzzed all at the same time. I could have picked Brody up and carried him to bed with no more effort than as if he were a kitten. I decided against it because he didn't seem like the kind of guy who would appreciate that.

"It's the magic in my blood that makes you feel satisfied. It's not like that with humans." That was reassuring to know, because for a moment there, I could empathize with the rabid vampires of old, drinking their way through whole towns.

The fact that I could empathize with such a horrifying notion filled me with shame, but I turned my face away so Brody wouldn't see. I wrapped an arm around his waist and helped him into the bedroom. He shed his clothes and hopped under the covers, allowing gravity to do most of the work.

I shed my nightgown and slid in beside him. We'd just dry humped each other into completion; the time for modesty was gone, in my opinion. I don't know what inspired Brody to offer himself like a lamb to the slaughter, but I was glad he did. I gave myself a pat on the back for my control, though the feel of it still scared me. I imagined it was how heroin addicts felt, always chasing that high. I worried that drinking bagged blood would never be satisfying again.

He spooned himself around me, and within

seconds, he was snoring away, his long black hair tickling my face. There was something about the quick beat of his heart that lulled me into a near trance state. Maybe it was like the purring of a cat, or the sound of the rainforest. Whatever it was, it calmed my racing mind. I closed my eyes, and let his warmth drag me down into a blissful sleep.

CHAPTER TEN

I was a woman obsessed. Not with Brody, though he did look positively delicious lying naked on my bed, his arms tucked under his cheek and his delightful ass bared to the world. His hair played over the muscles of his back, and I wanted to run my fingers through it.

No, what had me transfixed was the way his pulse ticked away in the long column of his throat. Thump. Thump. Thump. I couldn't drag my eyes away.

"You gotta stop looking at me like I'm breakfast," he grumbled, and my eyes shot to his face. Whoops. Busted.

"I, uh, was watching…" Yeah, I had nothing. "You just tasted really nice, and now I can't get enough."

He rolled over and stretched; finally, my eyes

moved from his throat considerably lower. Like real, real low.

"I take it back. You can look at me like that any morning," he purred.

Someone banged on the door, and Brody grinned. Well, that couldn't be good.

"Raine?" Walker's voice echoed around my apartment, and for a moment, I panicked like I'd be caught out cheating. Then I remembered he wasn't my boyfriend or my partner. He was my friend, at best.

Brody was still grinning, and I rolled my eyes. "You should get dressed before Walker uses you as a chew toy for debauching me."

Brody laughed, but he stood up, and I sucked in a gasp. Naked, he was glorious. "Babe, I'm pretty sure if anyone got debauched last night, it was me."

He leaned forward and kissed my lips, pulling his jeans on.

"Raine? Are you okay in there?"

Brody chuckled against my lips. "He knows your all good. He can hear us just fine."

He tilted his head and lifted a finger. As if on cue, Walker let out a disgruntled huff. "I sure can, fleabag. Get your ass out here, before I come in there and drag you out."

Brody grinned. "He's so uptight. Makes you wonder why?"

I dropped my voice low. "Isn't he dating Angeline?"

The shock on Brody's face was almost comical. "Angeline is married to the Doc."

No fucking way. "Doc Alice?"

Brody laughed loud, reverberating. "How many doctors do you think a town full of dead people needs? Come on, Raine. Better get out there before the old guy gets his panties in a knot."

I pulled on a dress and ran my fingers through my bed hair. I walked to the door and opened it. Walker stood there, out of uniform for once. He looked strange, like Mickey Mouse at Disneyland with no head-on.

He looked at my rose-colored cheeks, and then over my shoulder to where Brody was standing with a self-satisfied grin. His mouth opened and closed a few times, like a fish gasping for air, before he snapped it shut with an audible click. His jaw flexed as he ground his molars, and it was a little mesmerizing. It had to be bad for his teeth, though. I didn't know if Dark River had a dentist, or if they had to travel to one of the human towns. You couldn't pay me enough to stick my fingers into the mouth of a vampire, though. It was like flossing the teeth of a shark.

"It's time for your first counseling appointment. I thought I'd come over and escort you," he grunted. "I see you were busy."

I stared at his face, wondering if Brody was right. Was Walker so angsty because he had a thing for me? My belly flip-flopped at the idea. Walker was hot. If I closed my eyes, I could still imagine how his body felt beneath my hands when I'd almost nailed him in public on my second day in town.

Mika would be trying to get him on some kind of commitment lockdown, but I wasn't Mika anymore. I was Raine, a sampler of sexy supernaturals. Still a little high on Brody's blood, feeling bolder than I had any right to be, I stepped closer to Walker, until I was well inside his personal space. I looked up at him through my lashes and saw his nostrils flare.

"I was busy," I purred. If I stood on the tips of my toes, I'd be a fraction of an inch from his lips. His green eyes burned down at me, taking on that odd glow I saw on my very first day. The one he got when he was worked up. I felt my lips curl into a smug grin. Still smiling, I lifted and nipped his chin with my fangs. He shuddered, and I turned on my heel and walked away, human -slow. I could hear Brody's laughter following me down the back stairs of the apartment. I'd walked halfway across the square by the time Walker caught up.

I just raised an eyebrow at him. "Have a nice chat with Brody?" I had no doubt that he had been grilling his shifter friend.

Walker frowned at me. "You played a dangerous game with Brody. He is mortal. Well, mortal-*ish*, he'll live longer than humans. It is still definitely possible for you to rip his throat out. You are barely two weeks old. You shouldn't be trying mortal blood." He sounded like he was giving me the safe sex speech, and I rolled my eyes. There was nothing sexy about getting lectured. "Besides, I thought you were dating Judge?"

I stopped and turned toward him. "What does it matter to you who I am dating, Sheriff?" I looked at him straight in those glorious eyes, not giving him the opportunity to break away.

His jaw ticked. "I just want you to be careful."

I quirked my eyebrow again. Once again, I got into his space, pressing my body close until my soft curves were pressed against the long, hard lines of his body. He sucked in a breath, and my heart was thundering. "Is that the only reason, Walker?"

The part of my brain that was still a nineteen-year-old human was doing a pterodactyl screech of excitement inside my head. Walker was silent, but his chest was heaving. He leaned forward until I had no choice to look anywhere but at his eyes. "No. But this would be a gross misuse of my authority," he growled.

"What would be?" I whispered, not daring to hope he meant what I thought he did. In the next moment, my hopes were confirmed as his head dipped, his lips pressing softly into mine. He tasted like perfection, and I kissed him back and moaned when he sucked my bottom lip into his mouth, his fangs scraping against the tender flesh.

Then he was gone so fast that the red curls of my hair fluttered around my face. I stood there gaping like a fish, completely unsure what to do. What the hell was my life right now?

Someone was clapping from behind me, and I whirled to see Judge grinning like an idiot. Now I felt guilty. I might have talked a big game to Walker, but I'd actually slept with Judge, and now he'd seen me kissing another man.

"Judge…"

"Relax, Darlin'. Let me walk you the rest of the way to the Counsellors office." He put out his arm like a proper southern gentleman, and I placed my hand in the crook of his elbow. He leaned forward and sniffed me. "You smell like a shapeshifter. No wonder you had such a big smile on your face. Shifter blood is something else."

My face was flaming. Every drop of that shifter blood was now in my cheeks. "Judge-" I started, but he waved me away.

"Don't stress it. We are not, what's the human terminology now? Baes?"

It sounded so ridiculous coming out of his mouth, I couldn't resist the laugh that honked from my mouth.

"Let's never use that term again, okay?" I said, patting his arm.

He just grinned. "Done deal. As I was sayin', we aren't a couple. I know you were askin' Beatrice about me the other day."

I mumbled something incomprehensible, and he

just smiled wider. Geez, that grin was like a punch to the sternum every time. "I care for you, Rainy Day. But I'm not the kind of man you pin all your hopes for the future on. That's much more the good Sheriff's speed. I am a good time."

"Not a long time?" I quipped, even though I thought I was getting the 'let's just keep it casual' speech.

"That's the problem, Raine. We're here for a very long time. Not to sound cliche, but immortality can be a curse."

He was being serious. He never used my name. We walked in silence for a little while, until I was standing in front of another stone building that looked like a rich person's hunting lodge.

I turned to him and fell into the midnight blue of his eyes. I reached up and ran my hand down the hard edge of his jaw.

"I'm not asking for anything from you, only what you want to give. Just a warm body on cold nights. Believe it or not, not every girl is looking wants you to put a ring on it."

He laughed and kissed me hard. I'd kissed three hot guys in less than fifteen minutes. That had to be a record, right?

When he pulled back, he looked down at me with sad eyes. "I know, but some girls make you wish you could."

With that, he was gone too.

Jesus. I was definitely going to need therapy, and it had nothing to do with my turning. I pushed through the doors of the Dark River Counselling office. And stopped dead. The place looked like nothing I had ever seen. It was like a junk store had exploded, or someone had picked the most cliche thing from every decade and put it in pride of place. A hand-shaped swivel chair in electric green from the 2000s sat beside a floral couch, a crocheted throw in mustard and brown over the arm. Brass ducks from the fifties hung beside a replica of Andy Warhol's cans of soup. There was a lava lamp and a Persian rug. There was a hall, but the entryway was covered in a beaded curtain. A picture of Batman, the Joker, and Harley Quinn hung on the opposite wall. What the actual hell?

A laugh dragged my eyes back to the beaded curtain. The young guy from the Council, who had the presence of someone far more ancient than his young face belied, was there. "It is a bit much, yes? But what is the point of being ancient if I cannot fill a room with whatever I want?" His voice was young, and he had an almost American accent except for a hint of something else. But his speech pattern was overly formal, which led to me to believe English wasn't his first language. Looking into his swirling eyes, which were so dark brown that I wasn't sure they weren't black, made me feel the centuries that pressed down on his shoulders.

"Uh, sure. Sir. I'm here for my therapy session?"

He clapped his hands together. "Excellent. Given the circumstances of your turning, we thought perhaps we'd wait a few weeks before we started your obligatory sessions, allow you to settle in a little. I am sorry that it was marred by such violence." His face turned feral, showing every ounce of the violence he'd just apologized for, and I was glad it wasn't directed toward me. There was something primal and predatory about this guy. But he didn't make me feel unsafe. But then, no one had, and one of them was my maker and blinded me for forty-eight hours. I wasn't the best judge of character, obviously.

"Come on back. You'll have to see me once every two weeks for a little while, but I promise it will be quite cathartic for you." He led the way through the beaded blinds and back into the building toward what I assumed was his office.

As we stepped through the door, I swallowed back a laugh. If the waiting room had been a mishmash of different decades, this room was worse. An honest to goodness fainting couch in teal blue clashed with a thick pile green carpet. The walls were covered with nineties-style motivational pictures, and a barker lounger sat opposite the couch. There was a chrome and glass desk in the corner, with a MacBook on top. The walls were yellow. Like canary yellow.

"Holy shit."

The Council guy laughed. "It is something, right?"

"It's definitely something, Sir."

He laughed again, doubling over as he tried to draw breath. He stood and wiped at his face. "Please, call me Nico. Won't you take a seat?" He was still chuckling to himself. "Watching the first reactions to this room is one of the joys of my role."

I sat on the fainting couch and resisted the urge to swoon like a mid-century maiden. It was actually incredibly uncomfortable.

"So, how are you settling in to our little town?" Nico asked, relaxing into his comfy looking barker lounge. I eyed it longingly as I shifted around, trying to find a position that wouldn't result in my ass going numb.

"Everyone has been very kind. I really like working at the Immortal Cupcake."

"Hmm," he murmured contemplatively, scribbling on a notepad that appeared from nowhere. It had a picture of Hello Kitty on it. "Anything you'd like to bring up? Are you sleeping well? Sleep is very important, even when you are dead."

This whole thing was trippy. Nico looked about nineteen, and he was covered in tribal tattoos. If it weren't for the heavy presence of his gaze, it'd be like sitting on the therapist's couch with my younger brother.

Not that I would ever see them again. Pain shot through my chest at the thought that they'd be forever changed by my disappearance and apparent death.

"What is it?" Nico asked softly.

I shook my head, and then remembered he was meant to be my counselor. "I was just thinking of my family and how my disappearance would be hurting them right now."

Nico nodded solemnly. "It is harder to leave it all behind when you know you are loved. It is what most newly turned vampires struggle with."

I sighed, resting back on the arm of the couch. "It's not even that I won't see them again, though that's tough. It's the fact that this whole thing is causing them pain. That's what I'm most angry about. I want to kill my maker just for making them all hurt."

"Mmhmm," he mumbled again, writing more in his Hello Kitty notebook. "Do you want some icecream? I feel like ice cream right now."

He jumped up and pulled out two small tubs of Ben and Jerry's from a small icebox in the corner of the room I hadn't notice. Pulling two spoons plastic spoons from his filing cabinet, he handed me one of the tubs.

"Ice cream is the best invention of the modern age, in my opinion." He scooped a large chunk of ice cream into his mouth. "Raine, I have no platitudes to make you feel better about the loss of your life. In fact, I will not even encourage you to let go of these vengeful feelings toward your maker, because he deserves your ire. But just know, while you will never forget them, the pain of losing your family will diminish with time. As you build a life here, create intimate connections with friends, you will once again find happiness." We were silent for a moment as he let his words resonate. "Tell me about them. Not about how they would be feeling right now, but about them as people, as individuals that you loved."

So I did. I told him all about my Mom and Dad, about my little brother Christopher who was in Sophmore year of High School. He was an accident. I heard that when my Mom was pregnant and talking to one of my aunts. I'd gotten my ass whooped when I'd thrown it in Christopher's face when he nine, and I was fourteen, and he was being annoying. I told Nico all about my love of rock music because the boy next door used to tutor people in guitar for money during high school. I'd had the hugest crush on Tex since I was a kid. He was a couple of years older and had these beautiful lips that were almost too girly for his really rough face. He got his first tattoo at sixteen, and his parents had lost it. Hell, my parents had lost it. But I'd thought he was the best thing ever.

I told him about going off to college, and the fact that my whole family had come to wish me good luck even though I was moving less than two hours away.

I wasn't sure how long I sat on that terrible chair just talking like it was my last day on earth, but when the words finally ran dry, my ass was numb, and my voice was rough. Also, I was a little embarrassed. I hadn't been able to stop myself from speaking. I narrowed my eyes in suspicion.

Nico shrugged. "Sorry. It's one of my gifts, I guess. I am unable to control it. People like to tell me things with very little prompting. It is why I am the town counselor. It has its benefits."

"As an interrogator?" I said, disgruntlement coursing through me. Now I knew why they insisted on these post-turning therapy sessions.

"In the past, yes. In a much darker time in history."

I decided then and there that these little therapy sessions were going to be one way. I didn't want to know his past, all the dark, and sordid details. I stood and shifted uncomfortably. "I should go. I have a shift at the Immortal Cupcake."

Nico nodded. "Indeed. What is playing tonight?

"Dracula. The Francis Ford Coppola version."

Nico let out a burst of laughter. "You jest, yes?"

I stared him dead in the eye. "I never jest about Gary Oldman, Sir."

His laughter echoed around the room, and he wrapped his arms around his ribs. "I think you are just what this town needs, Raine. Perhaps I will come along tonight. What is the cupcake?"

"Red velvet brownie with a white chocolate lava center. The white chocolate has been dyed red. Honestly, I think Angeline might need the therapy. She has a terrible sense of humor." I pushed through the beads back into the eye-searing waiting room. Someone was waiting there, but I knew who it was by the sound of their heartbeat. Odd, right?

Brody inclined his head. "Nico. It is good to see you," he said. He did seem genuinely happy to see the ancient vampire.

"Ah, young Brody. How is your grandmother?"

Brody's eyes lit up. "She is well, Sir."

There was some fondness in Nico's eyes at the mention of Brody's family. Nico finally noticed my head ping-ponging between them. "Nico's grandmother was a child when we decided to set up Dark River. She used to sneak in and listen to the meetings of the Elders, as we negotiated our treaty over this land. She was a fiery one, even when she was no more than an infant."

Brody laughed. "Still is. Kicked my butt the other day."

Nico laughed and waved. "I shall see you tonight, Raine. Brody, give my best to your family."

Brody inclined his head and then opened the front door for me, like a perfect gentleman. Like I hadn't been sucking face with him a couple of hours ago. Well, sucking something anyway.

His hand rested on the small of my back as we walked across the square. Honestly. It was like a hundred yards. Why I suddenly needed an escort was beyond me. But anytime I went to walk anywhere, boom, one of them appeared.

"Not going to lie, Brody. I kinda expected you to be run outta town by Mr. Tall, Dark and Overprotective."

Brody laughed, his fingers curling around my hip and pulling me closer. "Eventually he'll pull the police issued baton out of his ass and realize he wants you, but until then, I'm going to soak you up," he whispered against my ear, and the scent of him overcame me. It was heady. Raw and earthy and completely freakin' delicious. "I think the real worry is your homicidal looking friend that likes to lurk in the shadows and pretend he only wants to hit it and quit it." He nodded in the direction of the small alley between two buildings. There, in the shadows, was Judge. He stepped out into the light and gave Brody the finger.

Brody laughed under his breath. "You may as well come over; otherwise, you are just going to seem like a creeper, dude." Brody didn't shout, but I knew he wasn't talking to me.

I could see Judge's jaw tense, but he was across the road and in front of us in an instant. Only it didn't seem so fast to me anymore. My sense of time was changing.

"So you're the juice pouch?" he asked, raising an eyebrow at Brody.

I groaned and covered my eyes.

"So you're the murderer?" Brody quipped back, and I wondered if I should stay to protect Brody when Judge ripped his arms off and beat him with them, or go get the Doc to sew his arms back on immediately. Vampire quandary.

Instead, Judge laughed, and Brody grinned, and I realized I'd never understand men even if I lived for a million years.

CHAPTER ELEVEN

They sat on my couch, drinking beer and watching the baseball. I leaned against my island bench, resting my chin on my hand and wondering how the hell this happened. I sucked on my blood bag, squeezing the medical plastic, and slurping it down like it was cheap wine.

"What is happening here? Are you guys in a bromance?"

For the last four days, they'd cohabitated in my apartment. First, it was one, and then the other, and then their visits would somehow overlap. Now, they didn't even bother leaving when the other arrived.

"What are you talkin' about, Rainy Day?" Judge said, swigging from his beer.

I came and stood in front of them. Honestly, they were almost snuggled up on the couch, not even six inches between them. Brody's nose twitched. I knew what he was smelling. I was hungry, horny, and angry as hell. While they were playing switcheroo, I was too nervous about doing anything in case one of them waltzed in while I was doing the naked mambo with the other. Which meant I was drinking bagged blood and sleeping alone. And now I was feeling meaner than a rattlesnake.

"Oh," Brody said in a growly voice.

"Yeah, oh." I tapped my foot. "You need to leave before I do something that will haunt my seemingly endless nights."

I wasn't exaggerating. The predator felt out of control tonight. She'd been denied too long. She wanted to hunt. And right now, Brody was looking more like prey than a friend.

"We talked about this. You don't have to resist with me," Brody said, standing, swaggering toward me with his eyes hooded. I hadn't drank from him since that night. His blood was too potent, too addictive. I wasn't sure I could go from lobster back to mac and cheese. And today, I wasn't sure I could stop, no matter what he said.

I backed away as he got closer, my fangs punching out. I felt wild. "I mean it, Brody." I breathed through my mouth because if I caught scent of his blood right now, I'd be on him, consequences be damned.

"I trust you, Raine."

My lip curled. "That makes you dumb as well as crazy." A slight breeze let me know Judge was now at my back. He pressed into my back, his hard torso molded against me. His fingers dug into my hips.

"How'd you let it get this bad, Rainy Day? Aren't you keeping up with your feeding regime?"

I scowled at him over my shoulder, even as I pressed myself tighter against his dick and wiggled my ass. He groaned. "Of course, I am asshole. It's not my fault you've been leaving me unsatisfied."

Brody sucked in a breath, and I saw the massive shit-eating grin on his face. I pointed my finger at his face. "Don't even get me started on you, butthead. Just make a move already!"

I stepped from between them and moved to the other side of the room. Why did I feel so jittery right now?

Brody cocked his head to the side. "You smell weird. I mean, under the scent of your need." He groaned. "Jesus, Raine. Come back over here."

I shook my head. I felt weird. My body was in control. "No." But even as I said the words, I was walking toward him. Judge moved toward the kitchen, plucking the blood bag I'd sucked dry moments earlier from the bin. He touched the tip of his tongue to the neck of the bag. Why the hell was that so hot?

"It's tainted," he said and grimaced. He opened the fridge and sniffed the rest. "They are all tainted. I can't tell you with what, but I'm pretty sure it's why Raine has that look in her eye. I think you might need to do what the lady says, Shifter, and step away."

Judge stepped forward, placing himself in between Brody and me. My inner predator growled. I growled.

The fucker just grinned at me. Judge didn't seem even the least bit perturbed that my inner vamp wanted to tear his throat out for getting between Brody and me. "You need to call Walker. Either this was a targeted attack on Raine, or the whole supply is tainted, in which case the town is going to go mad," Judge said with cool authority, though his eyes never left me. "Don't leave the apartment. You are one of the only things actually alive in this town, and if the whole place is drinking tainted blood, you'll be just a smear on the pavement by morning. This place might be a little Stepford, but I'm pretty sure that when your pack retaliates for killin' their golden boy, it won't be pretty for any of us."

Brody just grunted his assent, dialing Walker's number. I couldn't hear what he was saying over the steady thumping of the heartbeats in the room.

"Judge," I whimpered. I didn't know what I was trying to say, but desperation rode me hard.

"I know, Sweetheart. I'm gonna take care of ya', but just wait a second while Brody talks to the Sheriff."

The blur of Brody's words was just a buzz in the background until he appeared back in my peripheral and my head snapped toward him with freakish speed.

"Walker says that the rest of the blood supply is

fine. It's just Raine's that is tainted," Brody said slowly. "Doc Alice checked the rest of the supply."

I watched his mouth as he spoke, and I wanted to suck his full lower lip between mine and make it bleed.

"...suggest to counteract it?"

I shook my head from my bloodlust. "Just gotta ride it out. Or she said we could filter it out. The magic in my blood should help neutralize the toxin, but unless you withdraw it, the comedown is gonna be rough. The longer it's in her system, the worse it will get. At least, that's what Doc Alice said."

Judge's eyes hooded. "Well, Darlin', looks like its gonna be a long night. You have two choices right now. We can lock you in your bathroom until this shit passes. Or you can drink from our fine, furry friend right here, and then I can drink from you, and see if we can't satisfy another need or two."

Brody was whispering something at Judge, his heart going thump-thump-thump-thump in my head. "...ingesting the toxin yourself."

Judge just waved him away. "What do ya' say, Raine?"

He was in front of me, all of a sudden. The thump of his pulse in his neck making my mouth water, and the press of his body making my core ache. "I gotta know that this is what you really want? I think it's gonna get wild, and I don't want you to have any regrets in the mornin'."

I whimpered, no longer sure which need was more painful right now. "I don't want to hurt Brody."

He grabbed my chin, tipping my face up so he could see my eyes. "I'll make sure you don't hurt anyone, not Brody, not me and definitely not yourself. You trust me, Sugar?"

I nodded. Then he grinned, and my willpower dissipated as if it never existed. I jumped, wrapping my legs around his body as my mouth crashed into his. He kissed me back, but when I tried to bury my fangs in his neck, he pulled me back. "Nuh-uh, Sugar. Brody here is your magic ticket tonight, and aren't you lucky." He looked over my shoulder. "You cool with what's about to go down right now, man? I can take care of it if you need to leave. No harm, no foul."

Brody stepped closer. "No way. I got you too, Raine," he said as he peeled me from Judge, and I moaned. I latched onto his neck and groaned, coming hard from the magic in his blood.

"Jesus fuckin' hell," Judge groaned. "Take it to the bed, Brodes. It's gonna be a long night. Better to be comfortable."

Brody groaned in answer, lifting me up until I wrapped my legs around his waist and moving us quickly toward my bedroom. I didn't stop dragging hot mouthfuls of blood from his veins though. I rubbed my aching core on the hard bulge in his jeans and resisted the urge to beg. The taste of the coppery warmth coating my tongue was ambrosia. I dug deeper into his neck, but something intruded between us. I realized it was Judge's hand.

"Easy now, Sweetheart. Brodes is delicate, we don't want to rip his throat out, yeah?"

His words permeated the haze of desire that had fallen over me like a thick curtain. I unlatched from Brody's neck and pulled away. I looked down at his broad grin and slightly glazed eyes. "You okay?"

My words came out slurred. What the hell had been in my blood? He nodded, looking a little dazed himself.

Hands were stripping me out of my shirt, and my focus snapped to Judge. He tossed the piece of red fabric over his shoulder with a grin. Rolling off Brody, I wiggled out of my jeans, until I laid in front of them in just my underwear.

Then I stared, my hunger getting lost under the crash of longing that reared up when I saw them both naked before me, my eyes flicking from one to the other, unable to settle on either.

"Fuck, I love it when you look at me like that," Brody growled in a low voice that went straight to my ladybits.

Judge just laughed. "Like you're dinner?"

Brody shook his head, a lopsided grin curling his lips. "Like I am the most amazing person she's ever seen. It's really good for my ego."

His words trickled past the hunger, and I leaped. I

wrapped my legs around Brody's torso and covered his lips with mine, pushing my tongue between his lips and letting our teeth clash. Brody twisted us and slammed me into the bed, kissing me back with just as little control. Pulling back, he tore my underwear from my body and threw it in the direction of the rest of my clothes.

"While we are divesting you of clothing," Judge murmured, tearing off my bra and tossing it. I would be mad about them destroying my new lingerie later when I didn't think it was so damn hot. Brody pulled me toward the end of the bed by my hips, and I wrapped my legs around his waist.

"Ready, Raine?" He murmured, his eyes running over my face, then drifting down my body like he was memorizing it all for a later date.

"Please, Brody," I groaned, as the hard head of his cock pressed against me. He gave me another of those heart-stopping smiles and drove himself balls deep in one strong thrust. I let out a long, low moan, slamming my eyes shut as a wave of pleasure shot through me like a lightning bolt. I sucked in a harsh breath at a sting over my breast. Peeling my eyes open against the pleasure, I looked down where Judge had his fangs buried in the soft curve of my breast. Holy shit.

His eyes watched my face as the pleasure of his bite, combined with the pleasure of Brody's body between my thighs.

I let out another long, pained sound. "I am going

to come," I whimpered. "But don't you dare fucking stop." The last words were more of a growl, and I could feel Brody's chuckle even though his own small grunts of pleasure were echoing off my bedroom wall.

"No, Ma'am," Judge said, leaning over to take my nipple in his mouth and sucking hard, before sliding his fangs back in.

The orgasm that crashed over me was unlike anything I had ever felt. Screw fireworks, I saw the fucking Big Bang as lights danced in my eyes and my body gripped them both, holding them where I wanted them. The magic of Brody's blood, mixed with the pleasure of his body and the pure bliss of Judge's bite, and it was freaking apocalyptic.

Taking me at my word, they continued to suck and fuck my body as I whimpered, my body grinding into Brody's until he was slamming into me hard, only the steady weight of Judge across my breasts stopped me banging into my headboard over and over. Finally, Brody gave a primal roar that was completely inhuman and arched, his orgasm bringing me with him until our combined panting was all you could hear in the room.

Brody rolled off me with a groan, his fingers reaching out to touch me instinctively. I wrapped my fingers in his. I felt wrung out, but my blood was still electrified in my veins.

Judge lifted his head and grinned down at me, my

blood still on his lips. "We aren't done yet, Rainy Day. We are only just getting started."

The predator that shared my skin curled its lip. We were ready. She wanted more.

Brody's heart was still thundering, and it was the sweetest sound I'd ever heard. Pushing myself up onto my hands and knees, I crawled up his body until we were face to face. I leaned forward, pressing my lips to his in a hard kiss filled with every ounce of pent up emotion I had.

"Thank you," I whispered.

He grinned back. "You really, really don't need to thank me for that, Babe. Any fucking time."

Judge made a happy humming noise from behind me, and I looked over my shoulder. He was staring down at me, his gaze hooded with so much desire that I felt like I could come again just from his eyes caressing my body like that.

"Don't move, Rainy Day. This is perfect." His hands slid up my thighs, then over my ass, squeezing hard. He ran them up over my lower back, his hands spread wide until they curled around my shoulders and he pulled me up so my back was pressed against his chest and his hard cock was nestled against my ass. He leaned forward and nuzzled his face into the curve of my neck before his teeth pierced the skin and he took long, hard draws that felt like it was tugging directly on my clit.

I moaned like a hussy. My head started to fuzz, and my sight got blurry as I lost more blood.

Only Judge's strong hands were stopping me from collapsing.

Eventually, he pulled away and lowered me gently onto Brody's chest. "That should be most of the tainted blood, but she's going to need more of you," he said to the other man over my shoulder.

Brody must have said yes, but I wasn't sure he could have stopped me if he tried. My predator struck, but Judge's restraining strength was there again, holding me back. "Not in the neck, Darlin', you'll draw too quick, and Brodes will end up nothing but a husk. Take it from his chest, just above his heart."

He moved me where he meant, and I struck, not overly gently, which was something I'd feel horrible about later. I took a long, deep suck, and a part of my brain realized what Judge was saying. It didn't fill my mouth like it did when I'd taken it straight from his jugular. It was a slower release, safer for the man who'd given me so much already.

The contented noises soon turned to moans as Judge slid himself into my body with aching slowness. Such a contrast to Brody, who was wild and untamed. Judge was smooth and methodical as his hands adjusted my hips to get the exact right angle. Pleasure rode my body hard, making me suck harder and Brody moan as he ground his cock into the softness of my stomach. At that moment I was glad our bites were pleasurable because this was so damn perfect. I moaned against Brody's skin, the taste of him and the feel of Judge too much and I came again. And again.

Sometime around my eighth orgasm of the night, I felt eyes on my face. Looking up, I appreciated the long lines of Brody's face as his head was thrown back in pleasure, his eyes closed. And just past his head was Sheriff Walker Walton, watching us with true hunger contorting his face. Brody was so far gone, his movements ragged as he thrust in time with my sucking motions, that he didn't even sense Walker in the room. But Judge knew. He started fucking me harder, no longer happy with slow and methodical. He was making me his and driving me wild, taunting the good Sheriff with what he could have if he just pulled the stick out of his ass.

And the whole time, with the taste of one man on my tongue and another buried deep inside of me, I didn't take my eyes off Walker. Not until the orgasm crashed over me like a tsunami, forcibly closing my eyes against the sensations, Judge's groans sliding against my skin as he came deep inside me.

When I opened my eyes again, Walker was gone.

CHAPTER TWELVE

I woke up the next morning sinfully sore, and to the sound of someone dry retching. Bolting upright in bed, I looked around the darkened room. Brody was lightly snoring beside me, his naked body completely exposed. I took a moment to let my gaze travel downward, soaking in the picturesque view.

Then the heaving sounds echoed around my apartment again, and I was up and in the bathroom in an instant. Judge hugged the toilet bowl, as gutfuls of undigested blood poured from his mouth. His shoulders shook with the violence at which his body was expelling my blood.

"Was it something you ate?" I asked, and Judge looked over his shoulder, a small smile curling his lips before he keeled over, wrapping his body into a ball. I knelt beside him on the tiles as he moaned in pain.

"What's wrong?"

"It's the effects of the bad blood. Alice said the comedown is rough," Walker said from behind me, and I stood and turned. Then remembered I was naked.

Refusing to be embarrassed, I strolled to the hook on my bathroom wall and grabbed my robe, lazily tying it around my waist, but I was insanely aware of Walker's heated gaze on my body. I worked hard at playing it cool. The guy literally saw me being pounded by one guy and eating another. The time for modesty was probably gone.

I sat down beside Judge, pulling his head into my lap so I could stroke his hair. He moaned, nuzzling against my thigh and the femoral artery that sat there. He was so pale he looked almost grey, and he was sweating so badly that his skin had a light layer of moisture. "Will my blood help him recover faster?"

Snippets of Judge's conversation with Brody flickered into my mind. He'd knew filtering out my blood would have this effect, and he did it anyway. "You didn't have to do this. But thank you," I whispered to him, wiping at the hair that had stuck to his face away.

"Drinking your blood won't help him recover any faster, at this point he's just throwing everything up. It's his body's way of expelling the toxins. Eventually, he'll have to replenish what he's lost, but not from you. Your body is weak as it is."

I frowned at him but looked down at how my hands were shaking. My legs did feel weak, but I'd put it down to jello-legs because of, you know, the ridiculous amount of sex I'd had last night.

I looked down at Judge, who was staring up at me with big blue eyes that were wild and a little bloodshot.

"Are you okay?" I asked, even if it was a little redundant. He was very much, not okay, but I wanted to hear him speak, just to reassure myself.

"Fine, Rainy Day." His voice was rough and thready. I didn't like it one little bit.

"Okay, tough guy. Let's get you back to bed, and I'll get you a bucket, some saltines and a bag of blood. Just call me Nurse Raine."

He grimaced like he was in pain, and I moved away from his path to the toilet. But he didn't move. "Don't talk about role-playing when I'm weak as a kitten, Darlin'. That's just not fair."

I laughed and stepped away as Walker picked up Judge like he was a damsel. It was a testament to how ill Judge was that he didn't even protest.

"You carryin' me across the threshold, Sheriff? In some cultures, that'd make us hitched," he poked half-heartedly.

A ghost of a smile curved one side of Walker's mouth. "You aren't my type."

"What is your type?" He smirked. "Let me guess. Curvy redheads with a body that attracts the beast and a soothing innocence that attracts the man." The smile slipped from Walker's face as he dropped Judge none-too-gently on the bed beside Brody.

Brody didn't even stir. He must be really exhausted. If his heartbeat wasn't creating an enticing background noise to the drama, I'd think he was dead. Still, I reached out and stroked his hair from his forehead, reassured by the almost searing heat that emanated from his skin.

"I should get him a steak or an iron supplement or something. I took too much." The guilt in my statement hung heavily in the room.

"I don't think he'll be complaining, Darlin'. Hell, I haven't puked this much since I was a human, and if I had the chance, I'd redo last night all over again."

I leaned forward and kissed his forehead, completely aware of Walker's eyes, and more self-conscious of this small gesture of affection than I was of my nudity. If that wasn't my life, in a nutshell, nothing was.

Judge's eyes drooped as he desperately tried to hang onto consciousness, but his battered body refused to cooperate. When his ragged breaths became a muffled snore, Walker cleared his throat and tilted his head toward the kitchen. I stood, wrapping my robe tighter around my waist.

Walker moved around my kitchen like he belonged there, and maybe he did. Turning on my fancy coffee machine, he set a cup under it and turned to face me.

"Do you know what would have happened if Judge hadn't been here last night?" His voice was a low, angry growl, but I knew it wasn't directed at me. I was the victim here, the wronged party. Apparently, he mistook my silence as an indication I was a dumbass, he spelled it out for me. "You would have torn Brody to pieces. There would have been nothing left of him but gore on the carpet. You'd probably be dead too because you are a baby vamp and he is a shifter who has been training for decades to defend himself and his pack against our kind. You'd have the element of surprise though because he has feelings for you, so he would have let his guard down. I would have come here this morning, and instead of you getting..." he swallowed hard.

"Dicked to the nth degree?" I supplied a little unhelpfully.

He narrowed his eyes at me. "Instead of that, I would have been cleaning up your crime scene and mourning the short life of Raine Baxter."

I stared at him because there was way too much in that short statement for me to unpack. I didn't dispute what he said though. I remembered that feeling, like I wasn't in control of my own body, even as my brain struggled to deny the impulses of my nature.

Finally, I nodded and sagged into the chair. "It

was just my blood that was contaminated, wasn't it?" Walker grimaced but inclined his head. "What was his endgame? My maker I mean. Why contaminate my blood supply?"

Walker let out a shuddering breath. "You would have been sentenced to death. There are few rules that are sacrosanct in Dark River, but the one golden rule is not taking a life. It wouldn't have mattered to the Council, or to Brody's pack, that someone had forced you into your feral state. There is no leeway, no second chances. You would have been executed by a member of the Council."

I clenched my teeth so hard that my jaw hurt and willed myself not to burst into tears.

"So they are trying to have me put down like a puppy they don't want anymore? Baby Vamps are for eternity, not just for Christmas," I joked, even though I wanted to cry. Apparently, I wasn't doing a very good job of hiding my emotional distress, because Walker whipped out a hand and dragged me toward his chest. I wrapped myself in his warmth, soaking in his scent and the feel of his chest against my cheek.

"It means someone is getting close, and he's panicking. We will catch this guy, Raine. He will get what he deserves, and you'll get your justice. I'm missing something important, I know it, but it's remaining stubbornly out of reach. But I won't give up. Not until you're safe." He sounded so sure, so steadfast, that I almost believed him.

Well, I refused to be run out of town. Mika might have turned tail and ran away, but I was making the best out of this shitty situation, and I refused to lose another family to that psycho. I pulled away from the strength of Walker's arms and straightened my shoulders.

"I better get ready for work."

Walker looked like he wanted to argue. In the end, he sighed and shook his head. "You're right. As much as I want to make you stay here and keep you safe, you don't deserve to be locked away in here like a prisoner. Just promise me you won't go anywhere alone. Ask Brody if he can get Miranda to come over and ward the apartment."

"Miranda?" I asked, and tried not to let the little touch of jealousy I felt bleed through into my tone.

Walker looked uncomfortable as he picked up his Mount-Me police hat. "She's the billion-year-old Witch that wards the Pack lands against unwanted Vamp visitors. She makes me feel…vulnerable. But she is good at what she does. Locks don't keep this guy out, but a protective ward by Miranda will prevent even an ancient from entering."

I raised an eyebrow. I didn't think anyone could make the sexy, self-assured Sheriff feel jittery. I wasn't sure I wanted to meet such a creature. But I didn't want to accidentally cause a mass murder either. I'd talk to Brody when he woke up, and if Brody trusted her, then that was good enough for me.

I followed in Walker's shadow to the door. I wanted nothing more than to climb up on his body like a baby koala and bask in the safety of his arms all day. I didn't even care if that made me a sissy. We stood in the open doorway, and he turned, so he was gazing down at me. He was so tall, and broad it was hard to imagine anything could hurt him.

"Raine…" he said, then sighed. There was a lot of subcontext to that sigh. It could have meant everything, or nothing at all. Then he leaned down and kissed my cheek way too close to my mouth. Or not close enough, depending on if you were a horny vamp who had the hots for men in felt sheriff hats. "Don't do anything stupid."

Yeah, and then he went and ruined it. I rolled my eyes, gave him a jaunty salute. "Love you too, Sheriff."

Then I shut the door in his face. I walked back through the bedroom, gathering clothes from the dirty pile on my floor. I needed to wash sometime this century. I paused in the middle of my room and sucked back a laugh. Somehow, Brody had ended up spooned around Judge, the blankets bunched around their feet. My sexy shapeshifter had his arm flung over Judge's stomach and a leg over one of his calf muscles. Judge had his arm over Brody's, his fingers curled around his muscular forearm. If they weren't completely naked, I'd take a photo on my phone to show Angeline. Underneath how freakin' cute it was, and quite frankly how damn hot it was seeing their muscular bodies wrapped up like a Twizzler, the sight kind of made me feel a warmth that was a lot more in the area of my chest than my nether regions. Would they want to go back to how it was, or could this be a thing? Could I go to bed with them every night, and wake up beside them every morning without the threat of imminent death and the worst case of food poisoning ever?

Shaking my head, I headed for the shower. I was going to have to ice my hoo-hoo before I went to work, or I'd be walking like a penguin that had just had an enema for the rest of the day.

I SHOULDN'T HAVE WORRIED MUCH about heading to work, because when I got downstairs, there was complete silence. I'd left two bags of blood and a barely seared steak by the bed upstairs, just in case the guys got hungry before I went up for my lunch break, but I probably shouldn't have worried. The shop was empty. I saw a note on the counter.

"RAINE,

   Closed the shop for the day to help Alice pick up a new blood shipment, to be on the safe side. There are two casseroles and a dozen steaks in the fridge. Take them and feed your white knights. Speaking of white knights, Walker said he'd be around to check on you later, so I put one in for him too. While your white knights are out of action, maybe you should try riding him like a noble steed?"

I SNORTED. That woman didn't even blink an eyelid at the fact that I'd had some kind of hedonistic orgy for most of the night. But she was all about keeping things fair.

"THE SHOP WILL STAY SHUT for another night at least, so don't worry about coming in tomorrow either. Alice gave all the tested blood to Bertie and Beatrice, so if you need extra, head over there. See you bright and early Thursday. Angeline x"

I STOOD there in the empty bakery and felt a little lost. The store had given me a purpose, and without it, I wasn't sure what to do. I didn't want to go back upstairs, because despite what I said to Walker, the temptation of Brody's blood was still riding me. It felt like an artificial need, like the time I got the munchies after getting completely high with my roommate at college last year. But it was there, and it was hard to resist, and Brody needed the rest of his blood. I walked through the back of the shop, out through the kitchen and into the back parking lot. I'd head over to the diner. Maybe I could get a type-o float and this need riding me might dissipate a little.

But as I set down the footpath towards the diner, the streets that had once seemed quaint seemed awfully ominous all of a sudden. It was like I was waiting for the boogeyman, or the Witch Miranda, to pop out of the shadows. It was bad enough when I thought my maker just wanted me to keep my mouth shut. It had escalated, and now he wanted me dead, even if he was reluctant to swing the ax himself. My skin crawled like I was being watched. Paranoia – that's all it was.

Still, I used super-speed to get to the diner quicker. I burst through the front door like a woman possessed, and everyone turned to look at me again. Wow, that was some serious deja vu.

I lift my hand in an awkward wave at the people of the town who were no longer strangers and strode over to the long counter-top. Bertie was there, shining a glass like he was every time I saw him. I was beginning to think he had a serious compulsion.

"Hey Bertie," I said, and the man in question grunted, but he gave me a broad smile. He was a man of few words. I could appreciate that quality in a man. I opened my mouth to order, but before I could form a sentence, there was a Type-O float in front of me. Bertie moved incredibly fast, even for a Vamp. It was deceiving considering he looked about 65 and must have had a significant middle-age spread when he'd been turned.

I gave him a huge grin that showed all my teeth. "Thanks, Bertie, you're the best."

Beatrice came out and slid cheese fries in front of me, not even bothering to take my order. Apparently, even as Raine, I was a little predictable. But, you know, guilt-free cheese fries. I wasn't even mad.

"Heard you had a bit of a problem over at your place last night, Lass. The boys, okay?"

The entire diner was eerily silent, waiting for my answer. I wanted to say you could have heard a pin drop, but it was worse than that. It was the kind of silence that echoed in a room that was filled with people who had preternatural stillness. I should have just stayed home, pressed between the naked bodies of Judge and Brody. Quite frankly, that was even better than guilt-free cheese fries, and that's saying something.

"Yeah, they are fine. Recuperating, but I could use a couple of extra pints if you have them. And maybe another steak for Brody."

Beatrice nodded and then glared around the diner. "I'll make them to-go, shall I? Being stared at like a sideshow is bad for the digestion," she said huffily and gave the entire room a disapproving look.

Apparently, everyone was suitably shamed

because they went back to eating and talking quietly, but I'd lost my appetite. My name was a whispered curse that bounced off the memorabilia-laden walls, and I wondered if one day, I could just live a normal life.

Or just live.

CHAPTER THIRTEEN

"That is a fucking awful idea," Judge said, scowling at Walker. Brodie seemed content enough, holding me in his lap, and snuggling my hair like I was the unholy union between venison and chocolate.

"If you have a better suggestion, I'd like to hear it, Drifter," Walker growled, and Judge tensed at the moniker. "Unless you want to move in permanently and keep watch, then she needs some other kind of safeguard." He gave him a smile that wasn't friendly in the least. "But we both know that you are too selfish to put anyone else before your wandering. Raine is just a warm body to you, right?"

Judge stood, and Brody stiffened beneath me but made no move to stand too. "I ingested poison for Raine. You don't get to lecture me about the commitment to my girlfriend while you've done jack-fuckin'-

shit to find her killer. I am making progress. You're just sitting here in this town, spinning on the nightstick shoved up your ass, waitin' for the killer to what? Hand themselves in?"

I wanted to defend one of them, at this point I wasn't sure which, but my brain had stuttered to a halt when Judge called me his girlfriend.

Girlfriend. Maybe he meant girl friend. You know, with a pause in the middle. After the big discussion, we'd had the other day about Judge having an allergy to commitment like I had an allergy to the midday sun, it had to be with a space. I was his friend, who happened to be a girl. That's what he meant, I was sure of it. I could feel more than hear Brody's silent chuckling.

Walker whipped his furious gaze to Brody. Apparently, it wasn't so silent. "What do you think about this, Shifter? As you sit there with Judge's *girlfriend* on your lap and your dick pressed between her ass cheeks?"

I stood this time and got all up in Walker's space. "What are you implying right now, Walker? I know you are worried, and when you're worried it seems to make you a little bit of an asshole, but if you are insinuating I'm some kind of…" my brain scrambled around for a word that didn't taste bitter on my tongue, "…tramp, you can just take your sexy ass and your misogynistic views right out of my apartment and never return."

Walker had the good grace to look ashamed. "That's not what I'm saying at all, Raine. You know…"

"I know what, Sheriff?"

"That the idea of anything happening to you makes me physically ill. Because I care about you," he huffed out on a sigh. "Just as much as these two dick-wads." He indicated Judge, who was still scowling at the Sheriff, and Brody, who was grinning like an idiot. "I don't care who you, uh, take to your bed, as long as they treat you well and make you happy."

I wasn't sure if that was an apology, or as close as I was going to get to an apology, but I'd take it. I slid my eyes toward Judge, but he was pointedly, not looking at me. I wasn't sure I could let it rest. I shifted off Brody's lap, giving an imperceptible wiggle, but it was enough to make the shifter give a groan.

A mature person may have let it rest. A mature person would let Judge get away with his little slip and not pushed him about it. But I never said I was mature. "Am I your girlfriend, Judge?" I purred, sashaying toward him. Well, what I assumed was a sashay; hopefully it didn't look like I'd fallen in the shower and dislocated my hip.

Apparently, Judge wasn't one to let things go either, because he stared back at me defiantly. I wanted to know it was just a Freudian slip, a way to verbally mark his territory, or if he actually meant it.

His gaze burned into my own, a test of wills, a

battle to see who would look away first. I decided I now had a distinct competitive streak in my second life because instead of shifting my eyes from those piercing dark eyes, I leaned forward and kissed his full lips.

One point to Raine.

He leaned into the kiss, his tongue a searing brand against my mouth, and he got my bottom lip between his teeth and bit down hard enough to break the skin. The taste of my blood flooded my mouth, and I moaned as he sucked at it gently.

He pulled back and looked completely smug.

Okay, maybe one point all.

"Now you can update your relationship status to 'It's complicated' can we go back to what we were talking about?" Brody said, sounding amused. "I can set up a meeting with Miranda. I'm with the Sheriff on this one. I don't care how uncomfortable some little old lady makes you vamps, Raine's safety comes first. Besides, if you guys are all locked out of her apartment, more Rainey Time for me." He waggled his eyebrows, and I grinned back, shaking my head.

Judge gave him a mock snarl. "Watch it, Pup, or I'll put you in the doghouse myself." He let out a long sigh. "Fine, but make sure there's a way for us to get in too. I don't want Raine to trip and break her neck, and every person in town is locked out because we're all vamps."

I snorted but didn't comment. Mostly because he

wasn't wrong. I'd like to say that now I was an immortal badass, I'd left behind my dumbass ways. But if anyone could break their neck and starve to death on their bathroom floor, it would probably be me.

Walker nodded, his own lips twisted in a smile. "Make the call, Brody. I'll meet her at the edge of town and escort her in."

Brody gave him a jaunty little salute and pulled his phone from his too-tight jeans. They cupped his ass in a way that made my hands ache to do the same. He left the room, though it was a little redundant with all the supernatural hearing in the room.

"Hey Miranda," Brody said from the other room. Whatever was said on the other end made him give a deep, sexy laugh. He dropped his voice lower, and I couldn't quite pick up his words anymore.

Why wouldn't he want us to hear? Was I jealous of some old witch? I shook my head and looked at the other two occupants in my living room. "Have you both met this Miranda?" I worked hard to keep my tone nonchalant.

Walker nodded. "Yes, she fixed the wards around Brody's pack meeting place so I could attend. To do that, she needed a touch of my blood." He visibly shuddered, and I couldn't work out if it was because she was horrendous, or because she was a witch.

I looked at Judge, but he wasn't meeting my eyes again. "How about you, Judge?"

He lifted a single shoulder and looked bored. "I've met her once or twice."

My brows lowered. "Oh, when?"

"A few decades ago."

I gritted my teeth. "Are you purposefully making this as painful as possible?"

He just stared back at me, his jaw tight and his face expressionless. I turned away before I gave in to the urge to strangle him.

"We've worked together," he said, and the way he said it implied I'd extracted the information through some kind of mental torture. But it wasn't his tone that made me pause. It was the fact he'd given me even that tiny little window of his past. Judge would talk to me about his future plans, or the town and its inhabitants, sometimes about all the ways he'd like to taste my body, but he never talked about his time prior to coming to Dark River.

"What kind of work was that? Door-to-door vacuum salesman?" I said it lightly, not wanting to scare him off.

Brody laughed. "Well, one of them definitely sucked like a hoover. Knowing Miranda, maybe both."

What the hell did that mean? Before I had a chance to ask, Brody changed the subject. "We're in luck. She's in Vancouver. She can be here in an hour."

Vancouver was ten hours away. That was impossible. "Is her broom supercharged or something?"

All three of them laughed, but it was Brody who wrapped his arm around my shoulders and pulled me close. He was even more affectionate now that we'd been through the craziness of last night together. I wasn't going to lie, I lapped up his affection the same way I lapped up his blood. It was wonderful.

He leaned close until I could feel the brush of his lips over the shell of my ear, and a tingle ran through my body.

"Magic."

THE WOMAN who stepped out of a glowing slit, in reality, made my jaw drop to the floor like I was an animated cartoon cowboy with a big red mustache. The slit was one thing. That was fucking weird. Like some superhero movie with bad eighties special effects weird, it was like she was entering from a glowing red abyss.

But she was goddamn gorgeous. I mean, I wanted to strip naked and beg her to take me, and I was as hetero as they came. I mean, I was straight up strictly dickly. She was just that hot.

On the heels of that realization was Brody's joke about someone sucking like a Hoover. My eyes whipped toward Judge, but his face was completely impassive like he was carved from stone. The Fort Knox of expressions.

In the face of such beauty, that told me everything I needed to know. There was no hint of male appreciation, no spark of recognition. No nostalgic smile of meeting someone you'd long ago worked with. It was just stone-cold neutrality.

They'd been lovers. I knew this deep down in my gut, somewhere in the same vicinity as the acid of jealousy was currently burning.

I looked at Walker, who looked respectful, and in all honesty, a little petrified. That seemed like a logical response. The power that poured off her made me choke on the air.

The warmth in Brody's eyes wasn't lustful, but definitely friendly.

Miranda appraised us all in that silence. She gave Brody a small smile and wiggled her fingers.

"Sheriff. It is good to see you again."

Walker Walton honest-to-goodness tipped his hat. "You too, Ma'am. Thank you for coming on such short notice."

She waved a hand. "Not to worry. I was in town, and Brody has a way of convincing women to do what he wants." Her tone was teasing, but slightly disapproving. Apparently, the lack of attraction between the Brody and Miranda was reciprocated. They were both blind, obviously.

But when her eyes landed on Judge, there was

nothing platonic in them. Her eyes burned, and I couldn't tell whether it was with anger or with lust or with the fires of Hell.

"Judge. I didn't know you would be here." Apparently, they learned complete neutrality in the same vacuum salesman school, because I couldn't tell if she was happy to see him or not.

"I'm here for Raine," he said in a low voice that was nearly a growl.

Miranda raised a single eyebrow and looked at me appraisingly. I should feel offended, but there was nothing scathing in her gaze. More like professional interest. "Ah, Raine. So you are the fly in this little vamp commune's ointment. It is nice to meet you." She put a hand out to shake, and the good manners that had been drilled into me as Mika Mackenzie reared their head. I reached out to take her hand, but fingers around my wrist stopped me. I looked up at Judge, who'd moved impossibly fast.

"She can read your soul if you let her touch you," he growled, and I frowned at the beautiful woman. That was a damn sneaky trick.

Miranda let out a tinkling laugh, the kind that just made your heart happy.

"A bit dramatic Judge. Only your thoughts, not your soul. And sometimes, your desires." But still, Miranda let her hand drop. "Do you have my fee?" She directed this toward Brody, but it was Judge that held out an envelope.

It didn't look like it held cash, so I wondered what the payment actually was. I didn't want to ask in front of the Witch, though. Walker moved closer, subtly putting himself between me and Miranda, which was actually quite impressive considering we were standing face to face. There was nothing offensive in the gesture, and I now knew why the Council let him go on diplomatic visits to Brody's pack. He was effortlessly diplomatic, while still getting the outcome he wanted.

Miranda's lips quirked, and I had the impression she was a hell of a lot older than her early thirtysomething appearance.

"Welcome to Dark River. I regret the need for subterfuge, but at the moment everyone in town is a suspect," Judge said solemnly.

Another lip twitch from the witch. I couldn't even appreciate that my thoughts managed to rhyme. "Surely, not everyone?" Her eyes swung back to Judge. "Not your oh-so-revered Council?"

Well, you didn't need to be a diplomat to get the subtext in that statement. Judge narrowed his eyes, but Walker remained pleasant.

"Everyone is a suspect until proven otherwise. It is why we needed to call you in, I'm afraid. Shall we go?"

Miranda nodded, and snapped her fingers, disappearing.

"What in the Furby-loving-fuck?" I whispered.

Brody laughed, and Judge just tugged me closer to his body by my wrist. It was then I realized he'd never let it go. My Drifter was strung tighter than a rope bunny on BDSM night.

"She can glamor her appearance using her cloak." There was no awe in his tone, which I was pretty sure there would be if I'd said it.

"Like the cloak of invisibility in Harry Potter?"

The tinkling laugh again. "I like her. Let's go make sure she isn't murdered in her own home, shall we?" said a discombobulated voice coming from thin air.

As we all moved off from the town limits, I was left wondering if that was a threat or promise.

CHAPTER FOURTEEN

As we zipped back through town, I was wondering if the Witch Miranda would be able to keep up, or if she would just walk through another one of those slits. I needed to give them a different name. The more I thought about it, it was a little bit like getting rebirthed out a vagina. Mentally I changed the name to portal instead.

But when I opened the door to my apartment, she suddenly reappeared. She wasn't out of breath or glistening with sweat like she'd just run three miles at the speed of light. Hmm.

"Walker?"

I turned as Angeline and Alice came up the stairs from the cafe. Miranda turned and watched them too, her eyebrow quirked.

"Not so secret, I guess, Sheriff?" she said, slightly

disapprovingly. I bristled, but Walker maintained his bland, harmless expression.

"I trust Alice and Angeline above all in this town. Angeline owns this building and is Raine's friend, and Alice is the town doctor. They both need access." He made it sound completely reasonable, which it was. No part of me thought either Angeline or Alice had the capacity to take my life and then torture me like this.

I swear Miranda rolled her eyes. At Walker! Still she pulled a small knife from a bag slung around her hips, and a small vial of something. Eye of newt and heart of toad maybe. "So be it. I'll start with Raine. Give me your hand."

I hesitated, Judge's warning still ringing in my head. She let out an annoyed chuff and tapped her foot. "I can promise you, there is nothing in that pretty little skull that I haven't seen before. I still have four more vamps to do, and this is time-consuming."

I let out a long breath and squared my shoulders. I thrust out my hand, and she took it.

It wasn't a subtle feeling, having someone poke around in your head. I could almost feel her sifting through my memories, my thoughts, my desires. I felt her fingers clench on my wrist, and I can only assume she got to the part where Judge made love to me like my life was the only thing that mattered.

I watched as her jaw tensed, but then she relaxed. She pierced my finger in one long cut, dripping the blood onto the threshold. She chanted something in a tongue I didn't understand and sincerely hoped she wasn't about to turn me into a frog or curse me with an allergy to chocolate.

"Okay. The ward is set. You'll have to feed it your blood every couple of days to ensure it maintains its strength, but it shouldn't let anyone other than you in if you haven't given them prior permission. Now, you might want to pop that bleeding finger in your mouth before you give Judge an embolism."

I looked over at Judge, who's eyes were indeed serious. I went to do as Miranda said, but again Judge's hand stopped me by grabbing hold of my wrist. I stared at him as he lifted my bleeding finger and put it in his own mouth, sucking hard against the flesh.

The pull of his mouth went straight to my core, which made Brody groan and Walker look somewhere between angry and horny. Horngry. It was a thing.

I knew the feeling. I was horngry too. I pulled my finger from Judge's mouth with an audible pop.

"Whatever this is, leave me the hell out of it," I hissed, and went over to stand beside Alice and Angeline. At least they didn't send weird emotional signals. Also, they'd never seen me naked, and I didn't lust after their bodies.

I wanted to fold my arms and pout, but that would just make me look immature. Next, to Miranda, this powerful witch/sex goddess, I was having some serious inadequacy issues, and Judge wasn't helping. Brody walked over casually, kissed my cheek, and pulled me against his chest. That was it. He didn't say anything or try to one-up anyone. He could sense with his little supernatural nose that I needed comfort, and he gave it without expecting anything in return. It was never a power play with Brody. I sighed and leaned against him, ignoring the speculative expression on Miranda's face.

Shrugging, she looked at Walker. "You're up, Sheriff."

She repeated the ritual again, the words of the chant slightly different. She explained that she was only giving him permission to enter. Instead of dripping the blood on the threshold, she smeared a drop of Walker's blood on the back of the door. "Take good note where his mark is. To revoke his permission, you only need to wash it away and replace it with yours."

When she was done, she looked challengingly at Judge. "Are you going to suck on his boo-boo too?"

Judge narrowed his eyes, and as quick as a ninja, his hand whipped out, grabbing Walker's finger and sucking it into his mouth.

Walker's eyes opened comically wide, and he seemed frozen as Judge sucked the blood from his finger, his saliva closing the wound. The knitting flesh seemed to wake Walker from his shock, because he shook his head, pulled his finger out of Judge's grasp and scowled.

Angeline leaned closer to Alice. "I love you, Baby, and I'm pretty sure I am 1000% gay but watching the Drifter suck on the Sheriff's finger like that…" She fanned herself. Alice laughed, and I just shook my head.

Girl, same.

Fortunately for everyone, feeding the ward, both Alice and Angeline's blood went off without a hitch. Judge kept his lips to himself, and they excused themselves and got the hell out of Miranda's presence as quick as possible, even if Alice did shoot Walker an apologetic look on the way out. I couldn't blame them. Between Miranda's raw power and the tension in the room, it could suffocate a goldfish.

Finally, it was Judge's turn, and the tension in the room went to DEFCON 4. Or was it DEFCON 1 that was the bad one? Who knew, either way, it was enough to make my skin itch.

"Are you putting your blood on the ward, Judge?" She asked, and somehow the question sounded a lot more important than when she'd asked it of Angeline and Alice earlier. It now sounded like a challenge, or maybe a curse.

Never taking his eyes from the witch, he held out his hand. She frowned and gave him a feral grin, lifting the ceremonial dagger and cutting far deeper than she had with anyone else. I leaped forward, but Brody's restraining arm held me in place. Judge didn't even bat an eye as his blood gushed onto the floor between them, dripping over his palm until it was soaked red.

His lip lifted in a snarl as he slammed his hand against the back of the door, marking it with a full handprint, rivulets of blood turning the back of my door into a macabre splatter painting.

"Do your part," he growled at Miranda, who lifted a brow at his imperious tone, but started the same chant as she had done for the rest of us.

When it was done, Judge lifted his bleeding hand to his mouth and ran the flat of his tongue along the wound, smearing his face with blood. Not going to lie, the predator in me beat against my fragile control. I wanted to be tasting his blood, to push him down into the puddle of blood on the floor and fuck him senseless in front of the Witch until she knew who he belonged to. Luckily, Brody still had his arm around my waist, and Walker, who was a perceptive asshole, moved to the left to block my path a little more.

The two people in front of me, both as beautiful in their deadliness, maintained their standoff, neither of them willing to back down. Finally, Miranda laughed.

"It's good to see you fall, *Armastaja*," she purred, then opened her giant vagina portal and disappeared from the hallway completely. That was it.

I looked around the three men loitering in the hall. "Guess it's time to see if this works, right?"

I wouldn't say out loud that I didn't really trust the witch, just in case, she was omnipotent, or still hanging around the hallways like Christmas glitter in May. Or herpes after a trip to Vegas.

I went first, stepping over the threshold with ease. I don't know what I expected. A tingle of magic, some kind of viscous barrier. Instead, there was nothing. It was like walking over a normal threshold.

Walker went next, and with his entrance, there was a little tremble of magic that ran through my veins. Interesting version of a doorbell, but I could deal with it.

Brody strode in next, and I felt nothing. Obviously, because he hadn't been warded out at all. He could come and go as he pleased.

Finally, it was Judge's turn, and I found myself holding my breath. As soon as he stepped over the threshold, he dropped to his knees.

"Fuckin' bitch," he growled under his breath, but he was over the threshold and in the apartment. "She warded it, so it zapped me in the balls."

Brody laughed, and even Walker covered a chuckle. I threw them both dirty looks and strode over, pulling him to his feet and wrapping my arms around his waist. "You okay?" At his nod, I stood on my toes and kissed him gently. "Don't worry. Every time you get zapped, I'll rub them better," I dropped my voice low. "With my tongue."

Brody abruptly stopped laughing, and I could feel the low chuckle rumble in Judge's chest. "I'm going to take you up on that offer, Rainy Day."

WALKER LEFT, on the pretense of Sheriff duties. However, when Brody left soon afterward, saying he was happier I was safe now and had Pack duties to take care of, I wondered if they were just trying to avoid the inevitable fallout between Judge and me.

Because it was inevitable. There was the girlfriend (no space) comment earlier, then the obvious tension between him and Miranda and their unknown connection. Not to mention the fact that he used me as a weapon in their weird little game of headfuckery.

Judge sat on the couch, warily watching me as I paced around the living room.

"So, now we are a couple officially, should I clear you out a drawer? Maybe you should leave a toothbrush here. Maybe I can go to your apartment for once?"

He winced. "Raine…"

I held up a hand. "Unless you need to have some kind of passive-aggressive dinner date with the Witch Miranda, who I have to assume is some kind of ex-something. Girlfriend?"

He blew out a huge breath through his nose. "No, she wasn't my girlfriend."

The 'but' that hung in the air after his admission was so big, that even Sir Mixalot would have liked it. I quirked a brow, my lips pressed together so hard that I was pretty sure that I looked like my Great Aunt Dot. My dad always said her face reminded him of a cat's ass.

"We were lovers, once upon a time. Partners."

I threw my hands up in the air and marched into the kitchen before I did something stupid like punching him.

"No shit, Sherlock. Anyone with two eyes and two brain-cells they could knock together would know that. The sexual tension was so thick, I thought Brody was going to suffocate on it." *Deep breath*, I chanted to myself. "You're a vampire, Judge. You're old as dirt. I get it. Unless you were a monk before your turning, I'm pretty sure you wouldn't be able to count how many lovers you've had on a dozen hands. What I'm annoyed by is the fact that you didn't think you'd mention it, then used me as some kind of verbal ammunition to shoot around."

I strode back over to him and leaned down until we were nose to nose. "What I am infuriated about, is that she knows your past, and I don't even know your stupid last name. What I'm devastated by, actually heartbroken about, is that perhaps Walker was right. That I am a toy to you, a way to pass the years. I thought I was okay with it, really. But seeing you with Miranda today, I now know that you aren't allergic to commitment like I thought, just allergic to a commitment to me," I took a shuddery breath and blinked hard. "That hurts way more than I thought it would."

"Hudson. My last name is Hudson."

"Judge Hudson?"

He shook his head. "No. John. John Hudson. Judge is a nickname I...earned in my old profession."

I pushed. "What profession was that exactly?"

His jaw clenched, but he gave a tiny shake of his head. I sighed.

He lifted his hand up and cupped my cheek. "I care about you so much, Raine."

I rested my forehead against his and sighed. "Yeah, I know."

Then, because I was weak, I let him take me to bed and make love to me all night.

But I wasn't surprised when I woke the following evening, and he was gone.

CHAPTER FIFTEEN

I was that girl. You know the one? The one that needs a man in her life otherwise she's a ghost of herself? How the hell did I end up that girl? What happened to Raine, Badass Mother-Flipper who wasn't going to be tied down, that was going to flit from hot sexy paranormal to hot sexy paranormal, like a horny honey bee?

Apparently, I lost her somewhere between the Shifter snack pack and the paranormal sandwich. And now I was just hungry.

I flopped onto the couch in the library of The Immortal Cupcake and ate a huge slice of Angeline's Devil's Food Cake. Lucky my ass wasn't going to get fat because I'd basically eaten today's wages in baked goods.

When the bell tinkled overhead, I was surprised to see Cresta, Angeline, and Ella standing in the archway between the two sections of the business. They were dressed in outfits that were so spangly and shiny that they hurt my eyes.

"Is it 'dress like a disco ball day' and no one told me?" I said, shoveling more cake in my mouth.

Angeline looked at the other two women and inclined her head in my direction. "She's been like this all week."

"Tragic," Ella said, shaking her head sadly.

"Hey, I'd be gorging myself on cake too if I'd been loved and left by the Drifter. The man is-" Ella elbowed Cresta in the ribs to make her stop and held out a garment bag.

"Put this on. We are going out."

I scoffed. "Oh yeah? Is the diner having a seventies night?"

Angeline dragged me to my feet and pulled me toward the kitchen. I hadn't even noticed that the store was now closed. Once I was in the freshly scrubbed kitchen, they all stood around me.

"Strip, change into this sparkly little dress, and we are going to a nightclub in Calgary."

I froze, my fingers clutching the garment bag in my hands. "We are going to leave Dark River?"

Ella was already tugging at my clothes, making little tsking noises at the chocolate buttercream stains. "Yep," she said, popping the P.

I looked at Angeline, equal parts terrified and hopeful they were telling the truth. "There's no way

Walker would let me leave the safety of the town. I'm still too new."

Angeline gave me a look. It was part sneaky, part self-satisfied and all trouble. "Walker is coming with us."

Twenty-five minutes later I was jammed into Angeline's sleek black BMW, with Mr. Control Freak at the wheel. Angeline hadn't minded when he'd headed to the driver's door, just tossing him the keys and climbing in the back to sit beside an already giggling Cresta and Ella. Apparently, no one really got to go to the big city often, so they were even more excited about this than I was. Actually, I wasn't excited at all. I was a ball of nervous energy all wrapped up in killer heels. I finished the blood bag in my hand and no sooner had I put it down, that Walker handed me another one from the cooler in the footwell. Apparently the idea was to gorge me on blood on the way, and by the time I got there I'd be so full that the temptation of all those flitter-fluttering heartbeats would be dampened. This was pre-drinks to the extreme.

"Shouldn't we ease into it or something? Start with, like a cemetery?" I asked Walker in a low voice.

"Are you making a dead joke?" he stage whispered back. "It'll be fine, Raine. I won't let you do anything you regret."

I scoffed. The last time someone had told me that, I'd ended up doing tequila shots out of the navel of a freshman at a frat party. I reassured myself that the tequila probably sterilized whatever gross belly button crud had been living there.

Walker effortlessly maneuvered the BMW down the dark, twisty roads of middle-of-nowhere Alberta, as fast as the sportscar could go. His reflexes were impeccable, and we were all used to going so fast that the sportscar was almost hilariously slow. But I enjoyed the quiet purr of the engine, and the comforting smell of the leather, anyway. Quicker than would have been humanly imaginable, the lights of Calgary were in sight.

"Does the 'no biting' rule apply outside of Dark River?" I asked, wondering if Walker was here in his capacity of Sheriff as well as a babysitter.

"Yes. Though not quite as strictly enforced," he said begrudgingly. "While we promote abstinence completely, we understand that sometimes accidents happen. As long as you don't drain anyone dry and cover your tracks well, then it will be forgiven. Out here, you are under the purview of the Vampire Nation rules. If you fuck up, it won't be just me you are answering to. It's the Enforcers as well."

Again, the word Enforcer was a conversational anvil, quieting the chatter from the backseat. These guys must be some seriously scary mofo's if saying their name was like saying Beetlejuice one too many times. I really needed to look into the Vampire Nation again, and Enforcers. These were my people now, and living in blissful ignorance wasn't going to cut it.

We parked at the lowest level of an underground carpark, and as I unfolded myself from the front seat of the sports car, I couldn't help but notice how Walker's eyes took in the long line of my exposed legs. Exposed because Ella had given me a dress that was basically a long t-shirt. It sat just under my ass cheeks, and I would never, ever have considered wearing it as Mika.

But Mika was dead, and I put it on, along with the expensive hooker heels, and owned it. Now, seeing the heat in Walker's eyes, I was glad I owned it.

Cresta linked arms with me and dragged me along. I'd forgotten to tell Walker about Cresta's mind-wiping abilities, but I pushed the thought down. Cresta wasn't my maker/tormentor. She was a friend, and tonight I was out with people who liked me and wanted what was best for me. So I was going to enjoy the night, forget that my psycho maker was out there somewhere trying to passively kill me, though at the rate they were spiraling, probably aggressively kill me in the end. I was going to pretend to be a twenty-something human who just wanted to dance with cute boys, drink vodka that wouldn't work on me anyway and have some fun.

When we got to the club, the line zig-zagged down the pavement for three blocks.

The sound knocked me like a physical force. And

the smell. So much blood. So many heartbeats that thrummed in my ears like a siren's song.

"I'll take her from here, Cresta," Walker's low voice said from behind me, and he tugged me back to his side. He tucked me tight against his body in a move that would have seemed almost affectionate, if I didn't know he was just keeping me close in case I decided to go rabid.

I looked at the end of the line as the three vampiresses in front of me just strode straight past. They walked right up to the bouncer, who was looking at them like his eyes were about to fall out of his head.

I stared and tried to judge what he was seeing. If I looked at them as they were right now, all shiny and otherworldly, although a human wouldn't know that, they were a bit awe-inspiring. Cresta's hair was huge, her skin was golden, and her curves made her look like a bombshell. Ella looked like a model, straight up, and Angeline looked like a wet dream. I definitely couldn't blame the bouncer.

He opened the rope, and we all strode in like rockstars, right past the coat check, because we didn't really feel the cold anymore.

"Well, I can tick that off the bucket list," I said to Walker, though the girls could hear us too. "I always wanted to walk into a nightclub, like I was a celebrity. I think that the closest I was going to get."

"Never say never, Sweetie," Cresta said over her

shoulder and then squealed. "It's been so long! How long has it been, Angie?"

Angeline bit her lip, and if anyone had been looking close enough, they would have seen her fangs. "I think the last time was '78?"

Ella looked dreamy. "Disco. What a time."

I laughed. Looking at their outfits, I wasn't so sure they'd left disco too far behind. I concentrated on just Walker's scent, his slow pulse that was so different in comparison to the warm thrum of blood rushing through the club. I breathed through my mouth slowly and gripped Walker tighter.

"You got this, Raine. You have amazing control for a newbie. Brody is proof of that."

He was right. If I could stop myself with Brody, whose blood was like an orgy in my mouth, then a few humans should be fine. We walked to the bar, and Ella was pawing hot young guys like she'd been in a nunnery for thirty years. Considering she'd never said anything about having a bed partner, maybe she had been?

We got to the bar, and Angeline ordered five Bloody Mary's. Even though I was strung tighter than a g-string on a sumo, I couldn't help but laugh. "Really. Now we really are playing into the cliche." But I still gulped down a massive mouthful.

Ella walked over to a couch, where three kids who looked like they were high, or hipsters, were lounging as if clubbing was so basic and they were only here ironically.

"Move," she said pleasantly. One scowled and opened his mouth to argue, but instead he just nodded and left, and the other two followed, confused looks on their faces.

"Ella has compulsion. As her ability, I mean," Walker whispered in my ear. I stored that little factoid away in my brain as well. I wonder if she could only compel humans, or if she could compel other vampires.

I wondered if she could use it to feed on humans, whether they'd just offer themselves up as sacrificial lambs? I wasn't sure if I was envious or disgusted by the idea. Maybe a little bit of both, which was basically how my life went now. The constant war between my human sensibilities and the predator's needs.

No sooner had we sat that Angeline was standing again, dragging everyone onto the dancefloor. Walker just laughed and shook his head, but he moved to the edge of the dancefloor to watch. "Relax, Sheriff. We'll watch Raine. You don't have to be so uptight all night," Cresta said, laughing as she swayed to the music, kicking her legs out in a discordant rhythm that was as funny as it was oddly mesmerizing. I downed the rest of the Bloody Mary that was still clutched tightly in my hand and joined the circle of the dancers. I didn't know what it was about a group of dancing women, but all too soon guys were swarming the four of us. A guy danced behind me, his arms at his sides, completely respectable. My eyes looked around wildly for Walker, and as I met them across the dancefloor, I felt better. I danced back against the guy, enjoying the flood of music and pheromones. One song turned into another, then another and the vampire in my blood decided that this was some kind of primal release. Not as good as blood or sex, but there was something similar in the way your body just moved without thinking, the way it rolled with the people around you.

It was hard to pick the moment when it turned though. Whether it was the third or tenth or thirtieth song. But one minute I was dancing with a different guy, the third or fourth of the night, and another one joined in and rubbed his hand across my ass, and that was it. The predator snapped.

My body whipped around of its own accord, even as my eyes searched for Cresta or Ella or Angeline. I couldn't see Walker, but my body was wrapped around the guy in an instant, my teeth to his throat. I pulled hard at the reins of my control, drawing back, so my aching fangs didn't pierce the skin, even though they skittered along the surface. I stumbled backward, inhumanly fast, hoping that no one noticed that I was moving at a frantic, preternatural pace as I ran from the dancefloor.

I banged into a guy, almost knocking him over,

trying to escape the club. My hand whipped out and caught him, the heat from his skin searing my flesh as I let go as quickly as possible.

"Shit, I'm sorry," I mumbled, trying not to think how good he smelled. I ran past him toward the exit, ignoring whatever he yelled after me.

I burst through the exit doors into the back alley just as someone wrapped an arm around my waist from behind. I tried to spin in the hold, hissing as the predator finally got loose. And she was pissed.

"Hey, it's me. It's okay," Walker's soothing voice was beside my ear, and I shuddered with relief. But I was still so fucking hungry.

I spun in his grasp and latched onto his neck before he had a chance to move. The warm flow of his blood across my tongue made me moan so loudly it echoed down the alleyway. He let me push him back against the rough brick wall and press my self so hard against him, I could feel every inch of his body as if it were an extension of my own. I had no doubt that if he didn't want what was happening right now, he could have stopped me without a thought. Instead, he tilted his head a little more to the side and let me drink deep.

He tasted different to Judge, like a wine that was grown in a different region of France. Still amazing, but more subtle. Judge's blood was like a punch to the heart. But Walker was like a soaking warmth that you could drown in. I lifted my leg up so I could grind myself against his denim-clad thigh, almost the perfect height in these ridiculously high heels. The bottom of my dress rode up over my scant lace under-wear, but before the cold night air could even kiss my asscheeks, Walker had turned us both, pressing me back against the wall, preventing the world at large from seeing how badly I was soaking my panties. He groaned as he ground himself at the apex of my thighs, and then he slid a finger between my lips, released the sucking of my mouth at his neck and jumped away as if my vagina was electrified.

His chest was heaving, and I was basically panting like a bitch in heat too. "Are you okay?" I asked.

I rubbed my bottom lip with my finger, pulling away to stare at the remnants of his blood on my skin. Then I stuck it in my mouth and sucked hard. Waste not want not, right?

Walker looked physically pained and judging by the massive bulge in his pants, perhaps he was. Though he was also wobbling a little on his feet. Shit. I'd taken too much.

"Crap, I'm sorry. I didn't mean…" Well, that was a lie. I definitely did mean to suck on him like a straw. I cocked my head to the side, offering him my own neck and resisting the urge to rub myself on him at the same time.

Walker pushed me away another few inches. "If I take blood from you now, I'm going to fuck you against that wall like a rabid animal." He dragged in a shuddering breath. "Just stay over there, okay? I'm fine."

But his eyes were glowing, so I knew he was worked up. I resisted the urge to throw caution to the wind and insist he follow through with his promise, err, warning, and I couldn't even blame the now happy and sated inner predator for that. That was one hundred percent horny ass Raine right there.

But I knew Walker would hate himself for defiling me in a filthy back alley. I could resist to save his White Knight sensibilities.

I sighed heavily, cocking my hip against the wall.

"I want to go home, but I don't want the girls to cut their night short."

Home. Dark River was home now, even if a part of me still longed for my childhood bedroom with pictures of One Direction on the walls because all my friends had loved them.

Walker pulled his phone from his back pocket and swiftly texted someone, probably Angeline. Then he looked at his watch and nodded to himself. "We have time to run home."

I blinked at him. Then blinked again. "Excuse me? Are you suggesting we run fifty miles home? Is now the time I should tell you I failed gym class?"

He laughed, and I couldn't help but grin back, the high of his blood still coursing through me. "Relax, Raine. I'm not going to make you run in six-inch heels. I don't have to be a woman to know that is torture. I'll carry you."

Obviously, I was hard of hearing all of a sudden. "You want to carry me all the way back to Dark River. Are you insane?"

Walker stilled, checking out the dark pools in the alleyway. I went on alert too, waiting for an Enforcer or someone from the Vamp Nation to pop out and stab me in the heart with a stake for giving the guy on the dancefloor a killer hickey.

Eventually, he shrugged and refocused on me. "You say that like you weigh anything at all. I can jump small buildings in a single bound. You're barely more than a sack of potatoes to me. Now get on."

He showed me his back, and I laughed. Taking a running leap, I jumped on his back, wrapping my legs around his waist. "Okay, Superman. I give you ten minutes before you're out of puff and need to call a cab from carrying my jelly ass. Just FYI, comparing a girl to a sack of anything is not hot."

"What do I get if you're wrong and I can carry you all the way back to your apartment?"

I leaned forward, so my lips brushed the shell of his ear. "Whatever you want."

Wrapped around him as I was, I felt the small shiver that ran through his body. "Dangerous offer, Raine. You might not like what I want to take."

I chuckled and nipped the back of his neck. "I'm pretty sure I'm going to love whatever you have to offer, Walker Walton. Especially if you use the handcuffs."

He shook his head and took off at a speed I wouldn't have thought possible on two legs. In the back of mind, I thought we'd be constrained by the basics of biology. We are only designed to go a certain speed, right? Like you can treat your crappy Honda like a Ferrari, but eventually, the thing is going to blow up in a cloud of smoke.

Apparently, that didn't apply to vampires and their former human anatomy. We went from crappy Honda to F1 Fighter Jet. We were out of the city faster than would have been possible in a car even without traffic and fled into the darkness of the wild Canadian beauty. Apart from the frosting of my eyelashes, neither the speed nor the cold affected me, and the low heat of Walker's body shielded me from most of the oncoming wind. However, even with our superior hearing, the wind whipping by was too loud for us to talk, so I just rested my head on his shoulder and held on tight.

After an hour of running, Walker slowed and rolled to a stop. He let me down, and I stood on jelly legs. We might be able to run fast, but having my legs wrapped around Walker's waist for that long was hell on my thighs. I can definitely think of better reasons for having my legs wrapped around Walker for over an hour, and it had nothing to do with running break-neck speed back to Dark River. I shook out my legs, and Walker rolled his shoulders. "Carrying me like a baby possum getting to you, Sheriff?" I teased, and he quirked a brow.

"Pretty sure it was more than ten minutes, Newbie, so looks like I win our bet." He stalked toward me, looking every bit the predator in that moment.

"Oh yeah? And what do you want as a prize?" I purred back. The friction of the steady roll of his body as he ran had been pure torture. I was so revved, I was probably going to have to call Judge and see how fast he could get back into town.

A little spear of guilt spiked my chest, first that I was using Judge like that, and secondly because I was thinking about it when it was Walker who had gotten me worked up into this state.

"I want a kiss." Walker's words felt like a caress.

"Just a kiss? Where's your imagination?" I teased.

He hummed low in his throat. "I didn't say where." His voice was a low, seductive promise.

A thrill ran through me, and every part of me wanted to jump him there and then, except one little, annoying part of my brain that said that perhaps we should make him work for it. Oddly enough, that thrilled the new vampiric part of me too.

"Well then, Sheriff," I said, stealthily slipping off my heels. "I guess you'll have to catch me first?"

I laughed and took off down the darkened road, hearing his deep belly laugh, followed by the steady thump of his feet as he chased after me. I kind of expected the road to tear up my feet, but it felt so natural running barefoot down the road, the rocks no longer pricking my soft human flesh.

"Better run faster, little vamp, because I'm hot on your delicious ass," Walker said, and he sounded so happy that I just laughed and pushed myself faster. My eyes saw the darkness around us, in the same way, I saw the daytime as a human, with perfect clarity. I saw the nocturnal animals scatter as we ran past, not seeing us but sensing the real and present danger.

We went around all the smaller towns, skirting the edges of civilization until we were jumping rivers and rocky outcroppings. My dress caught and snagged on all sorts of things, and I sent up a silent apology to Ella. I was going to owe her big for this. Hopefully, Dark River had a dry cleaner I'd never noticed.

Finally, a sign that would be forever etched into my brain came into view.

Welcome to Dark River.

The population number had long ago been scratched out. Population 0. The irony wasn't lost on me. No one there was really alive anyway, no matter how we went on living.

When I rolled to a stop underneath the sign, I bent over and put my hands on my knees, panting like I'd run a marathon.

Walker stopped right behind me, and when I

looked over my shoulder, once I could draw breath again, I caught him staring at my ass.

"Are you looking up my dress, Sheriff? I'm going to have to call the authorities."

He strolled over like he had all the time in the world, and ran a hand down the curve of my spine and over my ass. "You should definitely call the authorities," he murmured.

He bit his lip, the points of his fangs dragging at the slightly pale flesh, reminding me that I'd fed from him and then made him drag me across the Canadian wilderness like a packhorse. Or a donkey. But he did have one fine ass.

I reached out and twined my fingers in his, and we strolled back into the town. Everyone was just winding down for the day, and the darkness was thick around us, heralding the dawn. "I think you should take me back to your place," I said into the silence with a nonchalance I didn't feel.

His fingers tightened around mine. "I want to, but I think it is a bad idea right now."

I resisted the urge to stomp my foot like a child. What was it about Walker that made me want to pout like a baby. "And why not?"

He pulled me closer as if to soften the blow. Or to ensure I couldn't run away.

"You are just lonely without Judge and Brody. They'll be back soon enough, and you'll have more than enough man problems."

I turned and punched him in the arm. "Are you serious? You think I want to fuck you because I'm bored without my playthings?"

He frowned, grimacing a little. "No. I know it's not that."

"Then?"

He didn't look at me as he sighed again. I seemed to make him sigh a lot. "I like you, Raine. A lot. You've overcome a difficult situation and flourished. And I want you so badly that sometimes I wake up in the middle of the night as hard as a fucking rock for the first time since I was a human teenage boy a long, long time ago." He shook his head at himself. "While there is this big black cloud threatening your safety, I feel like I'd be failing you somehow if I fell into bed with you right now and just got so caught up that perhaps I would let your maker have his way. Just let it go because it would mean you were safe and could stay with me. Because there is very little, I wouldn't do to make you happy."

Huh. I wanted to argue. I wanted to say that he would never do that, that his morals and conviction about the ideals of Dark River were what made him such a good Sheriff. But then I remembered telling him to drop it, and I knew how easy it would be to just let sleeping dogs lie and move on with my life. I also knew that Walker would hate that, and eventually, he'd hate me for making him give up his code of ethics just to keep me happy.

At least, I thought that's what he was getting at. Walker confused me sometimes.

We walked up the back steps of the Immortal Cupcake and came to a stop outside my door.

"After this is all over, and you've got the guy and exacted whatever shotgun justice passes for law out here, then we can see where this could go?"

He nodded slowly. "You have my word."

I stood on my tiptoes and kissed him gently on the lips. "That's good enough for me. We have all the time in the world."

He gave me that beautiful smile and my heart melted. "We have eternity."

CHAPTER SIXTEEN

There are some things that even the power of an eight stack of pancakes can't fix. The grief I felt when I thought of my family. The constant hunger that couldn't be touched by the fluffy pastry goodness. And the sound of absolute silence inside Bert and Beatrice's diner.

I don't know what it was about that silence, probably some underlying issues from that first night that I was yet to talk through with Nico in my therapy sessions, but every time it happened, I knew my world was about to change forever.

"Excuse me? I'm looking for a girl. I wondered if you'd seen her? She's blonde, American? I think she might have come through here recently."

My cutlery dropped to my plate as they slipped from my numb fingers.

"Tex?"

I thought I'd whispered it, but his head whipped in my direction, though he couldn't see me.

"Mika?"

His heartbeat registered, and I suddenly realized why everyone had gone so damn still. He was like a fucking chocolate cake at a Weight Watchers meeting. They might adhere to the principles of Dark River, but all it would take is one failed attempt at willpower, and my childhood friend, my fucking neighbor, the boy I'd had a crush on since I could walk, would be dead.

I was on my feet and standing in front of him in less than a blink of the eye. I stared at the vampires in the room, my fangs bared. "If any of you even fucking think about it, I'll tear you to shreds," I growled at my new found friends. I didn't give a fuck right now, as my protectiveness went into overdrive.

"Calm down, Lass. Everyone will behave. But may I suggest you call the Sheriff?" She was just diverting me because I could hear someone already on the phone with Walker now.

I still glared at everyone in the room, Tex pushed behind me protectively. His hand reached out and grabbed my hand. "Mika? What's going on? Is it really you?"

I shuddered as my eyes welled. "There's no Mika here. You should go. Dark River isn't a place for outsiders." I pushed the words out through the lump in my throat. God, I wanted to cry. Just lay on the floor amidst the rubble of the false wall I'd created around my heart.

"Mika, I know your voice as well as I know my own."

The bell over the door tinkled, and everyone was silent again. I whirled around to see Walker. "Guess we changed you enough that no one would recognize you, but apparently no one thought we'd need to change your voice." His eyes shot to where Tex was still holding my hand. "We should get out of here before your friend has problems." It was then he looks down and notices something that very few people ever spot.

Not because Tex hides it, but because the guy himself is just so...everything. He soaks up all the energy in the room. He's a mass of leather and tattoos and bravado. He is so hot that every single one of my teenage daydreams centered around him.

He's also completely and utterly blind. Had been since birth. The cane was the only mark that he is anything but a perfectly able-bodied bundle of twenty-something confidence.

I nod and walk out of the diner, human-slow. It was odd that I now had to physically slow myself to a normal speed. Tex held onto my hand like he was scared to let it go like I would just disappear into thin air.

The idea was tempting. I couldn't believe he was here…

"Why are you here, Tex? Your parents must be flipping out."

"They are too busy consoling your parents over the disappearance and death of their only daughter," Tex sneered, letting me see every ounce of his disappointment in me. I gasped and shuddered as if he'd actually stabbed me in the heart.

"You don't understand," I mutter, but it seems weak even to my own ears. "I'll explain, but let's just get you off the street already."

It didn't help his heart was racing a million miles a minute, and his skin was so hot against mine that it was like a brand. He made my own dead heart race, but not because I wanted to eat him. I wanted to protect him like a lion with a freshly downed gazelle.

Walker kept watching me for signs that I was about to pounce on him and tear his throat out, and I could have hugged him just for that. Because killing a human would break me, but accidentally killing Tex would destroy me completely.

I led him up the backstairs of the Immortal Cupcake to my apartment. I definitely couldn't take the pressure of leading him through the shop during the lunch rush. Once he was inside my apartment, and by extension the wards set by the Witch Miranda, I let out the breath I hadn't realized I'd been holding.

Then I gave into the other impulse that had been

hounding me since I'd seen him standing at the counter of the diner talking to Bert. I wrapped my arms around his waist and hugged him to me so tight that I was worried I'd snap him in half.

Tex and I had always had a friendship borne from proximity. He was two years older than me, which is a lifetime when you are young. He'd introduced me to rock music on his dad's old portable record player when he was ten, and I was eight, and he was going to be a rockstar. He took up the electric guitar, which was horrible for the first six months, and I'd hang out in his garage and listen to him play. Then he got better and hit high school, and there would be other girls hanging out in his garage listening to him play in the afternoons.

We drifted apart for a bit while we both navigated high school, and then I caught him smoking behind my garage when I was sixteen, and he was eighteen, and it was like all those years of barely speaking had slipped away. With Tex, I could tell him my fears, and hopes and dreams and he would tell me his in return. We weren't best friends, nothing like that. He was just the one place I could run, without running away. He leaned on me too, though I wasn't completely sure if it was because I could legally drive him places or not. When I'd driven him to a tattoo parlor, and he'd let his apprentice tattooist friend practice on him, I thought both his parents and mine were going to strangle me. It didn't help that it was a giant snake on his neck. His friend did a great job though, and Tex had been completely chill about the whole thing, even after he got chewed out by his parents.

"It's not like I'll have to look at it for the rest of my life, right?" was all he'd said. And that was just Tex. He was cool, self-deprecating, and the most honest person I'd ever met. He wouldn't stutter as he told you exactly how he felt.

When I was eighteen, and he was twenty, I'd given him my virginity, because I didn't want to head off to college being a virgin, and who better to give it to than the boy-next-door who'd been the fodder for every dirty dream I'd had since puberty? I'd climbed out of his window the next morning, headed off to college the following week, and that was that. With Tex and me, there was no awkward posturing. We both told each other what we thought, when we thought it, without the worry of hurt feelings.

Which is why I wanted to get this one good hug in before he literally murdered me for being such a bitch and faking my death. I pulled away as though it was physically painful.

"Look, Tex, I can explain…"

Well, kind of. I wasn't actually sure what I could explain that wouldn't result in him either being institutionalized or stuck here in Dark River with me until he died. I was a shit person because that was super tempting.

I looked at Walker, who was eyeing Tex like he

was something he couldn't explain. Which was fair enough, because how the fuck did a blind man find me in the middle of nowhere Canada when the cops from both the US and Canada couldn't?

"How did you find Ra… Mika?" he asked, suspicion overriding his normally pleasant cop tone.

Tex's head turned toward Walker and his brow furrowed. Not going to lie, that expression always made my heart skip a beat, and apparently being undead - er, re-alive - didn't change that fact. It drew my eyes to his piercing blue eyes, the ones that never saw me but were beautiful none the less. From there, you couldn't help but notice the dark slashes of his eyebrows, the almost blue-black of his hair that sat just too long around a jaw so sharp that you could cut yourself on it. And he'd gotten more tattoos, his arms were now covered in sleeves.

The predator stirred in hunger for the first time, but I tamped it right down. Now was not the time for any kind of lust to rear its head. I took a step toward Walker, and Tex turned toward me. I'd forgotten how acute his other senses were.

"Why was she hiding in the first place? Do you know your Mom has cried every single day since you were declared missing? Every time I go around to check on her, she opens the door with your name on her lips, convinced it will be you knocking .And you are here, doing what exactly? Would it have killed you to pick up the phone?"

I sob crawled up from my chest, snowballing until it was a cry of pure anguish when it passed my lips. I slumped to the floor and cried into my hands. I knew, deep down, that they would be devastated. But hearing about it from someone who witnessed it first hand, that was worse.

Walker came over, picking me up from the floor and wrapping me in his arms. I let my tears soak his shirt as I cried for the life I'd lost all over again. Tex had just ripped open the wound which has slowly begun to heal.

But Tex wasn't done. "I just knew, somehow, that you weren't dead. I knew it in my gut. Even when they'd found your backpack in the middle of fucking nowhere, and you were declared dead and we had a fucking funeral where everyone stood up and said what a good person you were, when I stood up there and said how you were the best person I'd ever known, you were actually here, living your life." He drifted closer to us, and Walker held me closer as if he could shelter me from the tongue lashing that Tex was dishing out.

"But I couldn't rest. I just knew that I had to find you. Dead or alive, I needed to bring you home. I followed my gut to Canada, even though my parents have basically disowned me for doing it, petrified that they'd lose me the way your parents lost you. I begged the cops for your file, and they gave it to me, because what could a blind guy find out that trained law enforcement couldn't, right?" He laughed mirthlessly.

"I followed your trail all the way to Calgary, and I've been trawling my way through nightspots, hoping someone, anyone had seen you. Then you bump into me because you were out partying? Having a goddamn good time?" He was furious now, the normal paleness of his skin getting flushed along the sharp angles of his cheekbones. "I followed you out into an alleyway, convinced I'd heard your voice. I thought I was going crazy, Mika. Then you and him," he points a finger in Walker's direction, "Yeah I recognize your voice, Buddy. You talked about Dark River then you were just gone. Into thin air. I thought I was going nuts, Mika. That your death had driven me insane. But what did I have to lose?"

The silence in my apartment was only disrupted by the sound of my refrigerator. I pulled away from Walker, wiping my face on my sleeve.

"Tex…" I threw a desperate look at Walker. I had to tell Tex that I hadn't just abandoned my family on a whim, but what could I tell him so he'd just go home and forget he'd ever seen me? My heart cracked at the idea.

Walker frowned. "Raine-"

The door was flung open, and I automatically stood in front of Tex, protecting him from the possible threat, my heart beating wildly.

But my shoulders relaxed slightly when it was just Brody. "Rainy…" His voice trailed away as he sniffed the air and frowned. "Why is there another shapeshifter in your apartment?"

CHAPTER SEVENTEEN

It took me a disturbingly long time to work out what Brody was talking about. My brain refused to make the connection, and then my head whipped toward Tex. Walker apparently had faster mental reflexes, because he took a step closer to us and breathed in deeply.

"I sense nothing."

Tex fidgeted away as if he could sense Walker is too close and scowled. "Does someone want to tell me what the hell is going on right now?"

Brody was in between Tex and me in a moment, inhaling deeply, his eyes narrowed.

"Who are you?" he growled, his teeth bared.

Tex glared back, his eerie unseeing stare seemed almost disrespectful if you didn't know he was blind. "What's it got to do with you?" he growled back, and I swallowed a groan, looking at Walker desperately.

"I'm Raine's boyfriend. And you are?"

Tex looks confused again. "Who the hell is Raine?"

It was all too much, and I felt like climbing the walls or screaming or something to expel all the tension that was crawling along my skin. Brody looked over his shoulder at me, always the first to sense my spiraling emotions.

He took a step away from Tex but didn't take his eyes off him. "Let's have a seat, and then we'll see if we can't untangle this mess." He grabbed my hand and pulled me toward the couch. I shook my hand out of his, and when hurt flashed across his face, I leaned up and kissed his lips.

"Tex is blind. This is a strange apartment," I said in a low voice. Tex would hate appearing weak in a room of strangers, but I didn't want to hurt Brody's feelings either.

I walked over and placed Tex's hand on my shoulder like I'd done a million times before today. It felt as natural as breathing. "There's an armchair two steps to your left," I whisper, and he squeezed my shoulder. I wanted to hug him again, but it was probably a good idea to get everything sorted out. Who knows if he'll even want to touch me again when he realizes I'm a monster now.

I pulled a chair from the dining table and dragged it into the living room. I didn't think sitting on anyone's lap would be a good idea right now.

"So talk," Tex said, and I could basically smell the anger and pain simmering beneath his porcelain skin. "Start with who Raine is."

He knew it was me. He just wanted me to say the words. "I'm Raine. It's the name I took after... after Mika died. Look, this is going to sound crazy, Tex. The whole thing. But you have to hear me out before you tell me I'm crazy. I want to go home, I really do. But I can't."

Then I explained the whole ridiculous, terrifying situation to him. Everything from the point I woke up in that stormwater drain. Even the fact I ran into him that night in the nightclub because I wanted to drain the guy on the dancefloor of blood. I didn't pull punches or sugarcoat it. I told him about how my maker was terrorizing me and how it was breaking my heart to think of my family in pain. I may have glossed over the Brody and Judge being my boyfriend's bit, and that Walker was definitely a massive crush. Telling that to my childhood beau seemed like some kind of awkward dating faux pas. Or maybe I was just a chicken shit. Whatever.

Tex listened to the story without interrupting, though his face went from disbelieving, to angry, to incredulous, and back again.

When I was finished, we sat there in that heavy silence again. Finally, he cleared his throat, awkwardly, filling the lull in the conversation.

"So, you're telling me you're a vampire. And we

are in a town full of vampires. And the guy that barged in here like he owned the place is some kind of shapeshifter? Am I getting all this correct?"

I winced. "Yeah. I know it sounds crazy. I wish I could show you…"

He gave a mirthless laugh. "Because seeing is believing, right?"

I sighed heavily. Yeah, it was. If he could see my fangs, or me zipping around faster than his human eyes could see, or see Brody turn into a fucking tiger like he's desperately wanted to do since I met him, then all this wouldn't sound like such a crazy fairytale.

I stood and walked toward his chair, and the other two guys tensed on the couch. I knelt in front of him and took his hand. "Yeah, seeing is believing, and that would make this whole thing easier. But feeling is believing too, right?"

I took his hand and put it over my heart, in the space between my breasts. I ignored Brody's grumble. Tex's skin felt hot, so I knew I would be a little cold to the touch, though not as cold as normal because Walker's blood still coursed through my veins. I could feel him waiting for the soothing thud-thud of my heart. But it didn't come. It would eventually, but not as often as that rhythm that we knew instinctively as humans. When it finally thudded against his palm after about ten seconds, he yanked his hand away like I was diseased. Which I kind of was, I guess, but it still hurt. I was suddenly glad he couldn't see the hurt in my eyes, or the tears glistening in their corners.

Clenching his jaw, he reached out and ran his fingers over the curve of my cheek, then his thumb dipped to my full bottom lip. He pressed it between my lips, and along the line of my teeth until he hit one of my fangs.

He sucked in a gasp but didn't withdraw his fingers. He got infinitely paler, but his thumb ran the other way across the straight edge of my teeth until he got to the second fang. He pressed it hard, and the sharp tip pierced the pad of his finger. The taste of his blood hit my tongue a moment later, and I moaned.

My hand shot up, grabbing his wrist, stopping him from withdrawing his thumb from my mouth. Walker was there in a moment, his hand around my own wrist, his eyes screaming a warning. I ignored him and sucked Tex's thumb, the hint of his blood coating my mouth, making me moan. Making him moan too.

Walker's cool voice pierced the lust-filled haze of my thoughts. "Take his thumb out of your mouth, Raine. You don't want to hurt him."

He almost sounded pleading, but I quirked an eyebrow at him. I didn't want to hurt Tex. I wanted to fuck him six ways to Sunday, but I didn't want to obliterate him until he was a bloody mass.

Still, I let go of Tex's wrist, and his thumb popped

out of my mouth with an audible sucking sound. Tex was staring at nothing, pulling his hand to his chest.

"If you are so dangerous to your family, why haven't you tried to maul me yet? If new vampire control is so very limited like you say." He didn't sound accusatory, well maybe a little, but confusion was there as well. I didn't know either.

I looked at Walker, and he shrugged. Brody raised his hand.

"I have the answer to that. Actually, it explains a lot if you disregard the fact that it should be a goddamn impossibility." Whatever he was about to say, he didn't seem overly happy about the fact. "Have you and Pretty Boy over there, ever, you know, done it doggy-style? Become the beast with two backs? As Marvin Gaye said, did you get it on?"

My face flushed, and I imagined I was now redder than my hair. "Uh, yes?"

I don't know why I framed it as a question.

"And is your boy -"

"My name is Tex, and I am not a boy," the 'boy' in question growled. Luckily, he couldn't see Brody's eye roll.

"Be nice," I mouthed silently, giving him a scowl.

"Sorry. Tex. Is *Tex* adopted?"

Now it was my turn to be confused.

"No."

"Yes." My head whipped toward Tex again.

"Seriously? I had no idea."

His jaw was tense, and I could hear his teeth grinding. "It was no one else's business. Mom and Dad are my parents in every way it matters."

"Except in one way. They are humans, and you are not. Well, not entirely. And when you, uh, slept with Raine, Mika, whatever, you made her your mate. And then she went and became a vampire."

I was somehow across the room and had my back against the wall before I even registered I'd moved.

"What?" Tex had gone so pale now I was worried he was going to pass out. My gaze ping-ponged between him and Brody.

"You're a shifter, Kid. Probably only half from what I can tell. Your scent isn't as strong as a normal shapeshifter, which is why the Sheriff over there is feeling a little inadequate in the nose department. Whoever your mama was, she did the best thing for you, because a blind kid in some of those US packs," he shook his head. "You'd be dead before you were five, for sure. Not everyone has my family's moral compass."

I noticed Tex's hands trembling, in shock or rage or fear, I couldn't be sure, but as if he could feel my eyes on them, he curled his fingers into his fists. But he remained silent, and Brody didn't elaborate further.

Finally, I couldn't stand it anymore and went to him, climbing into his lap and wrapping myself around him as if I could hold him together. I knew what it was like to have life-altering shit dropped on you by a random stranger. I'd been lucky, though.

Tex sat stiffly in my arms, but little by little, he thawed in my arms. Soon, his own arms slipped around mine, and he pressed his nose into my neck, a move so like Brody's that I couldn't refute what Brody was saying. Tex was a shifter.

We sat in silence for a long time, long enough for the sun to come up and the blinds to get pulled closed against the light. I led Tex to my bedroom, tucking him into my bed, and not resisting when he tugged me down beside him. I stared at his exhausted face and committed it to my memory. I clung to that little bit of home so tightly that I didn't know how I was going to let him go. But he had to go. I knew that deep down.

Our families wouldn't rest if they lost both of us to the Canadian wilds.

Brody crawled in later, wrapping his body around the back of mine, and stroking my hair. "Sleep, Raine. I'll watch over you both."

I think I might love Brody.

I WASN'T sure what the residents of Dark River did for entertainment before I was turned, but news of Tex was on everyone's lips. Every single one of the Council rocked up to my door and were not impressed when I turned them away, except for Nico, who seemed to find the whole thing amusing. The fact I'd warded my apartment wasn't earning me any brownie points either. Apparently it wasn't only Walker that the Witch Miranda scared the pants off.

A backdrop to all this eventfulness was a low hum of dread that Judge hadn't returned yet. It had been days. He normally never went this long without coming back to town. I was worried that my ultimatum had made him move on, but when I'd gone to the diner to pick up something that resembled a home-cooked meal for Tex, I'd asked Beatrice about it.

"I don't know what to tell you, Lass. I don't go into his apartment and invade his privacy, but his rent is still paid, and I haven't seen him walking out of there with any boxes."

I sighed, took the two giant lasagnas, and headed back to my apartment like my heart wasn't hurting. I'd pushed, and deep down, I kind of expected this as a consequence. I'd hoped so hard that I was wrong, but I didn't like my chances. At least Tex, who was a massive problem, kept my mind off the fact that Judge had rejected me. Cut and run. Gone for cigarettes and never returned.

I smiled, or maybe it was more of a grimace when Nico came out the front door of the Immortal Cupcake. I swear, I rarely ever saw any of the Councillors for months, and now Tex had turned up, they were everywhere. But I liked Nico the best.

He seemed the most relaxed. The youngest, though I had a sneaking suspicion that it went the other way.

"Hello, Raine," he said, giving me a fangy smile with too much teeth. "How is your pet human?"

From anyone else, I would take that as an insult against Tex. But Nico didn't seem to be saying it in a derogatory way.

"He's fine, thank you," I said, keeping my voice neutral and pleasant. 'Don't fuck with old vamps' should definitely be in the Vamps-For-Dummies guidebook. Nico turned and walked beside me toward the staircase at the back of the cafe.

"That is good. But he must leave your apartment sometime, and he presents a particular brand of trouble we have not had for quite a long time here in Dark River." I stilled, cocking my head to the side. "The rules are finite, but we are the Council, no? Sometimes the rules need to be broken."

A chill went down my spine at his pleasant words. The number one rule of Dark River was no turning humans, or was it killing humans? I mean, it is all the same in the end. Was Nico threatening Tex?

I looked at the young, tattooed vamp with eyes so old they made my bones ache. There was no malice, no vindictiveness on his face. His eyes challenged me, their amused light dancing in the darkness of the back alley. He was trying to tell me something.

"They are the unbreakable rules, but there are

very few agreements that are actually that." He raised his eyebrows at me and whisked away.

I stood there, shaking my head. He was...confusing. I took the stairs two at a time, balancing the trays and bread rolls, and the salad on top because sometimes you just needed a salad. I mean, I didn't need vitamins, but both Brody and Tex were human-ish.

I thumped on the door with my elbow and Brody pulled it open. He wasn't wearing a shirt, and my mouth watered. Then my fangs popped out, and I realized how long since I'd gotten laid, or tasted Brody's blood. The thought was enough to make a low rumble sneak past my lips. I'd been avoiding intimacy with Brody out of respect for Tex because quite frankly, it was just weird. I couldn't make love to Brody while the guy I gave my virginity to, my motherfucking mate, was sleeping on my couch.

I let out a huge sigh and stood on my tiptoes to kiss Brody's cheek. His eyes were hooded, he could smell how aroused I'd become at the sight of the hard planes of his chest. Dammit. I resisted the urge to pout.

Brody leaned forward, capturing my lips with his. "Soon."

I nodded, nipping his full bottom lip in that way that always made him groan. But I couldn't imagine when, because I couldn't send Tex home knowing I was alive and Tex couldn't live here with me in Dark River. Maybe if my maker hadn't been such a psycho, he could have mind-wiped Tex and sent him on his way, but when I'd suggested it to Brody, he'd shuddered.

"To have every memory of your mate wiped from your mind, but knowing that there was something missing from inside you. That's a fate worse than death to a shifter. Maybe he'd be okay, being only a half. But he followed you to the end of the world because he knew you weren't dead. And that was when he didn't even know you were his mate."

The absolute horror in Brody's voice made sure that option was firmly off the table. I could never do that to Tex.

Speaking of the handsome devil, somehow he'd lost his shirt as well, and my hungry gaze ate him alive. He was more tattooed then I remembered, his tattoos running up and down his arms and across his chest and back. The dark ink contrasted with the alabaster shade of his skin. It occurred to me that he looked more like a vampire than anyone else in Dark River. Oh, the irony.

His hair was mussed like he'd just woken up. Considering it was like three A.M., maybe he had. He was having trouble adjusting to the topsy-turvy schedule we all kept.

"I've got lasagna," I said, plonking the huge foil trays down on the kitchen bench. I needed two because between Brody and Tex, they ate like horses.

How Tex's parents had ever kept him fed without getting a second mortgage was beyond me.

I looked between the two guys, my past and my present and wondered if I had a future with either of them.

I dished up two plate-sized slabs of lasagna and placed the salad in a bowl on the bench. It was domesticated if nothing else. I left enough for Walker, in case he stopped by, which he usually did about now. I wasn't sure if he came over because he wanted to see me or to check I hadn't lost control and eaten both Brody and Tex into sexy, paper husks.

As if summoned by my thoughts, someone knocked on my door. He was predictable in the best possible way. I could depend on Walker, and I don't care what people say about bad boys, sometimes dependability was the sexiest thing in the world.

Smiling, I pulled open the door, and Walker was standing there in his uniform, hat, and everything, looking every bit as handsome as the first time I'd seen him. My eyes drifted past him, and my smile fell. Judge stood behind him, looking haunted.

"What's going on?"

Walker reached out and squeezed my arm. "Let's go inside first, hey?"

I moved aside and let them in, my eyes tracking Judge. He held himself stiffly, though his forehead creased when he saw Tex. His jaw tensed, but he kept silent. He moved through the room silently, but Tex's face moved with him as if he could sense the predator in the room. I wasn't going to break it to him; we were all predators.

"Uh, Judge. This is Tex. He's from… before." Apparently, you could fit an entire lifetime into those six letters. Before. Before I'd become Raine. Before Mika had died. Before I'd come to Canada. Hell, before I'd left for college without any idea what I wanted to do with my life.

"Tex, this is Judge, my… friend." I finished lamely. Jesus. Could this week get more awkward?

Judge nodded, though Tex wouldn't be able to see the gesture. "The Sheriff told me. A human found you here, in the world's most obscure town. I don't believe in those kinds of coincidences."

Brody stood and slapped Judge on the back affectionately. "I'm glad you're back, Bro. But I think Walker left out one vital piece of information." He raised his eyebrows at the Sheriff in question, and who just gave him a flat stare in return. "Not just a human. Raine's mate. Shifter mate. Guess Raine's harem is at two all now." Brody's grin said he wasn't mad about this change of circumstance at all, the competitive bastard.

Judge turned to stare at me, and I shrugged, glaring back. I hoped my stare said *Sucks when you are left in the dark, doesn't it?*

"Mate or not, he needs to leave." As I opened my

mouth to protest, he raised a hand. "For this conversation."

Tex crossed his arms over his broad, bare chest. He needed to put a shirt on while I was in a room full of men who can tell when I'm aroused or not. The tattoo that ran along his collarbone was an intricate musical piece, a swirl of words and instruments and musical notes. I ached to study it up close, to talk for hours like when we were young. But I couldn't see how that would ever happen again.

"He can stay. What more could you tell him that is more earth-shattering than 'hey, vampires exist, and I am one,' or my personal favorite, 'Yer a werewolf, Tex,'" I said in my best Hagrid voice.

Tex's lips twitched, probably because he was the only one young enough to get the Harry Potter reference.

"Shapeshifter," Brody corrected.

"How about the fact that you aren't the first back-packer to go missing in these parts, but you were the first one to stay dead?"

Okay, maybe that.

I blinked rapidly, and my eyes went to Walker for confirmation, but he wasn't giving much away.

"You mean someone is breaking the rules and drinking from humans?"

Judge rolled his shoulders, and I wanted to walk into his arms and never leave them. I didn't think he was ever going to come back, but instead, he'd been doing what he said he would do right back at the beginning when I first met him. He was investigating my murder.

Did I think he was avoiding me at the same time? Duh, obviously. I wasn't that much of a lovestruck fool.

He nodded solemnly. "It's not usually a big deal, but it's come to the attention of the Vampire Nation leaders. Tourist's disappearing for days on end, then reappearing with no memories, dirty and suffering from anemia? The human authorities have put it down to drug-taking prepper cult because they looked like they'd been attacked by leeches. Apparently, humans can be stupid." He raised an eyebrow at Tex, who sneered back, even if he couldn't see the condescending look on Judge's face. He could decipher tone just fine.

"Well, this stupid human found his missing person, so how about you go fuck yourself?" Tex growled out, and Judge's lip twitched.

I was going to drown in all this machismo one day. Everyone dreams about how amazing a harem would be, but in all honesty, that's a fuck tonne of testosterone all day, every day. Quite frankly, I was considering quitting them all, and asking Angeline and Alice if they want to make their duo a trio.

Pity I liked dick so much.

Sighing heavily, I prompted, "The Vampire Nation?"

"They've sent out Enforcers to track down the rogue vamp. Word is that they are getting close too. No mention of you though," he said, looking at Walker.

He shrugged but didn't elaborate. "They didn't need to know the circumstances of her turning. Neither Raine nor the town needs the scrutiny from the Leaders."

They all looked solemn at the thought, Walker's jaw clenching and unclenching rhythmically, and the muscle in Judge's cheek ticking in a rapid, discordant heartbeat. The Vampire Nation must really be something, and I, for one, was glad to be a dirty little secret just this once. "Word from who, exactly?"

Judge just shook his head, and I raised both hands and flipped him off. Twice. It was juvenile, but next to punching him in the nose, or angry sex, it perfectly portrayed my feelings about his attitude.

He just grinned, that perfect, charming fucking lady killer smile. Okay, so maybe angry sex wasn't off the table yet.

Heat flooded my cheeks. "Let's talk about this over food. No point in Bert's lasagna going to waste. This problem doesn't need to be solved in the next ten minutes."

Judge was still grinning at me, probably because the heat in my cheeks was matched by the heat in... other places. "Yes. Let's eat. I'm starving," he purred.

The way his voice growled out the word *starving*

made my panties damp. Everyone in the room turned to me at once, noses twitching. Even Tex.

"He's not talking about lasagna, is he? Jesus, Mika, how many boyfriends do you have in this boondock town?"

Brody laughed, and even Walker chuckled. I gave them all the evil eye. My face felt like it was on fire. I was waiting for my cheeks to melt off like overcooked mozzarella cheese. "I'm going to my room. Screw you bastards."

CHAPTER EIGHTEEN

Tex was getting restless being trapped inside my apartment all day. If I was honest, I'd been avoiding being alone with him for too long. It was too everything. Too sad. Too awkward. Too tempting.

But today, three days after he'd arrived in town, he was pacing around my apartment like a caged beast. Brody was out, and we were alone. And I was freaking out a little. I am woman enough to admit it. I still worried I would snap, and drink him dry, even though Brody assured me that was basically an impossibility because he was my mate. My freaking Mate. I hoped he was an ostrich because we'd both been sticking our heads in the sand about that little fact.

So I sat on the bench and watched him pace around the room in silence. I didn't have the answers to the questions that burned on his face. "Want me to get you a sandwich or something?"

"No." His words were short and sharp, like his temperament today.

"Want me to put the radio on?"

He shook his head again. "I want to go outside. Feel the sun on my face."

I let out a mirthless laugh. "Don't we all?"

His jaw tightened, and he began to pace more furiously. I sighed and wiggled off the bench. I had to do something. I walked to the old radio on top of the fridge and turned it on. I had it set to the classic, Golden-Oldies music station, also known as the only station I could get out here in the middle of nowhere, and the sound of someone crooning over the yowl of a trumpet blasted through the old speakers.

Tex stopped pacing, and I smiled. Even when he was an angry kid, raging against the injustice of being born blind, music could soothe him. Why hadn't I thought of it before? We used to dance around his garage, sometimes like Fred and Ginger, and sometimes like we were in a mosh pit at a Guns'n'Roses concert.

Eventually, we'd end up in a giggling heap on the floor though. Even as an eight-year-old, Tex moved like music was in his very soul. I, however, had as much grace as a baby elephant in roller skates.

Still, they were some of my most cherished childhood memories. Walking across the living room to stand in front of him, I was hoping it was the same for him.

"Want to dance?" I asked, trying not to wince out how husky my voice sounded. It would help if he wasn't so damn handsome.

He stared down at me, his hand coming up to touch my cheek. My body shuddered in relief at his touch. He slid his hand down from my cheek, along my side, his thumb just brushing my breast, and then curving it around my lower back. He pulled me close until I was pressed right along his body, and he let out a little sigh.

Apparently, I wasn't the only one feeling the relief of our connection. His other hand gripped mine, bringing it up and tucking it close to our bodies. Then he began to sway gently, doing a shuffling two-step in the middle of the living room. I was tucked under his chin, and I ignored the whoosh-whoosh noise of his blood flowing through his jugular. I focused on the thump-thump of his heartbeat instead, and the near searing warmth of his skin. He smelled like home, like all my happy memories.

"I'm sorry about this, Tex. I'm sorry about every-thing," I mumbled into his chest. It was easier talking to him like this. I could feel the heave of his breath as he sighed into my hair.

"Not your fault, Mika. You are a victim. I'm not angry anymore. I keep thinking that the other option is that you would be dead, and that is worse. The pain of thinking you were dead... " His voice trailed off like it caused him physical pain. "I just don't know how this is going to end. I don't want to leave. I can't leave. Even the thought makes me physically ill."

I shuddered at the rumble of his voice against my cheek, a wave of relief flowing through my body at his words.

"Still, I'm sorry I dragged you into this mess."

He huffed out a laugh. "I'm sorry I accidentally made you my mate."

I smiled against his chest. "I'm not," I whispered softly. But he heard. His body tensed up until it was almost vibrating with energy.

He pulled back, unthreading our fingers and sliding his hand back up to my cheek. "Mika, I'm going to kiss you."

I stood on my tiptoes, so my lips were an inch from his, clinging to his shoulders tightly. "Yes," I breathed.

As his lips brushed against mine, I realized my soul had been desperate for this contact. His lips pressed harder into mine, his hand slipping lower so he could pull my body impossibly closer. His tongue slipped past my lips, brushing along my teeth before tangling with mine. My hands roamed over his chest, over his sides, down along the curve of his spine as I tried to memorize every hard angle of his body, locking it away in my mind because he was right. I didn't know how this was going to end either, but just in case, I was going to commit this sensation to memory.

Finally, gasping for air, he pulled away. His chest heaved, and he tucked me back against his body, moving again to the music over the radio.

"I talked to Brody."

I resisted the urge to nuzzle his neck, in case he got the wrong idea. "Oh?"

"I don't want to go back. Brody thinks I could stay if I wanted. That he'd make me part of his Pack. I'd have protection."

I forced my body to keep swaying, even though I wanted to jump up and down in relief. "What about your parents? Your girlfriend?" I sounded way less invested in that question than I really was. What was I thinking? He was hot, talented, so fucking nice, of course, he had a girlfriend at home. And I'd kissed him, even subconsciously knowing that. I was a bad undead person.

He was silent, and I stared at the snake tattoo that curled as if to strike on his neck. I remembered when he got it. I thought he'd been the bravest person I knew. Maybe he still was.

He tangled his fingers in my hair. "Your hair always feels like silk," he murmured. "There isn't anyone else. Hasn't been since before you went to college. No one serious anyway. It never felt right. At least we know why now."

"Because my sexy skills blew your mind?" I laughed, and the grin on my face stretched wider when he chuckled too. It was low, and gravelly and so at odds with his baby face. He sang along to a Frank Sinatra song on the radio, and I tried not to swoon. Listening to him sing was like audio-foreplay. "Does it bother you? That I have... you know?"

"That you're dating half of Deadsville?" I snort-laughed. Deadsville. "It doesn't bother me as much as I thought it would. Brody is a nice guy, and the Sheriff seems alright, even if he is a bit uptight." Yeah, those three had bonded over the last couple of days, because both Brody and Walker were genuinely likable people. Judge, however...

"And Judge?"

"He's an asshole," he grumbled. "But he kind of makes me want to take my pants off."

I nodded knowingly. Same. Wait, what?

I jumped out of his arms. "Wait, what? I mean, I get that Judge makes you want to take off your clothes. Lord knows I've been there, but I mean, I didn't realize that you, uh..." I let out a silent scream and waved my hands around. I sounded like an insensitive douche canoe when I was really just surprised.

"You didn't know I was bisexual? Yeah, my parents are super conservative Catholics. There's a reason for that, Mika." He held out a hand, and I realized he was holding his breath. I took it quickly, and he dragged me back into his arms. "I figure, if you can remake yourself as an undead woman named Raine, I can at least come out, right?"

"Yeah, of course," I said too loudly. Honestly. My

brain had short-circuited. But hey, you try thinking about the seriously cut, sexy man of mystery that was Judge, and then add the nicest guy you'll ever meet, who was packaged like the kind of boy your mama warned you about. Got that image in your head? Now imagine them kissing. Hot, right? Now imagine them more than kissing. Yeah. This is why my brain wasn't firing well.

"Say something," he groaned.

I leaned up and touched my lips to his softly. "I was just surprised. It makes no difference to me who you find attractive. It only matters how you feel about me, right?" Gah. I sounded so dumb. What was it about Tex that just made me sound like an awkward thirteen-year-old all the time? "Is that why you want to stay? So you can explore this side of yourself?"

I drew back. I wanted to see his face when he answered. The dark straight lines of his brows drew together, but he was shaking his head. "I want to stay because of you, Mika. Because you are my mate, and that means something. I feel like half of a person, and I didn't even realize it until right now when I held you in my arms. It's learning to live without ever taking a deep breath."

We danced in silence for a little while longer, until the night started to edge out the light behind my heavy curtains. "So, you're okay with me having, you know, more than one boyfriend?"

Now it was my turn to wait on tenterhooks.

"Depends, are you willing to share them? Are they all as hot as they sound?" I laughed. I could definitely get used to having a bi boyfriend.

"Even hotter. But I'm not sure they swing that way." Well, Brody didn't mind sharing, but I didn't think he'd want to be the meat in the sandwich. And Walker, there was no way, I couldn't even imagine him being open to sharing me at all. Though he didn't seem to mind watching. Heat flooded to my core as I remember his face as he watched Judge bang me silly. Actually, Judge didn't seem so perturbed about Brody being in his space either. Maybe he was keeping more than one secret from me too. Apparently, I was oblivious to anyone else's attraction other than my own, Tex was proof of that.

I felt Tex's Adam's apple bob against my face. "What are you thinking about, Mika?"

Crap, crap. Couldn't at least one of my love interests have normal senses? "Nothing. I think you are out of luck with the Sheriff, and Brody might share. I'm not sure about Judge. He's a bit of a mystery in more ways than one. Can't hurt to ask, right?"

Tex scoffed. "The guy is a vampire. It could hurt very much to ask." He leaned down and kissed me like I was on the silver screen, slightly bent back, being devoured in the best possible way. It left me breathless, even though I didn't really need to breathe regularly. "What's he like? What do any of them look like? Sometimes I feel like I'm cursed. I mean, I only think I know what you look like. I'll never know the color of your lips, or your hair or what your face looks like when you come in my arms."

I sucked in a breath. "You might not know what color my lips are, but you know how they taste when you kiss me, and how they feel when I kiss you right here," I murmured, placing a kiss on the hard edge of his jaw. And then another one on his throat. His pulse beat against my lips, and I dragged in oxygen as I moved my aching fangs away from that spot. I kissed the edge of his collarbone that peeked out the neck of his t-shirt. "And you mightn't know what I look like when I come, but you know the noises I make when you give me pleasure, how I feel when my body shudders around yours."

"Mika..." he groaned, his hand dipping down to grab my ass. "I want you to bite me."

Someone laughed from behind me. "Well, that would be a freakin' terrible idea, Rainy Day. Especially not when Lover Boy just got interesting."

I whirled around, crouching, the predator ready to attack in defense of her Mate. But I relaxed when it was just Judge. "Geez, Judge. Make a noise next time. How long have you been standing there?"

Behind me, Tex was like a statue.

"Oh, long enough." Judge sauntered over like he was a big cat, all swagger and confidence. He stopped in front of Tex and grabbed his wrist. He wasn't gentle, and I held back a hiss. I didn't think Judge would hurt Tex, but I couldn't be sure. Judge was an enigma, his easy-going nature a facade that held a predator a million times more dangerous than mine.

A part of me expected him to break Tex's wrist or something, but instead, he lifted Tex's hand to his face. "You wanted to know what I looked like," he murmured, and I realized Judge had been standing there a lot longer than either of us knew. I held my breath as Tex held his hand stiffly until Judge's hand curled over the top. He moved it to the small scar on his cheek. "I got this scar in a knife fight. I won." He didn't sound cocky about it though. He moved Tex's hand to his nose, tracing his fingertips down the crooked bumps of it. "My wife in my human life broke my nose here. Hit me with a frying pan when I came home drunk one night." He shifted it down a little lower. "This one was from a fight with my neighbor." He moved Tex's hand to his jaw, to a puckered scar that I'd tasted with my tongue too many times to count now. "I got that one as a vamp. Ash blade when someone tried to behead me. I almost bled out, which is why it didn't heal properly."

Tex was still so rigid, but his face was heartachingly hopeful. God, I hoped Judge knew what he was doing right now. Judge moved his hand away, but pressed his cheek tighter into Tex's hand, a silent invitation to continue.

Tex traced his fingers over the hard lines of Judge's face. I found myself studying Judge harder, not just taking in the beauty of his face, but dissecting it. The peak of his hairline, the scars that littered his face, making him look dangerous and mysterious. When Tex ran his thumb over Judge's full lower lip, I almost came right there in my big girl panties. Judge slid his eyes toward me and raised an eyebrow, telling me everything I wanted to know.

He'd heard everything. I should feel annoyed that he'd invaded our privacy like that, but right now, lust was winning out against indignation. When Judge nipped at Tex's thumb, causing him to hiss, I was about three seconds from throwing myself at them.

I forced myself to stay rooted to the spot. Tex lifted his other hand, and pressed it hard into Judge's face, his thumbs running along the line of his cheek-bones, cupping the knife-edge points of his jaw.

"Are you satisfied now?" Judge said in a low, purring voice. Oh damn.

Tex shook his head. "Not yet."

Judge let out a chuckle that was one hundred percent sex, a hint of danger edging his words. "Hmm, what is stopping you then?"

I was watching them so intently that I could see the rapid rise and fall of Tex's chest as his hands drifted down over the columns of Judge's neck. They were similar heights, almost within an inch of each other, Tex just being a tad taller. He tentatively ran his fingers lower, barely brushing the muscles of Judge's chest, as if he was worried he would get burned.

I had to admit, this whole situation had the potential to burn us all.

Tattooed fingers drifted lower, over his pecs and when his fingertips brushed across Judge's nipples, the vampire hissed, making us all tense. He swallowed hard but nodded at me. I could see the heat in his eyes.

"Keep going. Can you sense how much this is turning our girl on right now? Rainy Day is about to live up to her name over there. Wetter than monsoon season."

I flipped him the bird, but I grinned because he wasn't wrong. Tex's hands slipped down Judge's ribs, and over his abs. Judge's nose flared, and he leaned into the touch a little, but that was the only sign he was being anything but hospitable. When Tex's hands got to the waistband of Judge's jeans, I was going to explode. His hands stilled their exploration, and we all stood there as if we were waiting for a bomb to go off.

Judge struck like a python, his hand gripped the dark strands of Tex's hair and slammed their mouths together.

Holy fucking shit on a dinner plate.

I sucked in a gasp as they kissed. It wasn't the way they kissed me, which was all soft and tender, even when Judge was being rough. No, they kissed like they were fighting for control like they were in a battle. Tex gripped the front Judge's shirt, and I couldn't tell if he was trying to push him away or pull him closer. It was frantic and feral, and I was about to come right on the spot.

As if he could sense the direction of my thoughts, Judge's hand whipped out and grabbed me, pulling me closer.

He dragged his mouth away, "Can you taste her need in the air, Human?" he growled.

I smacked him on the shoulder. "If you've sucked face with someone, you have to call him by his name," I chastised.

He gave me a look that promised me I'd regret my sass in the best possible way later, but still, he said, "Would you like to taste her need, *Tex*?"

Tex groaned, and his hands found me easily like I was a magnet. "Fuck yes. More than anything." He pulled me close, and then he was kissing me with just as much frenetic energy as he kissed Judge. I could feel the hard press of his cock against my stomach, and I might have been imagining it, but I thought I could taste Judge on his lips.

The man in question pressed against my back, and I could feel that he was just as affected as Tex. The mouths that had been battling each other seemed to have called a truce in the pursuit of driving me absolutely crazy.

Tex's hand slipped beneath my yoga pants and found my clit like it was a sixth sense. I moaned helplessly into his mouth, as he circled the swollen nub.

"She's so wet," he groaned. "So damn hot."

Judge's hands also slipped inside my pants, squeezing my ass, as he kicked my feet wider, and he slid two fingers inside my core, stretching me. I was so worked up from watching Tex's slow exploration of Judge that I was coming before I knew it, screaming into Tex's mouth. I sagged between them, and Judge wrapped an arm around my waist.

"Uh uh, Raine. We aren't even close to being done yet."

I looked over my shoulder. "Good," I growled.

He was out of his clothes so quickly, even my preternatural sight strained to catch it. But he held up a hand to stop me from doing the same thing. "Do you want to unwrap your present, Tex?"

I looked up into Tex's hooded eyes, his long dark lashes hiding the brilliant blue of his eyes. "I feel like I've been waiting a lifetime to do just that," he whispered, his hands finding the hem of my shirt. He pulled it over my head, the nails of his pinky fingers scraping along my skin and making me shiver. His hands traced the curve of my shoulder, the lines of my back, before curving around to take my aching breasts into his palms. When he brushed my nipples with his thumbs, calloused from the guitar, I almost shuddered my way to another orgasm. When he dropped to his knees and took them between his teeth, I did just that. I moaned and shuddered in his arms as he pressed his face into my breasts, his fingers gripping the waistband of my pants and peeling them down. Unfortunately, being a super badass, sexually aware vampire didn't give me better coordination, so I had to sit down on the couch beside Judge to toe them off over my feet. Then I wrapped my legs around Tex and pulled him closer.

"Fuck, you are so soft. You smell like everything good in the world," he whispered against my skin as his tongue traced a wet line down my stomach. His hands on my knees, he spread me wide and bared me to Judge's eyes. He was watching the whole thing intently, his hard cock already in his palm as he stroked it lazily.

Tex kissed his way up from my knee to my inner thigh, then surprised the shit out of me when he bit the soft flesh of my inner thigh hard, sucking it into his mouth. He was giving me a hickey on my damn thigh.

Judge reached over, flicking him in the forehead. "I'll do the biting around here," he laughed, and Tex grinned against my skin. But as his breath brushed against the dampness of my core, all the laughter left me.

As his tongue ran down my slit in one long stroke, I died and went to heaven. Well, I would have if I wasn't already technically dead. Judge moved over toward me and kissed me. "Is this what you hoped for when lover boy down there told you he batted for the other team?" he asked me softly.

All I could do is make an odd mewling sound as

Tex sucked on my clit, and my eyes rolled so far back in my head I saw the past.

Laughing, he kissed my nipple before sinking his fangs into my breast. Then I came like a freight train, the last little speck of my sanity reminding me not to clench my thighs together and accidentally crush Tex's skull like a sparrow's egg.

Tex pulled away, his tongue between his teeth. "I smell blood."

I gathered my wits enough to say, "Judge is drinking from me. Blood and sex are intertwined for vamps."

"Will one of you bite me?"

The question startled me, even though he essentially asked it of me before, but instead, Judge broke away, licking the wound in one long swipe that made me moan again. "Not today. There's plenty of time to fall down that rabbit hole. Come here."

He wrapped a hand around Tex's neck and pulled him up my body, kissing him hard, spreading the taste of blood between them.

I watched them kiss, my gaze flicking between the two of them. Well, it did until Tex thrust into me. My eyes slammed shut as pleasure washed over me like a tidal wave. But it was more than that. It was like something in my soul rippled. It was right. He began to move, finding the perfect rhythm like it was written into his very DNA, even though Judge was kissing him as if he owned him.

Judge moved away a little, and knelt to his full height, so his cock was level with Tex's face. I held my breath, well as much as I could considering Tex was moving like he wanted to wring every last ounce of pleasure from my body, waiting to see what would happen.

"You can't see her, Tex, but she has this look on her face when she looks at you like you're the only thing anchoring her to the world right now. Her eyes are shinin' like you are making her feel too good, and when you hit just the right spot, she gets this little crease between her eyes, and her pretty pink tongue pokes out between her teeth. It's fucking beautiful, and it's all because of you." Tex turned his head toward Judge as he spoke, and Judge took advantage. Holding his cock in one hand, he ran the fingers of his other through Tex's hair gently, a tenderness on his face when he looked down at him that made my breath hitch. But he didn't say anything as he pressed the head of the dick against Tex's lips, and waited.

When Tex wrapped his lips around Judge's cock, I came, like a tsunami during a hurricane, and Judge thrust deep into Tex's mouth. Tex wasn't done, continuing to pound in time as Judge thrust into his mouth, and soon he was making a muffled groaning sound. His thrusts got wilder, rougher, until finally, he thrust into me to the hilt, holding me with one hand as he came. Judge continued to slide in and out of his mouth until he pulled out and came on my breasts in hot spurts.

For a moment we all just lay still, absorbing what happened.

Finally, Judge moved away. He leaned forward, kiss me softly on the lips. Then, he moved back and kissed Tex equally as softly.

"I'll just go get a towel. Maybe run you a bath." He was gone in a rush of air.

Tex collapsed against my body, uncaring that his face was now in a pool of Judge's cum.

"So, that's what Judge is like," I said, running my fingers through his disheveled hair.

He turned his head and kissed my palm. "I'm beginning to see why you stayed in this town, Mika."

I let out a small, near-hysterical giggle. "I guess you better start calling me Raine."

CHAPTER NINETEEN

A kiss on my nose woke me, and I turned over and snuggled tighter into Tex's back. It was too early to be awake, but I guess he was still on human-time.

"It smells like a porn set in here, Rainey," someone whispered against my cheek. I opened one eye and saw Brody's grinning face. Groaning, I dragged him down until his body collapsed on mine. I banded my arms around his waist and nuzzled my nose against his neck. "Tex is bisexual. So is Judge apparently. It was wild."

Brody laughed and waggled his eyebrows. "Judging by the smile on your face, you got a little wild too."

I made a happy, humming noise. "It's too early, Brody. Come to bed."

He nipped my nose. "I would, Sweetheart, but the

Sheriff sent me. Apparently, they are making a decision about your boy-toy over there during the town meeting right about now. Figured you'd want to be there."

"They're what?" I said although it sounded a bit like a pterodactyl screech. Tex shot upright in bed. Judge was nowhere to be found, but I was used to that by now.

"Someone needs to stay with Tex," I said as I shot out of bed, dragging on last night's clothes. When Judge stuck his head around the door jamb, a mixing bowl filled with some kind of pancake batter in hand, I pinched myself. Surely I was still dreaming, right? That wasn't Judge playing domestic goddess?

"I'll stay with Tex. You go make sure they don't wipe him and send him home."

Tex's brows pulled together, his tongue darting out to wet his lower lip. I was momentarily distracted by the gesture, one leg half in/ half out of my jeans. So, so pretty. "They can't just decide that can they?"

I ran my hand over his cheek and resisted the urge to just climb back into bed with him. "They're the Council. They can do whatever they want. But we are going to make sure you stay where you belong. Wherever you want to be, I mean. If you want to be with us, that's-"

He kissed me to stop my inane rambling.

"I want to be here."

Brody slapped his shoulder. "Then, here is where you'll stay."

He led me out of the room and to the front door. "You should make our new harem mate feel welcome, Judge. I'm sure you know what he likes," Brody teased over his shoulder as we slammed the door behind us.

I elbowed Brody in the ribs. "I'm not sure how I feel about you calling yourselves a harem. Seems kind of derogatory or something."

"Cache of adoring men?"

"No!" I yelled, sprinting across the road toward the Town Hall.

"Multiple life partners?" he continued to tease as we ran. I wanted to just zip there, but I slowed my pace so Brody could keep up. That being said, we were traveling faster than any human could dream of running.

"I'm okay with multiple life partners," I said begrudgingly as we halted at the door of the Council building. It looked like every other hewn log building in town, though there were subtle hints at its importance. Heavy doors with iron filigree, marble floors that seemed to shine like ice, ten-foot statues of the founding vampires.

Seriously.

Inside the building was another set of double doors. I threw them open dramatically.

"I object!"

I was checking that one off my list. Hollywood

didn't lie about how satisfying it was to hear the doors thunk open, and every head turn to look at you. It was a diva moment. Look at me, ticking shit off my bucket list.

"You don't want Cresta to open a trade account with a hair extension company in California?" Nico said dryly, grinning at my theatrics. Everyone else seemed a little more annoyed.

"Uh, no, that's cool. Sorry Cresta," I whispered to the woman in question as I shuffled down the rows toward a couple of empty seats by Walker. When I thought I would be doing the walk of shame this evening, I imagined it would be because Brody and Walker caught me in bed with Judge and Tex.

Actually, in my imagination, it was less a walk of shame and more a stride of pride. And there was pizza. And Brody was wearing a thong. And it was the plotline of the only porn I've ever watched.

They wrapped up the business issues pretty quickly, and then Nico cleared his throat. "Now onto the issue that we are all dying to talk about," he said, grinning at me.

I leaned over to Brody, whispering low, though I knew that Nico could probably still hear. "Did he just make a vamp joke?"

I felt more than saw Brody's answering laugh.

"There is a human in the town with far too much knowledge of our kind. He is an issue, of course. He has seen the newest member of our town, knows her past life, knows that we are all vampire, knows entirely too much," Catherine said sternly. "However, I vote we take execution off the table."

I gasped, and it echoed off the walls. "Was that ever on the table? What happened to the town's ideals that you made me stand up there and swear to uphold?"

Nico applauded, and Catherine frowned. "Of course not." The guy who looked old as dirt, Tomas, although I still mentally called him the Grim Reaper in my brain due to his black cloak, looked like he wanted execution to be back on the table, just for me.

"We wipe him and send him home, it's the only course of action. Unless we give Raine the option to turn her former paramour?" Nico said, offering me something I'd only considered in the very depths of my soul. But I would never. Would I?

"That is not we are about, Nico. You should know. You made the rules," Catherine snapped.

Nico seemed unperturbed by her ire. "Sometimes, rules are meant to be broken. But I will bow to the will of the Council. Wipe him and put him on a plane home."

I stood up and leaped over Walker's lap. Well, I tried to at least. The Sheriff in question wrapped an arm around my waist and settled me on his lap. "Easy, Raine."

Brody stood up beside me. "I am authorized by my Pack to inform the Council that the Shapeshifter

Tex Flanaghan is now considered Pack and is therefore privy to the protection sworn between our two species when we allowed you to settle this land."

I stared at Brody, and at Nico who was grinning like I'd finally figured something out. Which I hadn't. Grim and Catherine were looking annoyed though, and finally, she bent her head in supplication. "Of course, we hold to our agreement. Are you sure the boy is a shapeshifter?" Brody quirked an eyebrow at Catherine, and she must have recently fed because her cheeks flushed with embarrassment. "But surely you agree that if that is the case, he cannot be allowed to go home?"

Oh. Now I know why Nico was giving me that look. He'd been telling me all along how to keep Tex. Find the unbreakable rules. An ancient pact would definitely be that. But why would he want me to keep Tex?

"I will press on the boy the need to stay. Or at least to keep his mouth shut. It is not just your colony that place a high value on secrecy." His booming voice was scathing.

I gaped at Brody. He'd transformed before my eyes, from playful, cheeky lover to someone who's presence filled out the room. I could feel the earthy energy that rolled off him, that made my skin feel too tight and made my dead heart race.

I leaned back into Walker's chest. "What the hell?" I whispered.

Walker chuckled. "It's always like that when he goes Alpha. It's like he transforms."

I turned and narrowed my eyes at Walker. "What do you mean Alpha?"

"He's the boss. The King of the Canadian Shapeshifters. Head Honcho. Ass Supremo," he murmured back, his lips brushing the shell of my ear.

"Holy fucking shit," I gasped, a little louder than necessary. Brody looked at me and winked.

They were still droning on up there about the need to prevent further incidences like this, and Nico insisted that it was a rare case, on and on it went. Finally, one of the other two Vamp Councillors, the woman with the sad eyes, snapped out of her trance. "Fine. Meeting adjourned. The human–"

"Shapeshifter," Brody corrected.

"Yes, yes. The Shapeshifter can stay. But he's your responsibility now."

Brody nodded and then turned and strode from the room like he was indeed a King. I scrambled out of the room after him, far less regally, barely stopping to say hello to everyone. I caught up with him in the middle of the square. I launched myself the last few feet and jumped onto his back, tackling us both to the ground. Somehow, by sheer skill, I'd ended up underneath him on the dewy grass.

"You got some 'splainin to do," I grumbled, as he nuzzled into my neck like rolling around on the grass was a completely legitimate and respectable way to pass the time. His hair tickled my shoulder, and his lips were tracing hot lines down the column of my throat, and I held back a moan. Screw respectable.

Luckily, Mr. Respectable himself turned up, standing over us and blocking out some of the street light. "Am I going to have to arrest you two for public indecency, or should you take it back to Raine's house?

I slapped Brody's shoulder, remembering I was a little mad. "You've been keeping secrets, Your Royal Anus!"

He stood, dragging me back up with him. He smoothed out my frown line with his thumb. "It's just a title. We are a democracy up there. I'm just the pretty face of the Pack."

Walker snorted. "Or the sharp claws, when needed."

Brody shot him a look but wrapped his arm around my shoulders. "If you'd met my grandmother, you'd have no doubt who was in charge. I'm a Poster Boy."

Yeah, I might have been reborn yesterday, but I knew a line of bullshit when I heard it. "That was a lot of power for a Poster Boy. The Axl Rose poster I had on my wall when I was thirteen, never shut down a room full of hungry vampires."

Walker laughed. "You had a rocker with big hair on your wall as a kid? Not Bieber?" When I raised my eyes at him in surprise, he shrugged. "We're in Canada. Not on Mars."

Having been in Nico's therapist office, I should have known better than to expect them to be stuck in the 1800s. But still, it was surprising to hear pop culture references from Walker.

"You can thank Tex for that. And his Dad's record collection."

As always, talking about home sent a barb of pain through my chest, but knowing when I'd walk through my front door, a little piece of home would still be there made tears well in my eyes.

However, when I pushed open my front door, it was to see Judge pushing Tex up against the fridge and kissing him like he wanted to eat him whole.

"Oh," Walker said, his eyes so wide it was almost comical.

Most people, when they get busted making out in someone else's kitchen, would leap away from each other. Maybe Tex would have, if Judge didn't have his hands pinned above his head, and his body essentially trapping him against the fridge. But Judge made no move to shift away, despite his new audience.

Walker was looking between them and me as if I was about to go into a Jerry Springer style rage. Instead, I sauntered over there, gripped Tex's chin and kissed him like I missed him. Which I had. Then I leaned over and kissed Judge.

I could hear Brody talking to Walker. "Apparently,

this is a thing now." He didn't seem at all perturbed by it. "We are all mutual life partners."

I looked over my shoulder and rolled my eyes at Brody. I held my breath and waited to see what Walker would say.

"Do you think they could be life partners a little more to the left so I can grab a beer from the fridge?" Walker asked, strolling across the living room.

And that was it. He'd accepted that Judge and Tex were both bisexual, that I intended to keep them both, and Brody too if he had anything to say about it. But that was just it. He didn't make any indication if he was included in that or not. Was it too much for him, all this sausage in the one McMuffin?

Judge finally moved away from Tex, straightening his shirt and smoothing his hair, and watching him give those small, sweet intimacies to someone else made me appreciate him even more. And to see him do it to someone he had only just met, despite the fact we'd all been naked together, it made me look at the mysterious Drifter a little differently.

Walker pulled open the fridge door, pulled out a six-pack, handing one to both Judge and Tex, before tossing one across the room like a football at Brody. He leaned forward and kissed my cheek, handing me a bottle as well.

"We should talk about your maker. Now we have Tex sorted, I'd like you and your harem of admirers to be able to live happily ever after."

Judge grabbed an entire tray of breakfast food from the oven and put it on the table. Pancakes, sausages, eggs, and some kind of little biscuit thing. Who knew he was so domestic?

Beer and breakfast seemed to be a very irresponsible life choice. Then I looked around at all the handsome men at my table.

Sometimes a little irresponsibility had wonderful results.

CHAPTER TWENTY

I stood at my front door, feeling anxious. I couldn't leave, because it was afternoon and I was still stuck in my tomb until sundown. I hugged Tex tight and breathed in the scent of him. I committed it to memory, just in case. Judge had been gone when we woke up this morning, his side of the bed cooling. Tex had looked forlorn ever since, like a kicked puppy, or someone who'd been picked last during gym class again. I squeezed his hand. "He'll be back. It's just what he does when things get too touchy-feely. It's not you."

Tex squeezed me harder. "Doesn't matter. As long as I have you."

I launched myself into his arms, and he grabbed me easily. I kissed him like he was leaving for a decade and not three days. I had separation anxiety now, apparently.

"Relax, Rainey. I'll take good care of him. We'll be back by the weekend, and you and Lover Boy can have all the crazy threesomes you want," Brody teased.

I pulled out of Tex's arms and walked into Brody's open ones. "Is that an offer, Alpha?"

He let out a little growl that rumbled in his chest. "I think I could get used to those words crossing your lips." He kissed me in that achingly soft way he had that made my toes curl. "I'd do just about anything for you, Sweetheart. I'm all about the orgies. But I draw the line at crossing swords with Lover Boy or Mr. Tall, Dark and Broody."

I laughed. "What about Walker?" It was my turn to tease.

Brody waggled his eyebrows. "He has handcuffs. I'd be tempted to make an exception for the good Sheriff."

We both knew it was an empty promise. Walker might be cool with whatever was happening between Judge and Tex and me, but he wasn't about to become the caboose to our train of love. I cringed at the bad euphemism.

With one more kiss, I sent them both out the door. They'd borrowed Walker's bike; apparently he had a Harley hiding in his garage, and that just made me wonder what else he was hiding in his cookie-cutter cottage; they were heading up to Packlands to get Tex properly sworn in. Brody was pretty tight-lipped about what that entailed, and if Tex knew, he was playing dumb. I stood at the door of my apartment until I heard the low rumble of the Harley rolling down the quiet streets of Dark River.

I was alone once again. But after being holed up with Tex for so long, going about my normal routine was almost a relief. I had to go have my Council mandated therapy session with Nico, which I was pretty sure only involved us eating icecream and him mining my brain for pop culture references to add to his office of horror, but I found myself looking forward to the bi-weekly ritual.

Dressed in some black skintight jeans that I never would have worn as Mika because they bordered on almost indecent, but damn they made my ass look good, I decided to head downstairs through the Immortal Cupcake and say hello to Angeline. I'd basically been ignoring everyone in lieu of Tex.

Guilt rushed through me as she lit up when she saw me. "Raine! I thought you'd died of dehydration up there. Just remember, you have the same vagina for all eternity, don't wear it out in the first year," she yelled, so not only would everyone in the store hear but everyone on the entire block. My face flamed so red, I could feel the burn.

"Jesus Christ, Angeline," I hissed back. "Say it louder, I don't think the people at the diner heard you."

When she opened her mouth to do just that, I

slapped a hand over her face. But the sparkling mirth in her eyes made a giggle bubble up in my chest, and before I knew it, we were both laughing hysterically while people stood waiting in front of the glass display cases to be served.

Finally, we both stood, wiping the pink-tinged tears from our cheeks.

"I'll help you catch up, then I have to head over to Nico's for therapy," I said, as I served the vaguely familiar vamp in front of me.

"That'd be great. Take him some of the unicorn cupcakes. They're his favorite." At this point, I wasn't even surprised that Nico liked cupcakes that literally looked like they'd been shit out by unicorns.

Nor was I surprised at the odd squee noise he made when I put them down on the desk in his office twenty minutes later. I *was* surprised by his ability to fit an entire cupcake in his mouth at once though. Multi-colored rainbow frosting extruded from the corners of his lips like a rabies epidemic in Equestria. That's where the My Little Ponies live. I was a Pony fan. Don't judge.

When he finally swallowed the cupcake in one large swallow, seriously it was as gross as it was fascinating, he finally greeted me.

"Hello, Raine. It is good to see you, and especially good to see you when you bring me baked goods."

I smiled and sat down on the stupidly hard chaise lounge. "I don't even care that I come second to one of Angeline's cupcakes. Totally under-standable."

In a gesture that was a dichotomy of innocence and exoticness, his tongue dipped out and licked the frosting from his lips. I followed the gesture like a moth to a flame. I blushed again, glad he wasn't looking as he sat on his inflatable ball chair.

Nope. Not going there.

"So, how do you feel about getting a little piece of home, right here in Dark River? With the bullet-proof protection of the Pack at that?" He asked lightly, as I laid back on the couch and stared at the ceiling.

I didn't think I could accurately describe my joy, at least not without letting on that Tex was also my Mate. "It's a little piece of bliss I thought I'd be denied forever. It's eased something in my soul," I said truthfully.

"And your other paramours? No one is upset about having a near-human in their midst?" He stuffed another cupcake in his mouth, devouring this one in two bites instead of one.

I almost laughed out loud. "Uh, they are all taking it well. Do you think it's odd? I mean, am I going to be stoned in the town square for having three boyfriends?"

"Three?"

Walker wasn't there yet. He was still holding back. I wasn't sure why, considering the way he kissed me outside the club in Calgary. I knew he wanted to solve my murder first, and I could respect that. "Three and a half?" I suggested, and he just laughed.

"To answer your question, no one has ever been stoned in the town square." He paused. "Actually, there was that one time Burt added marijuana to his brownies. I don't know who was more surprised about the effect on Vamps, Burt or the Council. It's like the effect on humans but knocked us out completely. There were a lot of stoned vampires in the town square that day." He laughed at the memory. Huh, I'd have to ask Alice why weed affected us and alcohol didn't. That was probably one for the vamp scientists though.

Nico continued. "But no one here will begrudge you any happiness. The rate of women turned to vampirism is far less than males, so our numbers are always at odds. It is not unusual for female vampiresses to have several lovers living in a nest together. Eternity is a long time to live alone due to a false belief in monogamy." His eyes grew sad, and I wondered if Nico had someone. He was so full of life for a man who had been dead for a millennium, and I hoped he did. The sadness was chased from his face by a grin. "From a Council perspective, closer ties to the Pack, because you are engaging in coitus with the Alpha, is always a boon."

I felt my eyes bug out. "You make me sound like some kind of sexual spy!"

He laughed, and the tattoos that encircled almost

every available inch of his skin danced in the light. It was hypnotic, like something you'd see on a snake in the wild before it opened its maw and swallowed you whole like Nico did with that cupcake.

"I'm fairly sure there are members of the Council that are convinced you are a spy for the Vampire Nation."

I laughed along, even though the idea perturbed me. "Hang on, wouldn't they be upset that you told me that?"

He shook his head. "Oh no, Raine. I am very certain you aren't a spy."

I crossed my arms and pouted. "I could be a spy. I'd make the perfect spy. Who'd ever suspect me? It would be like suspecting Burt." I'd done some stupid stuff in my time, but trying to convince an ancient vampire that I was a spy probably topped the list.

He didn't seem to be buying it though, walking over to sit by me on the chaise lounge. "I know it because it's my job to know these things." He gripped my chin and turned my head, so I was looking into his eyes. "I can compel the truth from you remember? Raine, are you a spy?"

"No." It was out of my mouth before I could stop it.

"Do you want the Sheriff to be one of your beaus?"

"Yes. Who says beau, though? This is the twenty-first century, you cad," I joked. None of this was revolutionary. "This is easy. I want to tell you this stuff. You're my therapist."

He grinned, and it was sly and a little alarming.

"Do you find me attractive?"

I desperately wanted to say no. I tried to make my lips form the words, pursing them tightly, pressing my tongue to the roof of my mouth. But when I opened it, all that came out was a squeaked, "Yes."

He grinned and moved back to his chair. He pulled out a tub of Ben and Jerry's and threw it to me. "This is how I know you aren't a spy, Raine. Maybe one day your mental shields will be strong enough that you could lie to me, but today isn't that day."

I just blinked at him, the ice cream tub chilling my fingertips. "So, I can't lie to you at all?"

He shook his head. "Sure, you can. You can tell me that you like the color scheme of this office, or that my taste in interior decorating is second to none, as long as I don't ask you a direct question. Try it."

I stuck the ice cream in my mouth. "Your taste in furniture is sublime."

He let out a small giggle, looking around at the room. No one would ever believe that was anything but a lie. "Raine, what do you think of my taste in furniture?" he asked softly.

"It looks like a yard sale threw up in a thrift store." I slapped a hand over my mouth. Oh my god. "I'm not sure I like this, Nico." He didn't need to compel me for the truth of that statement. The idea that I couldn't lie to him, not really, gave me cold sweats. Not that I'd ever felt the inclination to lie to him, but the security blanket was there.

I watched him scoop out the inside of one of the cupcakes and then spooned his ice cream into the center, creating some kind of icecream/cake abomination. "Yes, it is a rare ability that is both a gift and a curse. For instance, Raine, does my ability scare you?"

"Yes." That one didn't even need much compulsion.

"Did you ever think I was your maker?"

"Yes. But to be fair, I suspected everyone at first."

"Do I scare you?"

"A little bit."

"Would you ever let me take you on a date one day?"

"Yes. One day."

I don't know who was more shocked by my answer. I was at capacity for love interests. I couldn't do another one. Juggling four was more than any one woman had a right to expect. Nico gave me a sad smile. "And there is the curse of it, no? An answer coerced is no real answer. It's like your Google. The answers are all there, but the magic has left the world."

Obviously, he had never tried to get answers from Judge. But wasn't some of that dangerous mysteriousness what I found so appealing about my Drifter?

I looked at my watch. Our session was over, and I

probably could have survived without today's bit of show and tell. When I left the office, I'd convince myself that he was asking these questions not because he had any interest in me, but because they were the types of questions everyone wanted the answers to. Does Lawrence from Accounting 101 think I'm cute? Does Jimmy from second grade think I'm nicer than Sheila Lepkowski? It was natural to have a morbid curiosity for these things. It wasn't because the ancient vampire had a thing for me.

But still, as I left the room, I gave him a small half-smile. "Not today. But one day."

Then I ran out of there like the chicken with its ass on fire.

CHAPTER TWENTY-ONE

I downed my third Ruby Slipper, a vodka and raspberry concoction so strong that if you knocked them down fast enough, you got a light buzz. An overturned cupcake was sitting atop stripey witches legs with bedazzled red heels was today's cupcake. Tonight's movie was, you guessed it, The Wizard of Oz.

We had a bit of a crowd tonight, and I wasn't sure if it was because I was a zoo exhibit, or because movie night had been on a little hiatus while I sorted my life out. Either way, couples canoodled on the big leather couches, drinking and whispering under their breath. Four boyfriends, still alone on a Friday night. Wasn't that the story of my life?

Glinda was telling Judy Garland that there was no place like home, and tonight, I believed it. Homesickness was hitting me hard. Maybe because Tex was gone, and he'd brought all the guilt and pain back to the surface. And then he'd left.

Finally, Dorothy was back home, with guardians who didn't believe her tale and a life in black and white, and I'd never related so hard to a fictional character in all my life. What was the point of wishing I could go back? Could I give all this up? The knowledge that this entire supernatural world existed, and go back to the black and white of the human world?

Finally, the credits rolled, and everyone started to filter out of the Cafe, I switched off all the lights. I thought Walker would be by, but I guess I only had to climb the stairs.

I unlocked my door, surprised to see the lights on. I could see Walker passed out on my couch. My heart rate sped up when I saw Doc Alice leaning over him, though.

"Doc? What the hell happened?"

She jumped, looking at me with relief. "Raine! I don't know. He called me and sounded off. When I got here, he was out of it. I can't get him to rouse," she said, and I raced over.

I checked his temperature, which was stupid because he was going to be cold, he was a vampire, but I didn't know what else to do. "Walker? Can you hear me?" I shouted, but he didn't wake up. "Could it have been the blood supply?" I asked Alice over my shoulder. I shook Walker by his shoulders, but he didn't so much as flutter an eyelash. It was like he was really dead.

"I checked the blood supply, it looked fine," she said.

Walker's eyelashes fluttered, and I breathed out a sigh of relief. Thank god.

"Ra…" he whispered, fighting his way back to consciousness.

I smoothed a hand over his cheek. "Hey, I'm here. It's okay."

"Ra…" He breathed again. His eyes fluttered open, and there was fear in them. "Run," he gasped out, his eyes wide with fear. I stared down at him, confused.

But he wasn't looking at me. He was looking at Alice. "Run!"

I spun around, but Alice raised a hand. "Stop."

I froze. Physically unable to move from my crouch.

No, no, no, no. This couldn't be right. "Alice?" I whispered. I wanted her to deny it, for there to be another reason my body wouldn't move. Maybe some kind of paralysis pumped through the aircon system. "Why?"

Alice rubbed a hand down her face. "You know why, Raine. I'm your Maker. Which I'm really sorry about, by the way. I didn't mean…" she sighed heavily again. "I'm sorry that it came to this. I'd hope we would just accept you into the fold and then

Walker would let it go, but I should have known he wouldn't. He's that kind of person."

My legs were starting to cramp from holding the crouching position so long. My heart pounded, and I was scared. Beyond scared. I was petrified. "Why?"

Alice flopped down on the couch, looking totally defeated. But she didn't let me stand. She held me in that position, though my thighs were visibly starting to tremble. "It was an accident. Do you think keeping a blood supply to a town of vamps this size, without alerting human authorities or coming to the attention of the Vamp Nation, was easy? It isn't; it's hard and thankless work. So I decided I could borrow it from the human tourists. They donate for a couple of days, leave and go home to wherever, without being any the wiser. Until you."

I couldn't tell if she was remorseful or annoyed, but I was starting to whimper. Walker was still struggling to maintain consciousness, so he was no help. I tried to wiggle something, my pinky finger, a toe, something.

"You ended up going into hypovolemic shock. You died right there in front of me, and I panicked. I turned you, left you in the drain outside of Dark River where I could take care of you. But it didn't go like that. You wouldn't let it go, and neither would Walker. And then the Drifter started poking his nose into things, raising the suspicions of the Enforcers and now I'm screwed. You need to go. Walker needs to go.

Without him, the Council will let it drop to maintain the peace." It all ran out in one long, garbled sentence.

Tears began to run down my cheeks. She was going to kill me this time. Or wipe me and send me out into the world, where I would probably die. This was bad. She stood again, fidgeting as she walked to the kitchen.

"Raine, Child of my Making, feed from Walker until I tell you to stop." Finally, released from my position, my body leaped to Alice's command like it wasn't mine any longer. I latched onto Walker's throat, piercing his skin with my fangs and dragging his blood into my mouth.

I cried. I cried with every involuntary pull my mouth made, my tears running hotly down my cheeks until they pool onto Walker's shoulder.

"Shh, it will be okay," he whispered, as I dragged huge gulps of his blood, the predator thrilled to be feeding, even though I was trying to fight the urge with every ounce of my mind.

I wanted to tell him it wouldn't be okay. That we were both going to die. That I was going to murder him, and I couldn't stop myself. But I didn't say any of that as I drank him down faster and faster. Eventually, the blood spilled over my lips and onto his cheeks. The slow beat of his heart barely thumped anymore, and every time I waited, waited for the moment his heart wouldn't beat again.

"Alice…" his voice was whisper-thin now. "Stop this."

I slid my eyes to Alice, who was openly sobbing now as she saw the deathly paleness of Walker's skin against the vivid pinkness of mine.

"I'm so sorry, Walker. I am. But I have to do this. To protect me, and the town, and Angeline."

My brain screamed and screamed, and when she slid an honest-to-goodness stake in my hand, I wanted to wail at the injustice of it.

"Stake him, Raine," Alice said, her voice wobbling on the words. "Then stake yourself."

She turned her back, so she didn't have to watch the fucking coward. *Let go,* I commanded my fingers. *Drop the stake. Or better still, ram it into Alice's heart.* Instead of obeying me, my hand raised itself, and my sobs made me choke on Walker's blood. Good. I'd rather drown than be the death of Walker.

"Raine… Love…" he whispered, his breathing became a labored rattle, his eyes sliding closed. "Not your fault…" He was about to exsanguinate, and he was trying to make me feel better. Tears mixed with blood, and as much as I wanted to tell him everything I felt for him, that I would be with him soon, I couldn't.

I raised my hand, poising the stake above his chest. I begged any deity who would listen to smite me down and stop me from what was about to happen.

The door to my apartment flung open, and Judge strode in, the answer to every prayer I'd ever whispered. He took in the room in an instant, crash tackling me to the floor, tearing my lips from Walker's skin.

I still didn't release the stake, physically unable to loosen my grip, and the pointed tip tore across my chest.

"Alice. It's Alice. She's my maker. She wants me to sta—"

"Raine, I command you to stop speaking," Alice screeched as an absolute mountain of a vamp I'd never met barrelled into her, spinning her and pinning her to the ground in a movement so fluid and swift that I could barely follow it with my Vamp sight.

I opened my mouth to tell Judge that Walker was dying, but nothing came at. I opened my mouth in a silent scream and pointed at Walker, hoping Judge would know.

"Hey, hey. It's okay. I've got him," Judged soothed, prying the stake from my hand.

I scrambled across the floor like a crab, getting as far away from Walker as I could, the compulsion to break the leg from the chair and drive it through his chest riding me hard. Judge slashed his wrist and was feeding his blood back to Walker, who was so close to death he couldn't even suction his lips around Judge's wrist.

I sobbed in the corner. I cried and cried silently,

even my anguish was subjected to Alice's compulsion not to speak. The big blonde vampire had Alice on her feet, a contraption that looked a little like a ball-gag in her mouth. Tears streamed down her cheeks, and when Angeline burst into the room, I didn't think my heart could possibly break anymore. But when she took in the room, her eyes flicking between a near-dead Walker, me sobbing in the corner and Alice looking defeated, bound in cuffs, she sunk to her knees.

"No," she whispered, her face so pale I thought she'd pass out. Alice was trying to talk to her lover from behind the gag, but only garbled words came out. I dropped my head into my hands and wished the whole world would go away just so I couldn't hear Angeline's heart-wrenching sobs or Judge trying to coax a dying Walker to drink.

Who did we call? What did we do? Normally, we'd call Doc Alice and the Sheriff. But who do you call when the Doctor tries to kill the Sheriff?

When I heard shouting, I realized that the Council had arrived, but were still barred from my apartment, which only made me stare at the giant blonde man standing in the middle of my living room as if my ward meant nothing.

He caught me staring, and gave me a soft smile that looked totally foreign on his scarred, battered face. More yelling drew my eye to Caroline and Nico, who were standing at the threshold demanding answers. Nico's eyes were deadly. The absolute lack of humanity in his face when he looked at Alice chilled me to the bone. "We found the progeny's maker trying to compel her to drain your Sheriff." The big guy had a rough English accent. The kind of accent that was found in fight clubs and gutters.

"And you are?" Caroline said, her tone precariously balanced between haughty and hysterical.

"Oh, where are my manners?" the giant said in a tone that suggested he'd take his manners and shove them somewhere really uncomfortable. "My name is X. Collector of china teacups, savior of damsels in distress, and Vamp Nation Enforcer."

Well. Mic drop.

CHAPTER TWENTY-TWO

"X, stop being a prick and take her to the lock-up," Judge growled, drawing my attention back to them. I wanted to edge closer, to see if Walker was okay. I stood, but before I registered my body had even moved, I'd grabbed a knife from the butcher's block on my bench and was flashing toward him. Luckily, X was there even quicker, pressing my wrist until the knife fell to the floor, crushing me tight to his body until I was so immobile, I may as well have been in chains.

I screamed silently, as the tears slid down my face in hot, angry drops. "She's been compelled to stake him in the heart too," X murmured to Judge, who looked at me with more pity on his face than I'd ever seen. Even more than the night, he'd found me punching trees near the 'Welcome to Dark River' sign.

"It's all good, Sweetcheeks. I won't let you get all stabby on your boyfriend," X said in a low voice. He looked past me at Judge and Walker. "He looks better already. How about we get you out of here and let Judge finish what he's doing without worrying about you going all bunny-boiler on his ass?"

I nodded and shuffled toward my door. I needed out of this apartment. I didn't care if I never came back.

As soon as I stepped over the threshold, Nico pulled me to his side. "Are you okay? What happened?" He was using his compulsion, but I was unable to speak. I just shook my head uselessly. I wanted to go home. Back to my parents, and my boring life, where nothing was life and death. Where no one was more than they seemed.

"She's been compelled not to speak. Also, I'd keep her away from the Sheriff for a while," X said, returning to where he'd left Alice bound on the floor. "If someone will point the way to the police station, Judge suggested you guys like to do trials or some shit? I'm more than happy to end this right now if you like?"

And just like that, everyone in the room remembered that this guy said he was an Enforcer for the Vampire Nation.

I'd almost forgotten Angeline crying softly on my Persian rug. A Persian rug now stained with Walker's blood. "No," she said, leaping to her feet. "She deserves a trial. That's how we do things. That's why we made this town."

Neither Nico or X seemed particularly moved by her declaration, but I forced myself to look at my friend. I never wanted to look at her again, knowing her pain was in part my fault. When she met my gaze, I nodded. Alice deserved a trial, even if it was just as closure for Angeline.

Caroline sighed. "Of course. Alice will get a trial and a sentence."

Nico looked at Alice. "It would go a long way to your defense if you removed the geas on your prog-eny." The or else was barely veiled. When Alice just shook her head, I thought he was going to strangle her on the spot. "Do you have no remorse? You have been here for a century, and this is the legacy you wish to leave? You said you understood what we had created here, but you still flaunt the very rules we have lived by." His voice dropped to an octave so low that the primordial part of me, the part that had been born human and therefore prey, wanted to run and hide. "It is only because I believe in what you so cava-lierly flaunt that I don't reach into your chest and remove your heart."

Alice wailed around her gag, but X dragged her down the back stairs of the building, Caroline trailing after him. Angeline was a terrible sight. Guilt, pain, fear, and even hatred burned in her eyes when she looked back at me. I took it all. I deserved it a little. Without me, her happy Stepford life would have continued, unmarred by this ugliness. But still, I lifted my chin. I didn't ask to be kidnapped, used as a blood bank until I was accidentally murdered, and then unwillingly turned into a vampire.

Angeline was in shock. I got that. But I wasn't going to roll over like a kicked dog, especially when her lover had almost killed mine.

Angeline gave me one last loaded look and disappeared from the apartment building. Nico watched her go sadly. Then he bent forward and picked me up as if I weighed nothing.

"I will take her to the Sheriff's home. She will be comfortable there," he said to Judge over my shoulder. "I will wait with her until one of her other paramours arrive."

Judge nodded, though his focus was on Walker, one hand holding the back of Walker's head to keep him attached to his wrist. Actually, Judge was beginning to look a little pale as well.

I wiggled out of Nico's arms, ignored the flash of rejection on his face. I entwined his fingers in mine and lifted his index finger to my mouth. Scraping his skin with my teeth, I cut the very tip of his finger. When a single drop of his blood hit my tongue, it nearly knocked me on my ass. Holy shit. He was powerful. And so, so very old.

I blinked at him wildly, trying to take in everything his blood was telling me. I didn't have time right now, or the emotional fortitude. Instead, I took his still bleeding finger and pressed it to the door.

Then I pulled him across the threshold, still gripping his hand tightly. Grabbing an entire arm full of blood bags from the fridge, I opened one and held it to Nico. "You want me to see if she tainted the blood supply?" I nodded and held it out. He touched his tongue to the tip and nodded. "It is fine." I screwed the cap back on and handed him another one. We repeated this process for twenty bags, Nico never once losing patience. Instead, he tasted each one dutifully.

Finally, I put them all in a cardboard cereal box from my recycling and carried them across the room, using it as a shield from the overwhelming urge to smash the wooden picture frame and ram it into Walker's chest cavity. I clutched Nico's hand so hard that I was worried I'd crush his bones to dust. But he just squeezed back, holding me back and giving me support all at once. I stopped a few feet away, just to be safe, and held out the box of blood bags.

I almost started to cry again when I saw Walker's bright eyes staring back at me from the couch. He was going to be okay. I looked at Judge, who was giving me another sad look. I hoped I could convey everything I felt for him in my look alone because if I could speak, I'd say thank you. I wouldn't have been able to live with myself if I'd killed Walker, whether it was my fault or not. I would have told him I love him because he had my back always. I would have thanked him for taking care of Walker because he knew how much he meant to me.

I hoped he could see it all in my expression because I would tell him as soon as I could. I wanted them all to know how much they meant to me. I wouldn't waste another second.

"We will head to your home now," Nico said, addressing Walker, but it was Judge who answered.

"We won't be far behind you. I think we would all be more comfortable away from here."

My chest heaved in a muted, hiccuping sob. This apartment had been a refuge. I'd tried to rebuild my life here. I built new memories here. But now it was the scene of my almost death. A more permanent one. Instead of the memories of unpacking my life, of Walker handing me the keys or the first time Judge and I had made love or any of the other countless happy memories I'd made here, it would always be marred by ugliness. I knew at that moment that I could never live here again.

Nico nodded and scooped me back in his arms. I didn't fight him. I was done with today. I didn't have any strength left in me. He ran down the back steps, past the crowd that had gathered out the front of The Immortal Cupcake. I barely had a moment to register their shocked faces.

Nothing would ever be the same for the citizens of

Dark River either. I'd destroyed something beautiful, and I wasn't sure the townspeople would ever forgive me for that. Nico ran me past the police station and all the way to Walker's cottage.

Placing me down on wobbly legs, he jogged around to the back of the house. He reappeared, opening the front door for me. "I owe the Sheriff a back door," he muttered, helping me into the house like an invalid.

Instead of taking me to the guest room where I'd stayed when I'd first been turned, he took me down the hall to Walker's bedroom. He walked into the ensuite, and turned on the water, testing its temperature with a stern look of concentration.

When the front door banged open, Nico turned with lightning speed, his body taut and his huge fangs bared. When Brody ran around the corner, he stopped dead at the sight of the ancient vampire predator.

Unfortunately, or fortunately, Tex couldn't see the apex predator in front of him, and moved around both Brody and Nico, straight toward me as if I were a magnet. He had me in his arms, squeezing me impossibly tightly in seconds.

"Jesus, Mika. I was so scared. Judge called and said he knew who it was, and when we arrived at your apartment and all we could smell was Walker's blood. I think I aged a hundred years," he said, as he kissed every inch of my face. "Are you okay?"

I shook my head. I wasn't okay. I'd almost killed Walker, sentenced a woman I thought of as a friend to death, and destroyed a second friend's life. I burrowed my face deeper into his chest and cried. I could hear Nico speaking to Brody in a tone just low enough that I couldn't hear, but the growl that echoed around Walker's bedroom was in no way human.

I looked over to see Brody bowing at the waist at Nico. "Thank you, Nico, for caring for our Mate. We owe you a debt."

Nico waved away his words. "I didn't do it for you. I will stay in the locale for a little longer, but I will leave you with Raine. She needs rest."

Brody nodded, and Nico threw me a sad smile before disappearing. Brody came over and pulled me into his arms. "Oh, Spitfire. I'm so sorry. Let's get you cleaned up and tuck you up in Walker's bed. Everything will be better tomorrow," he promised. I wasn't sure it was a promise he could keep.

They stripped me out of my clothes, and then both hopped into Walker's tiny ensuite shower with me. I don't know how they knew that I needed to be surrounded by their life at the moment, but they did. They washed every square inch of me with tender hands, nothing sexual in their touch. They just took care of me as if I was made of the finest crystal that was sure to shatter at any moment. Maybe they were right. I did feel one more earth-shattering reveal away from falling apart. They wrapped me in one of Walker's t-shirts and put me into his bed.

Then they hopped in beside me, pressed me between them, stroking my hair, touching my skin, whispering sweet words into my hair until I drifted off to sleep.

I woke a few hours later as Walker, barely upright, hopped in beside me. I could see his profile in the darkness, and that of Judge. Brody and Tex were gone, but the sheets were still warm. "He's going to be fine, Raine. He just needs to rest beside our girl, and he'll be alright tomorrow. You both will."

I wanted to tell them that I wasn't alright. Instead, I just shook my head sadly.

Walker pulled me into his arms, curving his body around mine. "I almost lost you today," he said quietly, and the next instant his breathing had evened out into soft snores. I looked past him to Judge.

I patted the other side of the bed hopefully, but my heart sank as he shook his head.

He leaned over and kissed me lightly on the lips. "I wish Rainy Day. But I better catch up with X before he breaks the town. The Council have questions."

The Council weren't the only ones who had questions about how Judge was friends with an Enforcer, but I think deep down I already knew the answer. I just wasn't ready to face it. There'd been enough life-altering events for one day. Instead, I grabbed his hand. I gave him an imploring look.

He gave me a soft smile. "I'll come back to you, promise. I don't think I could stay away, even if I wanted to, Sugar."

He was gone with a light wind, and I drifted back into blissful darkness.

CHAPTER TWENTY-THREE

I woke wrapped in Walker's arms, mentally counting his heartbeats. I snuggled back into him, and just breathed him in. I realized I wasn't trying to stab him with the floor lamp. They must have gotten Alice to revoke the command.

But when I went to say good morning, I realized I was still mute. Panic rode me hard until I felt Walker's fingers tracing a circle on my back. I wanted to purr, to kiss every inch of him, to give him back everything I'd stolen. His skin was finally a healthy color, and I breathed easier knowing what Judge said was true. Walker really was going to be fine.

The man in question kissed the back of my neck, and I sighed soundlessly. "Still no voice?" he asked groggily, and I shook my head.

"That's okay, Sweetheart. You are pretty sassy normally. I think I could appreciate the silence."

I rolled over in his arms and gave him the stink eye. But seeing the life on his face, the laughter in his eyes, it broke me. For the three hundredth time in the last twenty-four hours, I cried.

Walker pulled me into his arms, letting me cry onto his chest. I hated that I'd almost lost him. Hated that I was no longer in control of my emotions, or my body. I hated that I'd had any control at all stripped from me.

I kissed his lips softly, hoping all the words I couldn't say poured from my mouth and into his, so he knew that it would have broken me if he'd died.

"Don't look so sad. I can take anything but your sadness, Raine. It gets me here. It has ever since you walked into the diner like a half-dead nightmare. But you are mine. I refuse to let you go, not in this life or the next. You got that?"

I quirked a brow at him, and he laughed. "Okay, you are ours. Trust me, I haven't forgotten that you seem to attract stray lovers wherever you go. But I have a feeling that it will take more than one of us to keep you out of trouble."

I wanted to frown, but all I could do was smile wider as he leaned in and kissed me, moving his body over mine, so I was pressed deep into the mattress, appreciating the hard length of his torso, and the feel of his morning wood against my stomach.

"I want to make love to you, to claim you as my own right now," he groaned, and I nodded fervently. I was totally down for that idea, especially when he was kissing that spot on my neck that made every single one of my nerve endings light on fire. "But when I do, I want to hear you moaning my name."

He rolled off me and back onto the bed. "Soon, Raine." He smiled as I pouted. "We should get up. We'll need to talk to the Council before the hearing."

I shuddered. I didn't want to relive yesterday. I wanted what Brody had promised me that today would be better. But I think he may have lied. Today was going to be a whole heaping pile of shit.

IN THE END, the Council needed very little from me. Their version of a trial was different from what I would consider a trial. It was mostly done behind closed doors, in front of the Council panel itself. There were no lawyers, nor a jury of her peers. It was just the facts, from as many different sources as they could find. The judgment would be handed down in the meeting hall area of Town Hall though. Maybe it was a blessing that Alice had stolen my voice like Ursula, minus the talk of poor, unfortunate souls. I couldn't tell them much, writing down what happened, and that was that. It may have been because of Nico, who dismissed me after I'd finished my statement, glaring at Grim when he'd tried to question me more.

Walker had been in front of them for an hour,

telling his side of the story. Apparently, Alice had called him, telling him she'd found me unresponsive on the floor of the apartment. He, in typical white knight fashion, raced over, only to be jabbed in the neck by an entire vial of some kind of neurotoxin that incapacitated him completely. Then I'd come home, acted like a completely trusting idiot, and the rest was history.

I hadn't been there for Judge's testimony, but apparently, he'd gathered enough evidence with the help of the even more mysterious X, that Alice's guilt was proven beyond a doubt. They'd even found where Alice was keeping her human victims; some dank cabin in the woods. Luckily, it had been empty. My death and subsequent rebirth must have scared her into stopping for a little while, which I can only consider a small mercy. Judge had presented photos, data, and all sorts of other irrefutable evidence. And he'd produced X. Proof that Alice had brought herself, and therefore the town, to the attention of the Vampire Nation.

By the looks on their faces, this was a more grievous sin than murdering me once and attempting to do it again. X had been strolling around town, scaring the locals and generally being menacing, all traces of the softness I'd seen yesterday completely gone. He was an enigma, and I wasn't sure if I wanted to solve him, or hope he went away and never came back.

Finally, they'd let Walker out. He still looked a little pale, but when he came over to pull me out of my chair, he did it with ease. Judge was somewhere babysitting X and Brody, and Tex were over at the apartment, collecting all my things. I couldn't go back there, and until I found a new place, I was staying with Walker. Although both he and Judge had offered to let me live at each of their respective places, I felt like I needed somewhere of my own. Mostly because I had a gazillion boyfriends, and my place would be neutral territory.

We walked out of the Council's chambers, and across the road to Town Hall. My chest filled uncomfortably full of something I didn't want to name when I saw my guys waiting for us in the square. They were all standing together, talking, Judge so close to Tex that when he waved a hand at the building behind them, his fingertips brushed Tex's arm. Brody smiled and laughed at something Judge said, and I wished I had my phone on me so I could capture the perfection of the scene. I looked around and noticed X was there, popping the heads off the daisies that bordered the path. No longer able to hold back, I flashed to the middle of the circle and wrapped my arms around them. I couldn't tell them how much I appreciated them in words, but I could in actions. I lifted my face and kissed Tex first, a sweet gentle kiss that hinted at all the promises I intended to keep. Then Brody whirled me out of his arms. "My turn, Pup," he teased Tex, dipping me into a long, almost porno-graphic kiss.

I was grinning wide when he finally set me on my feet. I turned and faced Judge, and the heated look in his eyes promised something better than a kiss later. Still, he leaned forward and kissed me hard, nipping my bottom lip with his fangs.

Walker finally caught up and nodded to the guys. "They're about to give the verdict. I'm glad you guys are here, for Raine."

Brody clapped him on the shoulder. "We're here for you too, Man."

We walked toward the Town Hall as a single, united front. X trailed along until he finally drew up to my side.

"Interesting little group you've got going on here. I mean, you got Judge after all. Do you cum rainbows or something?" My mouth unhinged and my brows raised so high, I was worried they'd fall right off my head. "Is there an application process? Because I don't even mind, you are mute. I like the strong, silent type," he laughed, and I quirked an eyebrow at him.

Judge reached around and pummelled him hard in the shoulder. "Stop talking to my girlfriend, Jerkoff."

"That's exactly what we were discussing in fact! I was wondering if she would jerk me-" The low, ominous noise coming from Brody made him snap his jaw shut, but he was still grinning. The dude was a massive, weapon of a guy. I was pretty sure he could take Brody. But still, I stroked my Alpha's arm, letting him know I wasn't offended. Strangely enough, I thought the Enforcer might actually think he was flirting with me.

Shaking my head, my high spirits sank to the floor as I entered the meeting room. I sat in the front, on the left, the guys filling out the row either side of me. The townspeople started to pour in as word got out that the verdict had been decided. I tried not to let the hurt show when so many of them avoided me alto-gether, choosing to sit on the other side of the room. There were five empty rows between me and the next set of people. Walker gave everyone the look. The look said 'I'm not mad, I'm just really disappointed.' I would have caved at that look. Angeline arrived, sitting in the front row. I noticed Cresta and Ella loitering at the back, and Cresta threw me an apolo-getic look. They weren't picking sides, and I appreci-ated it.

Burt and Beatrice however, came right on in and sat behind us. Beatrice squeezed my shoulder. "Don't worry, Lass. We all loved the Doc, but what she did was wrong. Rules are rules, and even if there weren't rules, there is still humanity. What she did went against those things. People will come to that conclusion eventually, even Angeline. She's just hurtin'."

I nodded, but still, my eyes filled with tears.

Walker clasped my hand tightly as the Council members filed in.

Lastly, Nico led in Alice and sat her in a chair before the raised dais of the Councillors. Her gag had been removed, and she looked awful. But I couldn't find it in me to feel sorry for her.

"Alice De Leon. You are charged with breaking almost all of our most sacred rules. You fed from unwilling humans; indeed, you fed us all from unwilling humans. Your actions brought us to the attention of the Vampire Nation." She glared at X. "You killed a human, and then turned her without accepting any responsibility for a fledgling vampire. When you joined this colony, you stood in much the same place as you are now, and swore to uphold our laws. Instead, you broke them in the most grievous way imaginable. Then, instead of admitting to your mistakes, you compounded them by first terrorizing your progeny, and then trying to kill her and the Sheriff of this town. A Sheriff that you considered your friend," Caroline spat the word as if she was appalled. Which she probably was.

"You had no defense for your actions. If you had come to us in the beginning, we might have been able to figure out some way to help you. Your intentions were good, even if your methods were bad. The Council would have appreciated that. You still would have been expelled from Dark River, but the conse-quences wouldn't have been so dire. Instead, you've hidden your mistakes and then proceeded to lose every trace of the empathy that had made you such a beloved citizen of our town. It is for that reason that the Council has decided to sentence you to immediate execution."

The gasp that went through the room was a tangible thing. Fear and outrage had a certain feel, and it was pressing in on me from all sides. Angeline let out a wail, and Alice just hung her head. I hadn't expected anything else. The Council ruled over the town with an iron fist. To show leniency here would be to invite mayhem among the predators who walked the fine line between civilized and frenzied every day.

Still, Angeline was my friend, and Alice was the great love of her life. For her, I stood. I wanted to make an impassioned plea for leniency, but then realized I was still mute.

Still, Grim looked at me, his parchment paper skin an oddly translucent shade in the unnatural light. Apparently, my intentions must have been clearly written on my face.

"Your protest is noted, but ultimately dismissed. We did not reach this verdict lightly. Alice has been with the town, in a highly respected position for almost a century. That is what has made this whole scenario even more of a betrayal. Our word is final."

With that, they stood as one. "Angeline, you will

have a moment to say your goodbyes," Caroline said, not unkindly.

Angeline was in shock. She was pale and shaking as she stood, walking toward Alice on unsteady legs until she fell into the other woman's arms. The whole room was silent so that only the sound of Angeline's tears could be heard. She was murmuring something angrily, and Alice was shaking her head sadly, then I dropped my gaze to my toes. I couldn't watch anymore. Couldn't deal with just the tragic waste of the whole scenario.

Walker sat beside me, as stoic as ever, but I could see his jaw working, his eyes bright with tears he'd never shed in front of all these people. I reached over and laced my fingers with his. I needed his support just as much as he needed mine tonight.

Finally, Nico went over to the two women, gently prying Angeline away. Cresta and Ella rushed forward, catching their friend before she could crumple to the hardwood floors. Nico lifted Alice from her chair, and walked her out of the room, the rest of the Council members following them. Their departure was like a vacuum lifting from the room. A cacophony of disbelief echoed off every surface, as everyone spoke at once. Cresta and Ella whisked Angeline away, and I was glad that she had them. Well, them and the rest of the town apparently.

I tugged on Judge's hand, looking at him imploringly and he nodded. "Raine wants to go home."

X stood up from the row behind us. "I will go and offer my services. No one should have to kill a friend." He said it with such sadness that I knew he was speaking from experience. The scar littered man was an intrigue. If he hadn't shown up at the most awful part of my life, he might have been a puzzle that I might have tried to unravel. But I didn't have the emotional fortitude to do anything at the moment.

Walker stood also. "I will come with you. I should be there," he said softly. God, he just broke my heart. I nodded and squeezed his hand one last time before he and X walked toward the door that the Council had just left.

I grabbed Tex's hand and led him from the building, letting his solid warmth ground me. I avoided the eyes of the townspeople, the accusing stares as if it were all my fault. I walked human-slow back to Walker's house because as much as I wanted to shut myself up in his spare room and never come out, I wanted to appreciate this night in all its terribleness.

We were at the end of Walker's street when magic tingled along my skin. "Oh," I whispered croakily, my voice rough from disuse. The geas had been lifted. Which meant…

I shook my hand out of Tex's and flashed the rest of the way to Walker's house, straight into the ensuite bathroom and locked the door. Turning the hot water to scalding, I stood beneath it and cried. This time my sobs were audible to everyone in the house.

CHAPTER TWENTY-FOUR

I hid in my room in Walker's house for four days. Four days they all let me wallow, steadily rotating their job as a warm body, soothing my nightmares, kissing away my tears. They took turns bringing me food and blood, even though I now know that some of that blood came from unwilling tourists.

On the third day, Tex had acquired a guitar, and he sat in the corner, strumming it softly and singing to me in a low voice that was mesmerizing and healing in equal parts. He sang me all my favorite songs from when I was a teen, and then a few he had composed himself. His dark, sexy voice soothed my frayed nerves. Sometimes Judge would join us, his body wrapped around mine as we both listened to the music that seemed to pour from Tex's very soul with the intention to soothe mine.

However, by the fourth day, they decided they'd

had enough of my wallowing. All four of them stood in the guest room, concern on their faces but arms folded across their chests. They kind of looked like they were posing for an album cover.

"If you guys are about to belt out some synchronized dancing, then I'm going to rethink our relationship status. I'm not dating the Backstreet Boys."

Tex was the only one who laughed. A hazard of dating men who were mostly born in the 19th century.

"You've moped around enough now, Raine," Walker said, his tone gentle but firm. "Nothing that happened was your fault."

Brody nodded. "Plus this room is starting to smell funky. You are starting to smell funky."

I let out a hiss of outrage. "I do not."

He pointed to his nose, his lips curved into a shit-eating grin. "Super sniffer. Trust me when I say both you and this room could use a quick rinse cycle." He gave me his most winning smile. "Don't stress it, Rainy. My wolf form likes to roll around in dead animals. I still think you're hot."

Tex couldn't hold back his laughter anymore, and soon, all four of them were giggling like Japanese schoolgirls at my expense. I flipped them the bird and strode around them, out of my self-imposed corner and into the bathroom.

I slammed the door and turned on the shower.

Then, because I couldn't help myself, I lifted my armpit and sniffed.

Super Sniffer, one.

Raine, zero.

I STEPPED out of the bathroom, dressed in clothes someone so helpfully left outside the door. Obviously, they didn't want to risk me crawling back into my hole for another four days. I strolled into the kitchen of Walker's house. His kitchen table was spread with breakfast. It looked like they'd ordered everything from the diner's breakfast menu. Pancakes sat in huge stacks, butter and maple syrup dripping down like it was the star of a syrup commercial. My mouth watered.

"How do I get her to look at me like that?" Walker asked as he put down a tray that held fluffy omelets.

"Bathe in maple syrup?" Brody suggested.

Tex snatched bacon from the passing tray with such accuracy, I would never have guessed he was sight-impaired. "What face is she making?" he asked around a mouth full of pork product.

Judge handed him another piece of bacon. "Her eyes are really wide, and her lips are parted in a way that just makes you want to kiss her. Then her little pink tongue pokes out and runs along her lip like she's tasting the sweetness in the air," Judge described easily.

Then he did exactly what he said, leaning over to kiss me, sucking the aforementioned lip between his. "She tastes sweet too. Not sure she needs these pancakes," he murmured, moving toward my pancakes.

I looked at Walker. "It's like he wants to lose a hand or something?" Walker laughed like I was joking.

Everyone appeared to be here, except for one blond giant. "Where's X?"

Judge wisely moved away from my pancakes. "He went back home two days ago."

I nodded. "So an Enforcer, hey? That's a pretty big secret," I said casually, slicing my pancake stack. Someone had poured syrup between the layers. I looked up, and Walker winked. A man who knew how I liked my pancakes? Bestill my heart. Someone was getting laid real soon.

"They bind us when we leave. It's one of the conditions," he looked almost apologetic. Luckily, my forced vow of silence made me appreciate his position just a little more than I would have a week ago.

I spent a minute in silence, just enjoying the fluffiness of my pastry breakfast, appreciating the view of all four of my guys at one table, sharing breakfast, wondering if this could be our future. That might be too much to hope for. They were four testosterone-laden males. If I thought they were going to play house nicely for all eternity, I was kidding myself. "What are we doing today? Is the town, I mean, are they mad?" I stumbled over my words as I forced them out. I didn't want to ruin the moment, but I needed to know. Needed to be prepared before I left the relative safety of Walker's house.

Walker sighed. "It's been tough. It always is, but no one blames you, Raine. You were a victim in every way. Angeline has closed The Immortal Cupcake and disappeared, but I'm fairly sure she's at home in the woods grieving. Cresta and Ella are keeping an eye on her. But we'll all move on, learn and grow from this situation. The biggest problem has been the blood supply. Alice hadn't set up any supply network because she was creating her own source." That was a very technical way to refer to the abduction and harvesting of humans. "Anyway, enough of that. We have a surprise for you after you're done making love to those pancakes." He quirked an eyebrow at where I was running my finger through the syrup on my plate. I guess it did look a little seductive.

I raised my finger and rubbed it over my lip. Brody groaned. I leaned over and kissed Tex because I didn't want him to miss out. He licked my lip with the tip of his tongue and made a happy humming noise.

"Is Lover Boy going to get all the kisses because he's blind? Because, that just ain't playing fair," Brody said, pouting. I frowned at him, hoping my expression screamed *you can't say that!*

Then Tex went and ruined it. "Suck it up, visually-able person. I'm going to milk the blind card for eternity. Get used to it."

Sighing, I sat back in my chair. "You said something about a surprise?"

They all stood as one, and I just knew it was going to be good, judging by the stupid smiles on their faces. "I think we should blindfold her," Brody said.

Judge punched him in the arm. "Still with the blind jokes?"

They tussled a bit more, although Tex came over and put his arm around me before Walker clapped his hands. "No blindfold, but you should close your eyes. It makes things more fun." He swept me into his arms, and I dutifully closed my eyes.

We weren't flashing, so it mustn't be far away. Maybe they got me a puppy?

I wanted to open my eyes, just a little, but then I thought of their stupid grinning faces and kept them closed.

After about forty seconds, they halted. Walker slid me down his delicious body, and part of me wondered if my surprise was an orgy. Not gonna lie. That might be even better than a puppy.

Judge squeezed my hand. "Okay, Rainy Day. Open your eyes."

I peeled one eye open, then the other. Then I gasped. I stood in front of the world's cutest cottage. Seriously, if Walker's looked like a Norman Rockwell painting, then mine looked like it came off the front of a cookie jar. Except it was black. Even the picket fence was black. The trim was all white, and the door was bright red. I loved it.

"It's so cute. Did you guys lease this for me?"

Brody shrugged a single shoulder. "Kinda." He pulled a set of keys from his pocket. "We bought it. It's yours now. We painted it while you wallowed."

I blinked. Then I blinked a few more times. They bought me a house? People didn't do that. I mean, I couldn't accept it, right? As if he sensed my upcoming protest, Walker pushed me toward the front door. "Okay, so maybe we bought us a house if it makes you feel better. Just you'll live here. And your name is on the deed. And you own it. Consider it like a club-house or something."

"Yeah, except instead of riding cool Harley's, we ride you," Brody teased. Freaking jerk. Sexy freaking jerk.

He said all this as he pushed me through the door. When I stepped in, the place was empty and filled with boxes. I assumed boxes of my stuff.

"We only painted the outside. We left all the hard work to you. I googled how to style the inside of a house, and they started talking about occasional tables. What the fuck is an occasional table? If you only use it little enough to call it that, what the hell is the point of having it?" Judge was grumbling under his breath. "What goes in here is completely up to you. This is your home now, Raine. You can decorate it however you want, paint it hot pink if that's what your heart desires. Let in whoever you want. Or no one at all."

I spun around the room, my eyes impossibly wide. "So this is mine?" I asked, waiting for them to yell, just kidding, and kick me out.

Brody hugged me. "Well, your's and Tex's. I figured you wouldn't want him too far away. But he can stay with Judge if you want your privacy."

His thoughtfulness made my eyes fill with tears. I wanted Tex with me, a safety blanket for us both. We still had so much to overcome, to worry about.

I looked at them, and a tear rolled down my cheek. "Are you going to cry again? Please don't cry again," Brody groaned. "I can't handle your tears. They're like my kryptonite or something."

I squeezed him tight. "Happy tears don't count." I shifted back and looked at them all. My eyes stuck on Walker. "Are you sure about this?"

I wasn't talking about the house, and we both knew it. I wanted to know if he wanted to dive into this craziness with me.

He reached out and pulled me away from a grumbling Brody. "Raine. Would you do me the honor of going on a date with me?"

"Absolutely."

Brody just headed toward the closest box. "About damn time."

. . .

FOR THE SEVEN millionth time since I'd been turned, I thanked the powers that be that I could no longer get fat. In front of me was a new creation made by Burt, aka my Deep-fried Overlord. He'd conjured deep-fried Oreos to tempt me back into the world, and who was I to turn down that kind of offer?

I sat in a booth, squished between Walker and Brody, Tex, and Judge across from me, and I felt perfectly content once more. Sure, there were eyes on me, and whispers that weren't soft enough for my vampire ears, plus Brody had already growled at a couple of nosy gossips, but generally speaking, life had gone on.

Walker wrinkled his nose at my plate of deep-fried cookie goodness. "That is disgusting. You are going to make yourself sick." He sounded as bemused as he was disgusted.

I leaned across and pressed a deep-fried oreo against Tex's lips. "Tex understands. He knows the glory that is the oreo."

Tex obligingly opened his lips, taking the whole cookie into his mouth, and then sucking on my fingers. I sucked in a breath as heat shot to my belly. Behind me, someone let out a distinctly feminine sigh.

Yeah, sister. I feel that.

"Nope, I'm with Walker. That's an abomination," Tex said, poking his tongue out. I kicked his shin under the table.

"Quiet. You'll hurt Burt's feelings, and then he

won't make me the double-fried apple pies he was talking about earlier."

Brody laughed, nuzzling my hair before leaning around to snag a bit of the cookie in my hand, the damn sneak. "You guys don't know what you're missing. Delicious."

The bell over the door tinkled, that dreaded fucking bell, but instead of silence, there was a sudden cacophony of whispered shock. I turned in my seat to see the grinning face of X.

He pulled up a chair and sat at the end of our booth. "Hello, Love. What's a nice girl like you doing in a place like this?" He grinned and took one of my Oreos. He bit down and gagged. "What the hell is that?"

I grinned. "Don't mind the taste, Love, just close your eyes, swallow, and think of Mother England," I teased, and he laughed, a few oreo crumbs flying across the table and onto Judge's plate, making the man in question grimace.

He flicked it off his plate and toward back toward the grinning Englishman. "What are you doing here, X?"

X stole a piece of Judge's toast, and Judge rolled his eyes. "You say that like you didn't miss me, Judgey Wudgey. Livin' it up in the new love nest yet?"

He waggled his eyebrows at me, and I blushed even as I gave him the finger. "Careful, Sweetheart, or

I might construe that as an invitation. I'm still waiting for the harem application form to come in the mail."

Brody might have mumbled something about waiting until hell froze over, but X just shook it off. "Nah, I mean it. It's good to see you up and about, not curled in a ball in your bed. That shit with your maker was nasty business. But between you and me, you're better off. Having a bad maker…" He hesitated, the roguish cheek draining from his eyes for a second. "Well, let's say it isn't a good thing now, is it?"

Everyone was silent for a moment as the weight of the past few months pressed down on us. But it was lessening. Soon, it would be a fading memory. There would only be happiness from this point on, I was determined.

So when X sighed and stole a sausage from Tex's plate, barely missing the knife that Tex slammed down with preternatural speed. "He's quick for a blind kid." Tex curled his lip, and X laughed. "Down Puppy. Look, I actually came with a warning, 'cause I'm kinda fond of this grumpy bastard," he pointed at Judge, "and I have a growing hard spot for Red."

He leaned forward, and we all leaned in closer. "The Vampire Nation is coming, so get your shit in order, because they are sending Lucius."

Judge let out a snarl that raised all the goosebumps on my arms. Who the fuck was Lucius? From the look on Judge's face and the fact that Walker's cheeks were completely blanched of color, I was going to assume it was no one good.

"Why?" Brody growled. Well, this was very, very, not good.

"Apparently, the little stunt your Good Doctor pulled piqued his interest in your little town, and the last place you guys ever want to be is within his interest. So I'd cross all your I's and bury all your skeletons because he's coming and soon."

A cold chill ran down my spine.

Apparently my happily ever after was going to have to wait.

ABOUT THE AUTHOR

Grace McGinty is eclectic. She has worked as a chocolatier, a librarian, a forensic accountant and finally a writer. Like her professional career, the genres she writes are also eclectic. She writes romance, reverse harem romance, fantasy, contemporary young adult and new adult books.

She lives in rural Australia with her crazy family, an entire menagerie of pets, and will one day be crushed by her giant piles of books that litter every room.

Keep reading for a sneak peek at the first book in my Hell's Redemption series: The Redeemable.

[f] facebook.com/GraceMcgintyAuthor

[twitter] twitter.com/McgintyGrace

[instagram] instagram.com/gracemcgintyauthor

THE REDEEMABLE

CHAPTER ONE

Today was a brittle day. My body felt like it would fall to pieces at any second, leaving me a gory mess of plasma and regrets on the pavement.

Almost home now, just hold your shit together, Ace said. Ace was complicated. Complicated in that she was merely a voice in my head. My calm voice of reason crossed with the attitude of the angst ridden preteen I'd been when I'd first heard her. Like an imaginary friend who bitched a lot, but had my back. The psych's said I'd developed her to cope with the traumas of my childhood and the combined blows of my parents' death. But despite the cocktails of drugs and therapy, she persisted, and deep down I was glad.

I pushed my way through the turnstiles and down the stairs to my subway platform. Groaning, I pressed my hands to my temples as I took in the scene. A fight had broken out, and the crowd had formed a circle around the dueling businessmen. This was New York, so fighting stockbrokers wasn't the weirdest thing I'd ever seen, but it was unusual enough to draw an audience.

I pushed my way around the crowd, desperate to make my train. The musty smell of the tunnel was gusting from the darkness, the silent harbinger of my train's imminent arrival. I edged way too close to the safety line, but there was no other way around the ring of spectators. People behind me jostled and shoved, and I plowed into the back of a man standing in front of me.

Despite the force of my meagre weight pushing into his back, the man didn't shift an inch. He didn't even turn, so I could politely ask him to move. Dammit.

He was huge and muscular, not someone I wanted to annoy, but he was in my way.

"Excuse me," I yelled over the shouts of the fight.

This time the man turned, and I took an unconscious step back. I took in his tense jaw, not-so-straight nose, and his flinty grey eyes. Small scars littered his face. His hair was shaved so close it may as well have been a five o'clock shadow to match his beard. It all added together to make him look rough and cruel.

Plus, he was a behemoth, must have easily been six and a half feet. Those gray eyes stared down at me with an intensity that made my sluggish heart beat faster.

"What?" he said, the words soft, at odds with his hard expression. I pulled together the shreds of my dignity and tried to stop staring.

"Excuse me. This is my train and I can't get past you. Could you please move?" I gave him a polite smile as my headache began to thump.

"You have to be fucking kidding me. You?" He looked over my head, towards the crowd watching the fight. "Ri, get the hell over here."

He still hadn't moved, and his eyes were back on my face.

"I'm sorry? Do I know you?" I was very sure I didn't. He wasn't someone you'd forget.

An equally large man joined him, but this one had caramel colored skin inked in dark black patterns from his neck down. Dark brown curls were cut close to his head and his eyes were the color of whiskey.

"Lux, what's up man? The fight was just getting good. One guy just hit the other with his briefcase." His voice was smooth and deep and his grin was guaranteed to melt the panties of any straight woman under a hundred.

"It's her," the behemoth said, and the new guy's face lost every trace of mirth as he looked down at me with the same intense expression as his friend.

"Are you sure?"

The behemoth placed a warm, gentle hand on my cheek, and I found it oddly comforting.

"Holy shit," the new guy muttered.

Snap the hell out of it, Arcadia. Random strangers are touching you in the subway. Do you not remember any of those after school specials we had to watch as a kid? This is not normal. Ace was beginning to sound very un-calm.

I moved my face away from the behemoth's outstretched hand as the whistle of the train echoed down the tunnel.

"That's my train. I really gotta go." I edged around the behemoth, but that just put me in front of the new guy, the one called Ri. The train blew its horn again and I could see its lights coming out of the tunnel over his shoulder as he moved to do the same thing as his friend. He reached up and put a hand on my cheek, his full pink lips parted as he just stared down at me, mute.

From what I can piece together, several things then happened at once. My heart began to thunder in my chest until the edges of my vision began to blur, and I could hear Ace yelling in my head to stay upright until I was on the train, but her yelling was only making my head thump more. Simultaneously to this small problem, the fight had shifted closer to me, and I turned at the last moment to see a briefcase connect with a face in a spray of blood, and the overly soft body of an office worker lurched toward me. As the office worker connected with me and my body toppled sideways towards the track, I remember thinking only one thing as the darkness replaced the bright lights of the train. There were worse ways to die.

I WOKE up on a leather couch that wasn't my own, a set of light blue eyes staring down at me from a chair placed beside it. My brain was foggy, but Ace was loud and clear.

You've been abducted. How the hell did we end up here? She sounded worried, but I just couldn't summon the energy to care.

"I need my meds." My voice was rough. The man beside me held up my pill bottle and a glass of water, helping me to ease into a sitting position. I realized there were more people in the room with us. Five more men to be exact.

Shit. You are about to become a late night repeat of America's Worst Crimes.

I scooted away from the man, and perched on the edge of the couch. I shook out a couple of pills from the bottle and dry swallowed them. They could've put anything in the water.

"What am I doing here? Where am I?"

"You passed out in the subway. If Lux hadn't grabbed you when he did, you'd probably be dead.

When they realized you wouldn't wake up, they brought you back here to me. I'm Dr Elias August. These guys call me Eli."

I finally noticed the stethoscope around his neck as he pulled it on and placed the end on my back. I took a deep breath out of reflex.

Great, a doctor. At least the cops will be able to appreciate the mark of a professional when they find your dismembered body in a dumpster.

"I'm Arcadia. Everyone calls me Cady. Who are those guys?" My voice was barely a squeak. So far the other people in the space had just been standing quietly at the edges of the room, staring at me with an intensity that was both confusing and a little scary.

"We'll get to them in a second. Don't worry, they are completely harmless to you." He placed the stethoscope on my chest. "Any pain?"

"No more than normal."

"Diagnosis?"

"Severe dilated cardiomyopathy."

"You're on the transplant list?"

I shook my head sadly. No matter how many times I repeated this bit, it was never any less of a blow to my soul.

"I'm in remission for Hodgkin's Lymphoma. The transplant board said no."

Eli placed his hands on his thighs, his fingers curling under and flexing hard. He had nice thighs.

A totally inappropriate thought to be having right now, in this situation, Ace groused.

"So you are dying?" Eli sounded stoic and professional, but someone else in the room sucked in a breath as if they'd been sucker punched.

"Essentially, yes. But hey, at least it wasn't today!"

"You can't be any more than eighteen." Eli shook his head.

"Twenty actually. I have a baby face." I gave him a tight smile and stood. "I better be heading home. Thank you for doctoring me," I said to Eli, and turned to find behemoth, or Lux I guess his name was. "Thanks for saving me." He was even better looking in this moment, his face less harsh now he wasn't under the fluorescent lights of the subway. I gave myself a few seconds to really drink him in.

"Didn't really save you, did I?" His voice was still a scary low growl though.

I shrugged. I knew the look he was giving me all too well. I'd seen it far too many times in my life. Frustrated hopelessness.

"You can't save them all, right?" I walked around Eli's chair towards the door. "Can someone point me to the nearest bus stop?"

Lux said something to Eli in a language I didn't understand and had never even heard before. "What language is that?"

"Latin," a voice said from somewhere in the

room. I peeked around the couch to find another guy lying on the ground behind the backrest, like a lost dollar. He had a full red beard, long hair that was tied in a messy bun on top of his head, and a red checkered shirt. He looked like a sexy lumberjack. His hands were linked behind his head and he was grinning at me without the intensity of the rest of the room's occupants.

I raised an eyebrow. "Who speaks latin, anyway?"

"Rich private school kids and those two. Definitely not me. I barely speak English with any kind of fluency. I'm Oz by the way."

"Cady."

"You're cute. Kinda like a pixie."

"Uh, you too?"

Eli and Lux finished arguing in latin, and Eli turned toward me. "Lux will drive you home. Is there someone there to take care of you? Parents? A boyfriend? A roommate?"

"Uh, no. My parents are both dead. But my friend calls me every day to check on me. She'll know if I'm missing."

Great save, Arcadia. Smooth. Let's not tell them that she's actually working in Somalia right now, nursing orphans or some shit.

Lux smothered a smirk, and Oz openly laughed from his spot on the floor.

"I understand, but I'm worried that if you have

another episode like the last one, you may fall and hurt yourself. Would you perhaps think of staying here until you are well? We have a big house and I promise you'll be completely safe. We would be over-joyed to have you."

Fuck no.

My automatic response was no too. They were strangers, and I was being reassured that they are good people by another stranger. Besides, I would never be well again. No was the right answer.

The only answer!

But I looked around and instead of feeling scared to be in a room of guys, I felt a level of comfort that was just bizarre. Earnest reassurance came off them in waves, and I I really wanted to say yes. I had two years left in my life, did I really want to spend them home alone watching HBO? Maybe I wanted to take this chance?

Have you gone mental? How are you even contemplating this? You might only have two years, but the wrong choice could make chemo seem like a resort spa. Haven't you ever seen the Saw movies? Ace was outraged in my mind, but lucky for me she was just a voice.

Seeing me so obviously vacillating, Eli came to my rescue.

"You don't have to make your decision now. Stay for dinner, Valery is a three hat chef. He's making something extravagant, I'm sure. No one else is allowed in the kitchen." He turned to look at a man who was leaning against the doorjamb. He was shorter than the other men in the room, but still inches taller than me. He had floppy blonde hair and a smile that made his eyes crinkle at the corners.

"Unfortunately, I was only making mac and cheese," he replied. His voice had a slight accent that I couldn't place.

Oz scoffed. "Mac and cheese with blue cheese and some other fancy shit. Not like you poured it out of a box, Val."

Valery smiled wider, dimples creasing his cheeks. He was very cute. Actually, they were all kind of hot. So weird.

I smiled back at him. "I'd love to stay for dinner. Thank you." They did save my life. It would be rude to turn down their dinner invitation.

How have you even survived this long?

Valery looked like all his Christmases had come at once. "Excellent. I shall be in the kitchen," he said and left, muttering to himself about bread and maybe pickles? His accent made him sound like he was saying 'keeshun' and it was adorable. Maybe French?

I took a better look around the room. There was a massive flat screen TV in the center of one wall, and the leather sectional sofa was positioned around it. A glass bookcase held a small collection of books, some very old judging by the cracked leather spines. Everything was tastefully minimalist in muted tones of silver and navy. It was definitely a bachelor pad. There wasn't a throw pillow in the place.

"Please, sit. Everyone can stop loitering around now," Eli said, and everyone converged toward to the sofa. "Oz, put on some music please." I leaned over the back of the couch to see Oz hadn't moved from his comfortable position.

"You aren't coming up here?" There was something about Oz that made me want to tease him.

"Nope, but you can always come and join me down here." He gave me a wink and I blushed. It didn't help that I could see a small strip of his flat stomach where his shirt had ridden up. "Mini-Oz, play 'Pretty Girl Dinner Party' playlist," he yelled at nothing, but sure enough, the sound of Frank Sinatra started to pour softly into the room from hidden speakers.

"That is seriously amazing."

"Voice controlled home management system. The pinnacle of technological laziness." He grinned widely at me and I grinned back.

"Well, I'm impressed."

"You shouldn't encourage him," a soft voice said from beside me. I whipped around to see the most beautiful man I'd ever laid eyes on sitting mere inches away on the couch beside me. He must have been hiding in a dark corner or something, because I definitely would have been dumbstruck before now. Thankfully the guy ignored my unhinged jaw and continued. "He's hidden the remotes, so now the channel can only change on the TV if he says so. It's super annoying."

I could only nod as I took in the man's midnight blue eyes, high cheek bones and ash blonde hair. He looked like a Scandinavian super model.

"I'm Sam," he held out one huge hand. I took it, and tried not to sigh contentedly as its strong, soft warmth enveloped by own.

"Cady, nice to meet you."

"The pleasure is all mine. I wanted to introduce myself before I had to head out to take Ri to work." He nodded toward the pretty guy from the subway station with the golden skin and the tattoos. And the voice like raw sex.

I gave Ri a little wave, and he smirked back. "Nice to see you with some color in your cheeks, Beautiful Girl. You scared the hell out of me back there."

"I'm sorry," I said, meaning it.

He gave me a sad smile. "Me too."

He picked up a leather jacket from the back of the couch and threw it over a black jeans and tight grey shirt combo that sculpted his body like a liquid. My mouth physically watered.

"Well, I better get to work, I'm already late. But if I turn up with the great Sam Sigurdsson, they'll forgive me once the pictures start hitting Instagram and Twitter. Free press."

Sam Sigurdsson. The name rang a bell. Hang on. "Oh my goodness. You're the Calvin Klein model from the side of the bus."

They all laughed, and someone muttered something about five foot junk.

"Hopefully you're still here when we get home. But if not, I hope to see you again soon. Take good care of yourself." Sam took my hand in his and kissed it. I forgot to breathe. Ri winked as he followed Sam out the door.

Now Sam had left, I could see the person sitting on the couch beside him. My mouth swung open again. "You're the Armani suit guy from the Times Square billboard. What the hell is this place? Mecca for models?"

Oz man-giggled from behind the couch.

The Armani model slid his perfectly proportioned body up the couch toward me. His face showed signs of a mixed heritage, but I couldn't guess what. He had beautiful golden skin, not quite as dark as Ri, a smooth square jaw and almond shaped eyes.

"Tolliver. Nice to finally meet you."

Odd choice of words, but then he smiled and I was distracted by the shiny white perfection of his teeth.

"Hi," I squeaked. "Aren't there any trolls amongst you at all?"

"Comparisons have been made between Oz and Bigfoot." Tolliver sounded amused, but he didn't crack a smile. "Would you like a tour of the mansion?"

Wait, mansion?

READ MORE: www.books2read.com/Redeemable

CPSIA information can be obtained
at www.ICGtesting.com
Printed in the USA
BVHW070226020822
643541BV00008B/1010